The Quality Street Wedding

Penny Thorpe lives in Yorkshire where she was the company archivist and historian for her local chocolate factory for more than a decade. She's worked in libraries, bookshops, offices, a Swiss school, a racecourse, a barber's shop, a church and a police station (to name but a few).

Penny is a recognised expert in her field, but still isn't quite sure how that happened. She has written about the history of confectionery for years and regularly appears on television and radio to talk about the history of Yorkshire, chocolate, coffee, Quakers and food.

To stay in touch with Penny, follow her on Facebook, Instagram and Twitter @penthorpebooks.

/penthorpebooks
@PenThorpeBooks

Also by Penny Thorpe

The Quality Street Girls
The Mothers of Quality Street

PENNY THORPE

The Quality Street Wedding

HarperCollins*Publishers*

HarperCollins*Publishers* Ltd
1 London Bridge Street,
London SE1 9GF

www.harpercollins.co.uk

HarperCollins*Publishers*
1st Floor, Watermarque Building, Ringsend Road
Dublin 4, Ireland

First published by HarperCollins*Publishers* 2021

1

This paperback edition 2022

A catalogue record for this book is available from the British Library

ISBN:
HB: 978-0-00-840686-8
TPB: 978-0-00-840687-5
PB: 978-0-00-840690-5

This novel is entirely a work of fiction.
The names, characters and incidents portrayed in it are
the work of the author's imagination. Any resemblance to
actual persons, living or dead, events or localities is
entirely coincidental.

Typeset in Sabon LT Std by
Palimpsest Book Production Ltd, Falkirk, Stirlingshire

Printed and bound in the UK using 100% Renewable Electricity by CPI Group (UK) Ltd

MIX
Paper from
responsible sources
FSC™ C007454

This book is produced from independently certified FSC™ paper
to ensure responsible forest management.

For more information visit: www.harpercollins.co.uk/green

For Scott and all his colleagues in the NHS.
Overworked, undervalued, underpaid,
and now overwhelmed.

Prologue

Easter Sunday 1938

'But why is this the *wrong* wedding?' The curate looked worried. He had agreed to perform the ceremony after receiving a personal entreaty which appealed to his sense of adventure, but he drew the line at illegality.

'It's not the *wrong* wedding – not in that way – it's just we thought it would be very different when the day came.' Reenie, realising that she had put her foot in it, tried to backtrack.

The curate quickly consulted his paperwork, 'These are the correct names on the marriage licences, aren't they?'

Mary hissed at Reenie not to ruin everything and then, rather too emphatically, assured the curate, 'Those are exactly the right names, and the right signatures; *everything* is above board.'

'And neither party is already married, or—'

Reenie bit her lip and brought up the matter she least

wanted to discuss. 'No, no; it's nothing like that. It's just – well, you of all people know about the *other* wedding.' She looked sadly at her friend Mary. 'We had just expected *that* wedding more than *this* wedding, if you follow me?'

'Ah . . . yes.' The curate appeared to be casting his mind back to the 'other wedding', a ceremony which had involved a literal shotgun – the story of which he was sure he would dine out on for years to come.

It wasn't just Reenie and Mary who had been taken by surprise. This was not the Easter wedding which any of the girls had been expecting to attend. The toffee factory that spring had been a flurry of expectation, educated speculation and then plain gossip, but the girls on the Strawberry Cream line had all been agreed that there would be wedding banns for one of them before the summer began.

'Well, these aren't the decorations I thought we'd be having.' Reenie poked her head inside the doorway of the chapel and sighed at the brightly coloured embellishments which had been left there by some other person, for some other purpose; Eastertide was very much in evidence. It was a shame they couldn't have done things differently, but the wedding was going ahead and that was all any of them cared about now.

'How long do you think we ought to wait?' Mary was kicking at her shoes because she was wearing them without socks and her feet had slid down to the toe uncomfortably.

'Why?' Reenie asked with just a hint of friendly sarcasm. 'Did you have somewhere else to be?'

Bess giggled. Bess often giggled.

'What's so funny?' Mary was determined to treat the

occasion as a solemn one and her sister's silliness was getting on her wick.

'You kicking at your shoe.' Bess chuckled quietly, just sensible enough that she shouldn't let the curate inside the door hear her. 'You look like Reenie's horse when he's been given a job he doesn't fancy doin'. He's always kicking his shoes off.'

'I'm not kicking them off, I'm just trying to get my foot straight. The insole's all over the place.'

All three girls turned to see the curate emerge from inside the chapel looking more nervous than they did, if such a thing were possible. 'Ladies, this is really most irregular, I do think . . .' The curate's voice trailed off as he realised that he had no objections left to make. It was the other girl he needed to speak to – the one who was beautiful and terrifying. These girls were here at her express instruction and she had made the arrangements with him – only she could reassure him that this was all above board, despite appearances to the contrary.

For months the toffee factory workers had been laying bets on who the next factory wedding would be. The smart money was on Reenie Calder who, though still only seventeen, had been courting a very sweet Junior Manager from the Time and Motion department for nearly a year and, according to rumour, had been negotiating with him on the terms of an engagement. Reenie's friend, Mary Norcliffe, would not have seemed a likely candidate for matrimony a year before, but then life had wrought its changes and Mary was no longer known as 'The Bad Queen' behind her back because her bad temper had given way in response to the kindness she found in new friendships in the factory. Now that she had been given the chance to work in the Confectioner's Kitchen and work closely with the handsome young widower who ran it, some (including her flighty younger sister, Bess) whispered that she might make a suitable stepmother to the Confectioner's two small children.

Meanwhile happy-go-lucky Bess, still known as 'Good Queen Bess' in the factory because her kindly nature never changed, was possibly the Quality Street girl who everyone hoped would wed; Bess was friendly and obliging to a fault, and her sister Mary was convinced that if she wasn't guarded round the clock, she would get herself in the family way by obliging rather too much. There were always a few semi-serious suitors ready to take pretty Bess to a dance, but Mary was clinging to the hope that the new home which awaited her sister would be one where she could settle down in comfort – and give Mary's blood pressure a well-earned rest.

Then there was Diana Moore, but she was now so old by the standards of the factory girls that no one had seemed to think of her in matrimonial terms – and that was the way Diana had liked it; being the talk of the town lost its appeal for her years ago.

Now the morning of the wedding was here and it had come in an unholy hurry.

Reenie was resplendent in a satin gown and light fur cape which had been a gift from her young man's parents when he'd told them they were to be engaged. Reenie was glad of the cape in the chill of the church and she felt sorry for Mary who shivered a little beside her while they waited just inside the nave door. Reenie was not surprised to see that Mary's dress was of a slightly old-fashioned cut; it had echoes of a dress she'd seen

Mary wear on another occasion to church, and she remembered how it had transfixed Albert Baum, the factory confectioner; it seemed fitting that Mary would choose something that he would have liked had he been the one to choose it.

That more assertive factory girl the curate had been waiting for appeared at the bottom of the steps in a chauffeur-driven car and made her way quickly up toward them.

'She isn't coming.' Diana did not sound disappointed. 'The wedding can go ahead.'

'Who isn't coming?' The curate found this whole situation most suspicious and he would have raised more vocal objections if a very large, ornate special licence signed by his superior's superior had not persuaded him to go along with it. 'Is this a person who knows of some lawful impediment why—'

Diana cut him off before he could waste any more time. 'There is no lawful reason why this marriage shouldn't take place. It was a personal reason and I have dealt with it.'

Mary looked a bit scared of Diana when she said that, but Reenie knew better and breathed a sigh of relief. A spring morning was warming the rooftops of Halifax and it was nearly eight o'clock; in just a few moments it would be legally late enough in the day for the wedding to begin.

Chapter One

Two Months Earlier

Mackintosh's toffee factory was invisibly falling apart. The bricks and mortar were sound – much of it new, thanks to rebuilding efforts throughout the preceding year – and money was pouring in to help with preparations for the war which everyone feared was coming. But *workers* weren't pouring in; instructions for how to use the money, or how to prepare weren't pouring in; *help* was not pouring in.

If this war had appeared on the horizon ten years earlier – or maybe even two – they'd have been better equipped to tackle it, but it was January 1938 and the board of directors had decamped to the posh offices of their well-to-do chocolate factory in well-to-do Norwich. The experienced staff who had weathered the storm of the last war had been put out to pasture, and Major Fergusson – not just head of the Time and Motion

Department, but also the glue which held so many departments together – was convalescing in a cottage hospital, leaving a power vacuum in the factory which had been filled by chaos, confusion, and the conflicting ambitions of rival managers.

Reenie Calder – seventeen years old, and barely seventeen months on the payroll at the toffee factory – found herself in charge of a new toffee production line and new machinery which needed bedding in. She had received special dispensation from the factory manager to keep a group of talented married women on for this very task, but nothing else. This was the argument which always raged in the corridors of power at Mackintosh's: could married women be allowed to work? A casual bit of seasonal work in a lowly production line job was just about tolerable, but married women couldn't possibly be permitted to take the permanent place of a man who might need that job to provide for a family. The company had made an exception the previous year when they were rebuilding their factory after a catastrophic fire, but those had been exceptional circumstances and it had been all hands to the pump. Circumstances were different now; they were returning to normal and the marriage bar had to be reinstated. It didn't matter how talented the female worker, or how incompetent and unwilling the male who presented himself at the gate, jobs must be given to men at all opportunities.

Single women could continue to work, of course – they needed to support themselves without a husband – but they had a choice to make: keep the job which gave them joy, a feeling of belonging, and a tremendous sense of purpose with self-worth – or marry and start a family, and hope one day that they'd be allowed to return briefly during some seasonal rush, to wrap Easter eggs in tinfoil, or some other such triviality, far below their skill and dexterity, and smell the burnt sugar in the air again, and remember when they were seventeen and had felt like this could never end.

'Where's Doreen?' Reenie was hurrying around her toffee production line, fretting to get everything right. Doreen was a talented worker, but not the most reliable of her married ladies and Reenie was worried that Mrs Starbeck would find out and disapprove of Reenie's decision to keep her on. But what else could Reenie do? She was working such long hours at the factory that she thought she was seeing spots in front of her eyes; she certainly didn't have time to ask Doreen why she was so often late. 'Is she here?' Reenie asked the clutch of women she thought most likely to know. 'She's not late again, is she?'

Siobhan Grimshaw said something convincing about the other woman being out on an errand and Reenie nodded. 'Starchy Starbeck is coming to inspect this line today and I don't want her to have anything to complain about.'

Doreen Fairclough was late for her shift and, unbeknown to her, she had a small toy soldier caught in her hair. She had missed the earlier tram to the factory because she'd had to spend fifteen minutes crawling on her front among one and a half inch tin replicas of the 92nd Regiment of Foot. She had been trying to prise her eight-year-old out from under the bed, then, just as she had got him into his shoes and coat, she realised that his sister had vanished and had wriggled into the same hiding place as her brother in an attempt to avoid compulsory school attendance.

There was always some battle to be fought with those two and she decided that there wasn't time to demand that they tidy up the toy soldiers – that she'd managed not to scratch herself on any of them as she'd wriggled out from under the bed, was mercy enough.

All the way to work on the tram she'd caught people giving her funny looks and wondered if they knew she was late and were thinking ill of her. She hated being late and wished she was more like the other mothers whose homes ran like clockwork. Doreen dashed through the factory gates too quickly to see the watchman's raised eyebrow and when she reached the cloakroom the other women had already departed for the start of their shift. Doreen changed hurriedly into her overalls, all the while cursing herself for being one of *those* people to whom *things* were always happening. If the kids weren't hiding under the bed, then they were shaving the dog or eating a bee, and she was always late – and these things never happened to anyone else. Doreen hurriedly pulled her mobcap over her mousey hair that was lightly greying at the temples and sidled through the doors as unobtrusively as she could, entirely unaware that the painted tin leg of one of her son's Gordon Highlanders was sticking out from underneath the elastic of her white cotton cap.

'Where have you been?' Siobhan hissed to her friend as she made room for her at the starch-moulding rack where molten toffee was deposited from the copper boiling pans behind it. 'We've been up and running fifteen minutes already and Reenie Calder has been asking after you.'

'I couldn't get away in time for the tram,' Doreen said with evident remorse. 'I had to pull both kids out from under the bed to make them go to school.'

'And how long does that take?' Siobhan did not sound unkind, but she was exasperated by Doreen sometimes.

'What did Reenie say? Am I for it?'

'Just keep your head down and look busy. We've got an inspection from the Time and Motion manager today.'

Doreen looked more anxious than ever. Mrs Starbeck – who was, of course, not married, but was senior enough in the factory management to be given the honorific title 'Mrs', had a reputation for arbitrary perfectionism. She liked all her workers to be young, pretty, tastefully made-up, and to look as much like each other as possible. However, the production line Siobhan and Doreen worked on could never aspire to this level of symmetry; they were mothers and grandmothers who had about as much time to spend on their hair and make-up as they did on writing epic poems or learning classical ballet. Mrs Starbeck would always find them wanting, but this didn't stop young Reenie Calder from scurrying around the line in advance of a visit, helping her ladies to tuck loose strands of hair into their mobcaps, or straighten their overalls. It was on one of these rounds of inspection that Reenie Calder screamed, '*Spider!*'

Doreen froze. Reenie was looking directly at the back of her neck and she had an odd feeling that something had shifted underneath her mobcap at the same moment that Reenie had screamed.

'Doreen,' Reenie said, with slow, deliberate reassurance, 'you mustn't move. Stay completely still. It's a big one. I can see its leg just under the edge of your cap. Stay perfectly still and I'll swat it out with my hand.'

Doreen's neck and shoulders became rigid as her muscles tightened in fear; she hated spiders and they sometimes saw exotic species of spiders and other insects in the toffee factory, creatures which had travelled there from foreign climes in the sacks of imported cocoa beans and Brazil nuts. These insects usually all died out in the winter, but it was warm in the factory and this might be one of the bad ones. Doreen held her breath and she could see Reenie do the same thing as she raised her arm and swatted tentatively at the back of Doreen's mobcap.

'It bit me!' Reenie looked down at her fingers where a little drop of crimson blood was blooming on a tiny scratch.

There was a pause as they looked at one another in shock, then Doreen shrieked and began frantically flicking at her hair and shaking her head wildly while hopping from one foot to the other in panic. Then a chorus of shrieks rang out through the production hall as the tiny offender, exotically coloured and with multiple limbs, whizzed through the air and landed with a plop in one of the open vats of molten toffee which were about to be poured into starch moulds.

A hush descended on the workforce, a hush just low enough to allow them all to hear the squeak of a door as Starchy Starbeck entered to perform her inspection at the newly-created production line. She did not look happy.

Chapter Two

'We can have these sent on to your workroom, you know. Or your manager.' The freckled youth who manned the service hatch of Mackintosh's factory post room had long since grown tired of Mary Norcliffe's thrice-daily visits, and wasn't shy about showing it. He'd have forwarded her letters on to Timbuktu if it meant he didn't have to check for her blasted foreign letters three times a day.

'Thank you, no.' Mary was tight-lipped and determined. A pulse beat hard in her throat as it always did when she went to wait for word from Albert Baum.

'Happens my superintendent wants to know what's in these letters of yours.' And the freckle-faced youth called out into the office behind him, 'Mr Pinkstone! She's 'ere again!'

Mary's blood ran cold and she gave the lad at the service hatch an icy look. 'You don't need to know what's in my letters. It's confidential Mackintosh's factory business and I've got permission.'

Mr Pinkstone, a balding, snivelling sneak who spent his days griping about improperly wrapped parcels, sniffed his way over to the service hatch where Mary waited.

'What's all this?' He wrinkled up his nose as though the smell of caramel and sweet roasted almonds which wafted in from the factory corridor offended his finely tuned olfactory sense which could tolerate only the delicate aromas of gummed envelopes and brown paper. 'I need to know what's in all these letters. You get too many for company purposes, so they must be illicit.'

Mary noticed that the freckled youth was smirking in triumph and she clenched her teeth as she said, 'You know what's in my letters, sir; it's company correspondence. I've been coming here to collect it for the past ten months. My head of department is stranded in Düsseldorf and he sends me my instructions by daily airmail.' Mary's voice wavered as she thought of the last letter her manager had sent her. It had read, '*My darling Maria, I beg you not to think of propriety, but to write as often as you can. Your letters are the sunshine to my darkest of days.*' Mary's letters might have started as business correspondence, but if they were opened they wouldn't pass scrutiny now.

Mr Pinkstone sniffed. 'Stranded, is he? Stranded in his own country?'

'Herr Baum has been appointed as the Head Confectioner of this factory and as soon as the Home Office grant his work permit he will return. Until that time you'd do well to show his correspondence the same respect you'd show that of any other head of department.' Mary gulped down an angry sob. She was sick and tired of hearing people

14

talk about her Albert with derision because he was foreign, and Jewish, and powerless. He was the only person in the world who could make her worries melt away with a glance and he was worth ten of Mr Pinkstone.

'Well, it's my job to see to it that people don't abuse the system. It costs a lot to send letters abroad and I must safeguard company funds. I've left your letter with Mrs Starbeck at her request—'

'You've done what!' Mary's anxiety bubbled over into indignant rage and her voice was loud enough to startle some factory workers in the next corridor. 'You have no right. Those letters are addressed to me and to me alone.'

'Well, if you've got nothing to hide you won't mind a senior manager looking—'

'She's not even remotely my manager, she has no jurisdiction in my department!'

'Well, as long as your manager is away in his own country I must air my concerns to *someone* in a senior position.'

'Then talk to the employment Department; talk to Mrs Wilkes, or to her secretary Diana Moore.'

'Your *friend*, do you mean?' the freckled youth offered the unwelcome heckle with another triumphant smirk.

'Don't think I don't know that you only went to Starchy Starbeck because she's *your* friend. Don't think I don't know that you're all in the same nasty little club, with your uniforms and your political meetings. I know this isn't about postage, it's about Herr Baum being a Jew and you being one of Oswald Mosley's stinking lot. You're fooling no one!' Mary was crying with rage now and she didn't care who saw her. She stormed down the factory corridor towards the workroom where she knew she would find her friend Reenie. Only Reenie could help her now, because Mary knew, without having read it, what would be in that most recent letter which was with Mrs Starbeck – and it wasn't Mackintosh's company business.

Chapter Three

'All these notices can come down.' Cynthia Starbeck waved a hand in the direction of a staff noticeboard where the factory medical department had put up posters warning workers to be vigilant against seasonal outbreaks of influenza. 'It only encourages girls to make a meal of things if they're under the weather. Nine times out of ten it's a common cold; and if they're weak enough to catch *real* influenza, they weren't constitutionally fit to work here in the first place.' Starbeck looked to her assistant who was nodding vigorously, but doing nothing. 'Well, take them down, Dunkley; don't just look at them.'

Verity Dunkley, who preferred to be known as Dolly and was constitutionally averse to work of any kind, looked in surprise at her manager. 'You want *me* to take them down?'

'Yes, you; take down any nonsense about influenza. These noticeboards are for advertising the Time and

Motion Department's piece rates, not medical scaremongering from Nurse Munton. She's got her own noticeboard outside the factory sick bay, that's enough for her. I'm not having her taking over all of mine.'

Dolly looked mortified at the thought of having to undertake any task more strenuous than agreeing slavishly with her manager and moved to take down the notices, pin by painstaking pin.

Mrs Starbeck was evidently not impressed by her assistant's snail-like progress. 'Come along, quicker than that, stop dawdling. Take down the rest from the corridor and take them to my office. Quick about it, Dunkley, come on now.'

Young Dolly Dunkley, her face screwed up into a scowl, stomped out of the factory workroom, more like a thirteen-year-old sulking at their mother than a twenty-year-old who owed their promotion from the factory floor to Mrs Starbeck.

Cynthia Starbeck pulled back her shoulders, pulled straight the cuffs of her cream satin blouse, and surveyed the workroom. The workroom was much quieter than usual and something was clearly amiss. She knew they were expecting her for a scheduled inspection of the new production line, but this was not the hush of expectation. The rows of women who wrapped sweets from dawn until dusk were whispering to each other, while the conveyor which brought them naked, glistening sweets was silent and still.

The line had clearly been shut down and Mrs Starbeck could see a commotion in the far corner of the hall where a gaggle of staff were anxiously pouring out a whole copper boiling pan of toffee with exaggerated slowness. This was just the kind of time-wasting inefficiency she was there to stamp out.

'What is happening here?' Cynthia Starbeck's tone was bright as pear drops and her almond-shaped eyes crinkled at the corners in a smile that was almost maternal. It was a manner which fooled plenty of people who hadn't encountered her before, but the women on the experimental toffee line were not so green; they held their breaths.

'We're looking for a spider, Mrs Starbeck,' Reenie said, careful not to suggest the involvement of any other colleague by name, although Doreen Fairclough and Siobhan Grimshaw were clearly implicated by their proximity.

'A spider?' Mrs Starbeck's smile was still fixed in place, but its warmth dropped by a degree or two. 'And what would a spider be doing in a twenty-four gallon copper boiling pan of molten hot toffee?'

Reenie cleared her throat. 'It flew in, Mrs Starbeck.'

'It flew in? Do spiders usually fly? Would you think me unreasonable if I said that I suspect you left a window open – contrary to factory regulations – and allowed a bluebottle to contaminate the toffee and are even now attempting to conceal your misdeed with a false tale about a spider?'

'No, really, Mrs Starbeck,' Doreen implored, 'there was a spider. It bit Reenie and made her finger bleed. It had crawled up my neck and got onto my hair and she tried to swat it off. If it hadn't been for Reenie it might have poisoned me.'

Siobhan nodded earnestly, with the plausibility of a thirty-something mother of four; this was not the nonsense of young girls, it was the serious claim of grown women. 'I saw it too. It was a big bugger, and colourful. It moved too fast for me to get a good look at it, but you could see that it was something tropical. We thought perhaps it was one of those foreign ones come in on the crates of Brazil nuts for Quality Street.'

Mrs Starbeck's attitude abruptly changed. The appearance of tropical pests was not unknown at the factory and they had a strict code in the circumstances. 'Have you sent for the factory pest controller?'

'Not yet.' Reenie still looked half afraid of the senior manager. 'We thought we'd get it out of the toffee first so we've got something to show them. For identification, like.'

'Well, I doubt it will be in a recognisable state after it's been boiled in sugar. Reenie, go and use the telephone to summon the pest controller immediately.' Mrs Starbeck nodded to the man who had been holding back the last of the molten toffee and he resumed the task of lowering the edge of the copper pan in its frame, and gently pouring a thin ribbon of caramel into a one-gallon tin tray waiting below. The tin tray filled, the man pulled back the edge of the pan, replaced the tray with another empty one, and began again. The women waited and watched in anticipation for what could only be an unpleasant sight among the dregs of the sugar solution – the spider would surely be in pieces – but the tin tray was replaced again, and then again once more, and still there was no sign of the broken body of the dreaded tropical spider.

Reenie ran back across the workroom to where the copper was almost empty and said, 'The pest controller is on his way as fast as he can; he's bringing a couple of men from the laboratory to analyse it – see if it's poisonous – and a nurse from the sick bay to see to our bites.'

Mrs Starbeck frowned into the pan. 'This is turning into a very expensive enterprise for the company, but I'll grant it's necessary given the foreign intruder.'

Another tin vessel of molten toffee was drawn away and the women edged closer to see what would be revealed in the last dregs of sugar.

It was a leg that appeared first, sticky and brown with toffee, but straight as that of any soldier in the British Army. Then an elbow appeared. Finally the torso of a tiny child's toy emerged in one piece from the tide of toffee and, poured over the lip of the pan, landed in the waiting tray with a plop.

Mrs Starbeck took in an angry breath through flared nostrils. She reached over to a nearby workbench, seized a pair of steel tongs and plunged them into the one-gallon tray of toffee. It was only a moment before the tongs re-emerged, grasping the offending article. Mrs Starbeck squinted at it in disgust, before turning her beady eyes on Doreen Fairclough, who had so ill-advisedly admitted that the tropical spider had been flicked from her hair.

'Is *this* a tropical spider?' Cynthia Starbeck hissed in a deliberate whisper.

'No, Mrs Starbeck.'

'What is it?'

Doreen did her best to meet the manager's eye, but it was not easy, 'It's a Gordon Highlander of the 92nd Regiment of Foot, Mrs Starbeck.'

'And why is it in a factory workroom?'

'I-I think it must have got caught in my hair when I was crawling under the bed, Mrs Starbeck.'

Mrs Starbeck's lips curled in contempt. As she launched into a merciless dressing-down of the assembled factory staff, she failed to notice that Mary Norcliffe had appeared at the door and almost as quickly vanished again in the direction of Mrs Starbeck's empty, unguarded office.

Chapter Four

Diana Moore was watching the clock on the office wall and she could have sworn its hands had gone backwards. She was not usually one for clock-watching, but on this occasion she had good reason. She needed to leave the office exactly on time if she was going to be able to fit in a bath and a change of clothes at her boarding house before she went on to the charity dinner she'd been roped into.

Diana had never thought she would be the sort of girl to attend posh charity functions, or to sit at a smart desk in an important office, or to worry about 'dressing for dinner', but as life had taught her, people will do all kinds of things for love. In Diana's case it was love for the seven-year-old everyone believed was her sister.

Diana usually rattled off her work at a fair speed, but that afternoon had been something of a blitz. She had dealt with all the factory memoranda from her in-tray (mostly other departments boasting about their own achievements and easily ignored); typed up all of her managers' meeting minutes (even the ones she hadn't been permitted to attend because the discussions were too secret for secretaries – who did these managers think typed up their secret minutes?), and delivered her correspondence to the factory post room by hand (so that Mr Pinkstone couldn't claim it had arrived too late for the last collection). The plants were watered, the inkwells emptied and cleaned, the pencils sharpened and their shavings binned. It was five minutes until close of business on Friday afternoon and, if nothing else landed on her plate, she would be able to clock out her timecard and make a dash for it. For once there was no great crisis engulfing the toffee business and she was not required to find thieves, poisoners, or miracle workers in order to save the business from collapse, so she was reasonably confident that she would be leaving on time. The clock ticked the passage of another minute away, and Diana heard the heavy rumble of running feet in the plushly carpeted hallway outside her door.

'I'm in a lot of trouble!' Mary was out of breath and she slammed Diana's office door behind her with the caution of someone who feared they were being pursued.

Diana did not lift her gaze from the clock on the wall. She did not move in her seat, she did not register surprise, she did not so much as raise an eyebrow. She simply sighed. She was used to Mary. 'What is it this time?'

'I've just stolen something from Mrs Starbeck's office and she's going to know it was me.'

Diana's head snapped up and she looked at her friend with undisguised astonishment and more than a little admiration. This was not like Mary Norcliffe. Her sister

Bess, perhaps; their friend Reenie Calder almost certainly, but not Mary. Mary feared rule-breaking the way that witches were meant to fear water. Diana pushed her chair back from her desk, rose without undue haste, and moved to drag a chair over for her visitor to sit on. Diana's office was more of an ante-chamber to the office of her head of department, but it was better than any other 27-year-old factory girl at Mackintosh's could boast. There was a fat iron radiator which belted out heat behind her; a frosted glass chandelier providing steady electric light above her; and a portrait of the late John Mackintosh – the Toffee King – before her on the wall to provide the only company she needed while she worked. Diana liked this new, quieter working day. She wasn't entirely solitary – there were meetings to attend and dictation to take – but after a decade on the factory floor, wrapping sweets with scores of rowdy – and frequently melodramatic – girls, she was glad of the change.

Mary had been one such of those melodramatic girls with whom Diana had wrapped toffees. So too her sister Bess and their friend Reenie. Diana offered Mary the seat in front of her; Mary took it for a moment but then sprang up again as though the seat was on fire and only pacing the room would put it out.

'Out with it, then. What is it you've taken?' The telephone rang on Diana's desk with a shrill chirrup, startling Mary and irritating Diana; she disliked the rude intrusion of the telephone into her otherwise quiet office. It rang out once and then stopped as abruptly as it had started; perhaps the person at the other end of the line had lost the courage they had briefly raised to telephone Mrs Wilkes's notorious secretary. Diana shrugged and returned her attention to Mary. 'Be quick, I haven't got all day.'

Mary held up a letter, but didn't offer it to Diana. 'It's from Herr Baum. I went to collect it, but the post room said that Mrs Starbeck was going to check my post to make sure my mail from him is legitimate company business. I went to talk to Reenie, but when I got there she was tearing a strip off some lady toffee wrapper because she'd dropped a toy soldier in a vat of Harrogate Toffee—'

'What, Reenie?'

'No, Mrs Starbeck. She was on Reenie's line, throwing her weight around. So I knew she wasn't in her office and . . .' Mary swallowed hard. 'I went straight there, looked through all the letters on her desk until I found mine, and then I took it back. I came straight here after that.'

Diana glanced at the clock. Why was nothing involving Cynthia Starbeck ever simple? 'Did anyone see you?'

'I passed Dolly Dunkley in the corridor, but no one saw me in Mrs Starbeck's office.'

Diana considered a moment and then said, 'Although I don't like her interfering in the work of every department in the factory, I think it would be wise on this occasion to put the letter back before she notices so you can't be charged with the serious offence of stealing.'

'No, I won't let her see it!'

'I know it's galling, but I can speak to Mrs Wilkes first thing on Monday and she can take her to task for you. She'll make sure it never happens again. In the meantime, you've got nothing to hide, have you?'

Mary said nothing, but her expression said everything.

Diana supposed she ought to have predicted something like this would happen. She didn't ask what was in the letters and she dreaded to think. The only matter of importance to Diana at that moment was to postpone this problem so that she could leave the office on time.

'All right, then, take the letter out of its envelope and give the envelope to me. I'll tell Mrs Starbeck that it was delivered to this office and that she must have bundled it in with her memorandums to me by mistake. I'll say that I opened it, but I won't tell her this until Monday. That gives you a full weekend to either forge a run-of-the-mill letter in Herr Baum's hand, or find an earlier letter from him which would pass for our purposes. Either way, you need to bring me a letter to show her first thing on Monday morning which shows that you have nothing to hide and that she was wrong to suspect you of unprofessional conduct, and so she had no good reason to intercept your post; do you think you can do that?'

Mary nodded.

'Good.' Diana rose and picked up her coat from the stand by the door. 'Come straight here on Monday morning – and for God's sake don't get caught again. Now, if you'll excuse me, I have a dinner engagement.' She slung a new leather satchel over her shoulder and opened the door for Mary and herself before another thought occurred to her. 'Oh, and write to Herr Baum as soon as you can and warn him that his letters are not private if he sends them to the factory; if you must carry on with him, have him write to your home.'

But there were to be no more letters from Herr Baum. Diana could not have predicted that Mary was holding the last one . . .

Chapter Five

Cynthia Starbeck despised her assistant Dolly Dunkley – and Dolly Dunkley hated her manager Cynthia Starbeck. They made one another's lives unpleasant day after day, word after word, and only their mutual dependence prevented them breaking into open hostility.

Dolly had applied for a position in Mrs Starbeck's department at a time when a trained Shetland pony would have been given a job at Mack's if it could hold a broom and follow an order, but at any other time in the firm's history Dolly would not have made the grade. Coincidentally, Dolly had joined the British Union at the same time, just when their numbers had been dwindling and they were glad of any recruit and Cynthia Starbeck's great passion in life was the cause of Oswald Mosley's British Union of Fascists and National Socialists; this had been part of the reason she had taken Dolly under her wing. But the factory no longer had a shortage of staff and the British Union's membership had doubled in a year. In its swell of popularity, people like Dolly were becoming an embarrassment and Mrs Starbeck wished she could get rid of her somehow.

'Dunkley, why are there still posters about influenza on the walls outside my office?' Mrs Starbeck's sweet, sugary tones were slightly impeded by the fact that she was clenching her teeth.

'They're not on the *walls*. They're just on one wall.' Dolly appeared to think that this was a get-out-of-jail-free card and she pressed on. 'I took them down from the side of the wall I was walking past. You didn't say you wanted me to walk down *both* sides of the corridor.' Dolly whined as easily as she breathed, perhaps a little more easily because a congenital nasal obstruction tended to give her something of a waking snore.

If Mrs Starbeck hadn't had Reenie Calder in tow she might have given Dolly a sound ticking off, but as it was she merely said, 'Go and take the rest of them down and bring them here.'

'Why can't Reenie do it?' It was the same old complaint; Dolly was from a good grammar school, had obtained the Higher School Certificate, and felt personally cheated that someone of a lower social status should be allowed to achieve advancement in the factory through a combination of hard work, innate gifting, and heroism in the face of blazing danger as Irene Calder had. Dolly knew what trigonometry was and could recite chunks of things which she didn't understand in ancient Greek which meant, in her mind, that *she* should be in charge. Mrs Starbeck knew that, once in charge, Dolly would be just as ungrateful, but Dolly was greedy and she wanted everything she saw, whether she could make use of it or not.

Mrs Starbeck gave her a steely look. 'It is not your place to question your manager, Dunkley.' She watched Dolly stomp out of the office, and then directed Reenie to sit while she removed the white coat and mobcap she always wore when she visited the factory floor, revealing the neat, glossy rope of golden plaits which were twisted tightly round the crown of her head like a halo.

Mrs Starbeck's office in the Time and Motion Department was spartan. She didn't permit work spaces to become cluttered with evidence of the daily grind, personal mementoes, distracting family photographs, or rogue plants. Perhaps, deep down, she was trying not to settle in the Halifax factory; she wanted to return to her émigré's life in Düsseldorf where she had enjoyed a lively social calendar and an unprecedented amount of power over the day-to-day running of the factory. She would go back to her friends and her fascism in Germany if it weren't for the cost. Financial constraints now meant that her departmental manager position in the factory was a necessity rather than a hobby. Little reminders of her old life remained: a notebook cover bound in Austrian calf skin and monogrammed in gold; a box of new pencils wrapped in marbled paper that she'd picked up on her way through Florence last spring; a letter opener with the insignia of the British Union of Fascists emblazoned on the bone handle – a gift from a Greek admirer. Yes, there was a good life to return to on the continent as soon as she'd settled her affairs in Halifax once and for all.

'I'm shutting down your so-called "experimental" line' Mrs Starbeck said once she had made herself comfortable in her own seat of power. 'Allowing a foreign body to contaminate raw product is unacceptable.'

'Oh no, please don't do that, Mrs Starbeck! My ladies really do work so hard and they have done such a good job setting up a whole new line from scratch and getting it running without any fuss at all.'

'I hardly call stopping production on an entire line while you cry wolf about a dangerous tropical spider to be an absence of fuss.'

'Please don't blame them for that – it was my fault. I was the one who said I thought it was a spider and they weren't to know. I was tired and I couldn't see properly, and I mistook the leg of the tin soldier for—'

'I don't have time for this, Irene. You have not only wasted my time today, but also that of the factory pest controller, the factory laboratory, and the Mackintosh's nurse. Not to mention the time lost by shutting down the line while you drained an entire vat of toffee, which now has to be incinerated as unfit for consumption. You leave me no choice but to shut down—'

'But what about Mr Johns?' Reenie blurted out the question against her better judgement, and cringed at her superior's reaction.

Cynthia Starbeck was frosty. 'What about Mr Johns?'

'Well . . .' Reenie hesitated as she embarked on a dubious course of action. 'I just thought that if he's still acting head of our department, then . . . because shutting the line down would mean putting so many ladies out of work and losing us so much production time . . . he'd have to be notified and give due consideration . . .' Reenie looked as though she were trying to suck all of her words back into her lungs and expunge the horrible echo of the veiled threat she had just made against Cynthia Starbeck, a manager far more senior than herself.

'Give due consideration? And what do you think a disciplinary panel would decide if they had the opportunity to give due consideration to your histrionics over an imagined spider? I do hope you appreciate that I am treating you very leniently by not taking this to a disciplinary hearing?' Mrs Starbeck waited for a reply and then prompted, 'Well, do you?'

'Yes, Mrs Starbeck. I'm sorry, Mrs Starbeck. I only wanted to save the jobs of my ladies.'

'Yes, well, I suppose if they're good workers I might be able to use some of them. I will agree not to take the foreign body incident to a disciplinary on the condition that you don't make any trouble while I take over the running of the experimental line myself. As a particular kindness to the women on your former line I will give them a one-week trial to see if they can work according to my methods.' Cynthia Starbeck waited a moment while Reenie looked at her like a rabbit caught in headlights and, once she was confident that the girl was not going to mount any challenge, she ushered her out. This was how Cynthia Starbeck annexed new territory in the power game she played at Mackintosh's Celebrated Toffee Factory.

Chapter Six

Kathleen Calder wanted to be the first woman to sit in the House of Lords. The fact that she was thirteen years old, still shared a bed with her sister Reenie, and lived on a sheep farm in rural West Yorkshire, were merely temporary obstacles to her plan to reach the elevated status of the highest in the land. So too the fact that a woman had never been allowed to sit in the second chamber; there were women in the House of Commons as Members of Parliament, which meant – as far as Kathleen was concerned – it was only a matter of time before a woman of wealth and ambition bought herself a peerage and got the rules changed.

Kathleen Calder was one of those strange combinations of vaulting ambition mixed with pragmatic fatalism. Where her older sister Reenie would invest great energy into forcing an outcome, Kathleen was ready to watch, anticipate, and play the long game.

Kathleen's plan centred around her starting a successful

business empire and becoming High Sheriff of Yorkshire. To the sister of Reenie Calder this did not seem such a stretch in the twentieth century; after all, Violet Mackintosh had started her own business selling toffees on a Saturday in Halifax and now her family were rich as Rockefeller and her eldest son had received a knighthood in 1922 and had become a baronet in 1935. Their business was worth making a particular study of as far as Kathleen was concerned and the most obvious way to study them would be to get a job at Mack's, but here were her first two major obstacles: they didn't take girls under fourteen and her sister Reenie – who already worked there – had explicitly told her she didn't want her getting a job at *her* factory.

Reenie, however, hadn't reckoned on Kathleen finding a loophole, and on Friday after school Kathleen went to assess its potential.

'Excuse me, Mr Hebblewhite?' Kathleen assumed her most Shirley Temple-esque expression of polite and well-meaning innocence. 'I've found some litter outside your shop and I was just wondering if you'd allow me to put it in your wastepaper bucket. I do *so* like to try to leave places looking better than I found them.'

Kathleen had chosen her mark carefully; Mr Hebblewhite not only ran the only Mackintosh's misshapes shop in town, but he was also vain about his shop premises. Any young person who showed an enthusiasm for the shabby little place under the bridge, and the presentability thereof, was likely to do well with the old man.

'Yes, well,' Mr Hebblewhite sniffed with a resentment which concealed a weight of pride, 'quite right too. Young people these days, they come round here on a Saturday and mob me like gannets, then leave the place looking like a bomb's hit it.' Mr Hebblewhite shuffled his hunched old shoulders around the cramped shop counter in search of a wastepaper bucket, and when he returned – proffering it with long, arthritic fingers – he was waving it in the direction of the door to demonstrate that he expected Kathleen to extend her Good Samaritan work even further and go back outside to pick up even more of the litter which had gathered around the shop under the bridge.

The bridge was no mean lean-to; it was a mighty iron construction the Victorians had put up. It had statuary, supporting towers in carved stone, streetlamps and gaudy paint. It crossed the river and the railway line in grand style and it left one tiny surviving relic of the old days and the old bridge nestling beneath its east span: Hebblewhite's Newsagent, Tobacconist, and Fancy Confectioner. As far as Kathleen could tell, the refuse of the entire town had blown down from the bridge and gathered at the feet of the old man's shop and he hadn't lifted a finger to sweep it away for weeks. Kathleen was not keen on picking up other people's rubbish as a rule, but if this was her way to secure a job – and a job which got her one step closer to Mackintosh's – then she'd willingly push a broom.

'They've left it in a terrible mess this time, Mr Hebblewhite. Would you like some help clearing it all up?'

'There's no free sweets in it for you, if that's what you're thinking!'

'Oh no, Mr Hebblewhite, I just offered to be public-spirited. I've not much of a sweet tooth; I'm bookish.'

The fact that the two didn't need to be mutually exclusive did not come up.

'Hmm . . .' Ropey old Mr Hebblewhite growled as he thought aloud. 'More youngsters ought to show an appreciation of local landmarks like this one. Oldest building in town, this is. Older even than the Oak Room.'

Kathleen knew her local lore; she'd even been to the Halifax library at Belle Vue to do an extra bit of reading on it in readiness to impress the shopkeeper if she got the chance. There had been a bridge over that part of the River Hebble since the last years of King Edward I, that miserable, warmongering, Hammer of the Scots. In those dim and distant days of Edward Longshanks the town had been little more than a cluster of huts around a brook, but they'd had a wooden bridge all the same, and it must have been well-used because it was eventually rebuilt in good Yorkshire stone.

'You're too right, Mr Hebblewhite.' Kathleen gathered up handfuls of old paper bags and discarded bus tickets to stuff into the bucket which waited. 'I heard tell your shop used to be a chapel, back in the time of the Wars of the Roses, like?'

'That one fell down.' Mr Hebblewhite pulled his ratty brown woollen shawl a little closer in at his throat and turned to go back into the shop, his bucket now full. 'This one were built in 1490 with roof beams as could last till doomsday; just look at those roof beams. Solid elm, they are.'

From her reading in the library Kathleen had gathered that, in the age of knights and damsels, it was common to see little chapels at the end of bridges. They weren't true churches with Sunday services and a regular congregation who'd be hatched, matched, and dispatched under the auspices of one priest; they were just little shrines where folks who'd travelled a long and dangerous journey to get to a town could stop and give thanks that they'd reached safety. Now that same little chapel had lost what symbols of religion it might once have borne and was papered from floor to ceiling with advertisements for Rowntree's Clear Gums, Dairy Box chocolates, and Mackintosh's Toffee Deluxe.

'I'm very interested in the history of your premises, Mr Hebblewhite.' Kathleen hoped this sounded plausible; her entire plan hinged on him believing that she was a budding antiquarian. 'I should be most grateful if you'd be good enough to tell me about them.'

The old man made a show of reluctance, but talked at length while Kathleen got a good look at this shop which was once a chapel. The chantry – so this type of chapel was called – at the end of a bridge was a small place; it only needed to be large enough to hold a handful of travellers for a short mass, then the rest of the time a monk would rattle around it on his own, offering up prayers for the safety of all those who might be coming to, or going from his little chapel. The old chantry had survived not only the Wars of the Roses, but also the ravages of West Yorkshire weather. Even those loyal subjects of King Henry VIII, who went about tearing down so many examples of piety, didn't touch it either; they ignored it and let the locals use it as a warehouse and then as the local gaol. After changing hands too many times to follow, it became a little grocer's shop, and then metamorphosed like a butterfly from a grub into the solidly successful sweetshop Mr Hebblewhite thought of as his home away from home. Its success was down to one thing, and one thing alone: it was the only store in town which sold the cheap misshapes of Mackintosh's toffees.

It seemed peculiarly fitting that the goods which were surplus to requirements at Mackintosh's should be sold from a building which had itself always been surplus to requirements – chapel, gaol, warehouse, shop. Like the broken confections it sold, the shop had a gnarled and bobbly appearance. What had once been gargoyles and decorative flourishes carved into the outside walls were now weathered to lumpy outcrops of sandstone, worn down by wind and rain to stumps like lollipops. Yes, Kathleen Calder thought she could make something of the old place.

'You know, I think it's a terrible shame that this history isn't written down somewhere, Mr Hebblewhite. You know so much, but will it all be lost to the next genera- tion? I'd consider it an honour to come and work here on my Saturdays and keep the place tidy if you would tell me all you know and let me write an account of it to put into the public library.'

Mr Hebblewhite lifted his chin the better to ponder her request. It was true he did know a great deal about the history of the building – who knew it better? – and it was only right that a young person should take an interest in it. But 'Aren't you a bit on the young side for a job?' he asked.

'Just means I'd cost you less, Mr Hebblewhite. And I know all these young kids by name, so I could threaten to tell their mothers on them if they got too rowdy on a Saturday.'

'How much less is less?'

'Five shillings a week.'

'For one day's work? Highway robbery!' He sniffed. 'I'll gi' you three shillings.'

They shook on it. Kathleen could now move on to the next stage in her plan.

Chapter Seven

'We're not going to the pictures tonight, then?' Peter might not have meant it to sound like a recrimination, but the fact that he'd been sitting on a bale of hay in the chill and the semi-darkness of the old factory stable waiting for Reenie – and she was much later than they had agreed – made her feel a pang of guilt.

'I'm sorry.' Reenie moved quickly to untie her horse, Ruffian, and ready him for the ride home to her parents' farm. 'We had an accident on the experimental line, and—'

Peter leapt up from his makeshift seat in a panic. 'What sort of accident? Are you all right? What happened?'

Reenie, worked up from her confrontation with Mrs Starbeck, began to cry in exasperation and disappointment.

'Are you hurt, Reenie?' Peter cupped her face in his palms and anxiously looked for any sign of injury. 'What happened?'

'No, no, I'm all right, really; it wasn't that sort of

accident.' Reenie sniffed and buried her face in Peter's shoulder, hugging him to her. She was so very tired and she felt that she had got everything wrong all over again. 'Something got into one of the toffee vats by accident. It was nothing, really. I had it all in hand, but then Mrs Starbeck turned up and it became this big palaver, then she threatened to close down my experimental line and then she said she was taking it off me.'

'She can't do that.' Peter sounded certain. 'It was a company director told you that you could do it. She can't go against a director.'

'But where are the directors now? They're all down in Norwich in their fancy new offices and they never come here any more. Major Fergusson's not going to be back any time soon, his replacement still isn't here, and no one knows who's in charge. Sometimes Diana's manager pulls rank on Mrs Starbeck, and sometimes she doesn't; it's all such a mess.'

'Well,' Peter huffed in thought, 'there's always Mr Johns; we could go to him. He's *technically* her manager – I think . . .'

'Yes, but where is he? No one's seen him at the factory for a fortnight and I've sent letters to the Norwich factory and had no reply.' Reenie rested her cheek on Peter's lapel, listening to his heart beating strong and steady, taking comfort in his warmth. He smelled of roasted hazelnuts and creamy caramel. 'What are we going to do, Peter? Where are all the grown-ups?'

'I was thinking the same thing. But it's Friday night and there's nothing you or I can do until Monday.'

'I'm sorry I made us late for the cinema. I know you wanted to see the newsreel of the rugby.'

'I shouldn't worry about that. I saw the results in the paper the other day.' Peter made light of it, but Reenie knew that he'd been dying to see the highlights. It was an international match and reading about it in the paper was very different to seeing five whole minutes of moving footage in cinematic black-and-white, bold as day.

There was another reason Reenie had wanted to go to the cinema; privately, she was very conscious that whenever they had a chance to do something romantic together it was she who got in the way of their plans. They spent plenty of time together – they worked in the same department, Peter went to Sunday dinner at Reenie's parents' farm, and they visited their old manager Major Fergusson in the cottage hospital together. But these weren't the routines of a courting couple and Reenie felt a little relieved every time she avoided one of these close, intimate evenings, and then guilty that she was a little relieved. She told herself that she didn't need to think about what it meant – they were only young and there was plenty of time to dwell on it later, when they were older. For now, she told herself that she didn't really like the cinema because Pathé always showed so many things on their newsreels which worried her: they showed the destruction of the war in Spain which Peter had very nearly run away to fight in; they showed millions of gas masks being made in London in case Britain went to war and they found themselves cowering under gas attacks; they showed Oswald Mosley strutting around talking as though he'd be the dictator in Britain soon enough, just like they had dictators in Italy and Greece and Germany and Spain and Romania. Worst of all, people acted as though none of this was really anything to worry about, as if the sky wasn't falling in.

'There was one good thing happened today, though.' Peter gave Reenie a hopeful smile.

'Really, what was that?'

'I got your friend Bess a job in the factory canteen and she didn't burn it down, flood it, or fall in love with the porter. That's a factory first for her. I don't think there's a department she's worked in yet that hasn't had to take out extra insurance to indemnify them against "Acts of Bess".'

Reenie laughed and wiped at her tears with her handkerchief. 'I'm so glad you didn't go to Spain, Peter.'

'I don't know if I'm glad or not. Maybe if I'd gone with my cousins and helped them at the port they'd have arrived without a hitch. Maybe we'd all be there doing some good.'

Reenie couldn't help but think of the newsreels they'd seen of shattered towns and cities all over Spain and hated the thought of Peter caught in all that hopeless chaos. 'It's not your fault they were arrested. They knew the law when they set off, knew they were taking a risk, and you don't know that you'd have made any difference. I think we've got enough to fight here.'

Reenie had no idea how much.

Chapter Eight

Mary returned home to the little one-up one-down back-to-back house she shared with her mother and sister Bess. She was angry at the thought that Mrs Starbeck should be allowed to poke her nose into her correspondence at all, let alone that she should have to provide her with a suitably businesslike letter from among the stash of correspondence she had saved. It was galling, and a sign of just how chaotic the factory had become that there was so rarely anyone there to stand up to Mrs Starbeck when she began interfering in departments outside her own. However, Mary hoped there might be an early letter from Albert which she could give to Diana and pretend was recent, but she knew in her heart that there were very few, if any, which solely mentioned work.

Mary sat beside the stove in the parlour, waiting for the flames which licked the coal to fully catch and make them glow so that she could boil water and make the tea. Now that she was alone and wouldn't be over-looked, she took Albert's most recent letter from her pocket, unfolded the sheets of neatly-written Germanic script and read them for the first time.

My Dearest, My Darling, My Maria,

I sat up until dawn rereading your letters. Your words were so like your voice that I could almost have imagined you were here beside me. The morning took me by surprise because when I am thinking of you it is as though no time has passed at all. If only all people in Germany were loved as dearly as I know I am by you, there would be no more anger here.

Maximilian and Greta ask to be remembered to you. They do not go to their schooling any more, but they are content to read at home with my sister and ask every day when they will come to England to meet you. They have drawn more pictures for you, and Greta has changed her mind again about which doll she will bring when we leave here. Maximilian remains faithful to his fireman's helmet. Their bags have been packed for months in readiness to leave, but still no word comes. The waiting is unbearable.

Our neighbours are still missing and there is no news of them. It is now six weeks since they were arrested, and we still do not know why. It is awful that this is normal here now.

I must keep reminding myself I am one of the lucky ones; I have not been barred from working. If I had worked in the civil service or one of the

*professions we would be destitute by now. There
are so many learned professors turned out of
work. The factory, however, it is permitted. I work
still, and we keep our apartment. I am not
permitted to work in the confectioners kitchen any
longer, but Mackintosh's keep me in the technical
library at the factory and I make a useful
researcher for my old colleagues.*

*I count myself lucky because I have work, I have
a home, I have my sister to care for the children,
and I have hope. I have the hope that soon we
will all of us leave for a new life in England. I
count myself lucky because I know that you are
waiting for me there.*

*And so now I come to the good news which
I had saved until last: by the time you read this I
will be on my way to you. I have watched for
morning because I know that I leave at first light.
I have a short permit from the Home Office to
allow me to come to Halifax and sign a lease on a
house and complete preparations for our arrival.
Laurence Johns has made arrangements, but I
will explain them all when I see you again, and
I will see you very soon.*

You are all my thoughts and more . . .

Mary choked back tears. After all the anger and injustice she'd felt that day, this was the most wonderful news
she could have imagined. They had been apart for so
many months and although this was only a temporary
permit, it was hope. It made her want to read his letters
again and again until morning and cry with relief because

she couldn't believe she would finally be able to see his face again.

Mary climbed the small, narrow flight of stairs to the bedroom she shared with her sister and was so lost in her excitement and her thoughts and her letter that she almost didn't notice Bess sitting on the edge of their bed. Then her brain deciphered what her eyes were seeing, and she gasped.

'You're going to spill that all over the floor if you're not careful!' Mary said sharply, frowning at her sister's precarious arrangement of books piled up on their lumpy bed and topped with a water basin.

'I'm propping up the basin so that I can read my colour magazines while I'm washing my hair.' Bess was clearly about to soak their bed in violet-scented water, but foreseeing the consequences of her actions had never been one of her strong points.

'Why don't you leave it until I can wash it for you? You know you always get the Amami powder in your eyes.' Ordinarily Mary would have forcibly intervened in this clearly doomed enterprise, but she was intent on her own occupation. Under the loose floorboard on her side of their creaky bed was her secret hoard of Albert's letters. She took out one at random.

One day I shall take you to see the place where my grandmother taught me to sail. There are lakes here which would take away your breath. I remember thinking, as a boy, that there could be nothing so beautiful in all the world as the lake where my grandmother lived, but then, as a boy, I had not seen you.

At first – when there were only one or two letters – she had kept them with her in her pockets all the time, but within a matter of weeks the volume of correspondence had become so large that she needed to select which of the precious epistles she would leave at home and which she would carry closest to her heart.

If I live to be one hundred and nine, and you to one hundred and one, we will look back on this short time apart and wonder why it troubled us so. But I am not yet one hundred and nine, and you are not one hundred and one, and I am troubled, Maria. You are so far away and I feel the distance like a knife.

The bundles of soft blue envelopes which Mary had amassed since June were as perplexing to Mary as they were precious. When her manager, Mr Albert Baum, Mackintosh's Head Confectioner, had left his post at the start of the summer he had told her that he would try to come back, that he would try to return for her; however, he hadn't said why. At first Mary had spent a great deal of time turning that moment over in her mind and chastising herself for speculating that Albert Baum's motives might have been anything more than professional.

When we are together at last will you promise to write me letters each day still? When we are apart I miss you, but when I have you with me always I think I shall miss your letters.

He had taken his leave of her at the last possible moment before he left for his old life in Düsseldorf and, at the time, she had assumed that this was because she was the last on his list of priorities, not because he wanted to hang on to her until the last possible moment . . .

I think of you without ceasing. I think of the work
we will embark on together, I think of the things
I will invent and name in your honour, I think of
the places we will go and the things we will see.
I think of the great partnership we will forge,
unstoppable and unmatched in the whole history
of sweet makers. We will make a sweet pair, you
and I.

It wasn't easy; he was a German Jew who wanted to move to England with two small children and his sister in tow and the Home Office were not well disposed to allowing foreigners into the country at all, but for some years they had shown a particular mistrust of Jewish immigrants, particularly Jewish immigrants like Albert who had a tenuous claim on Polish citizenship through a grandparent. The suggestion was always the same: 'Go back to Poland', even if he had never seen Poland, and never known the grandfather who hailed from there.

The British government had allowed Albert Baum onto their shores on a three-month work permit, but if he wanted to return with his family he needed to apply again in Germany and that was where he now resided, writing to Mary from the Mackintosh's Düsseldorf toffee factory. Mary's letters by return were all passion and fury, for she was anxious for his safety and that of his little family and she was enraged by the way he was treated in his own country, was frustrated to the point of tears by the Home Office in England who sent back application after application, with never a reason why. Albert told her that he loved her for it; he had never known anyone care so much as she did. *I care too much,* she had told him, *everyone says so.* And he had replied, *Not me.*

Mary was lost in her pile of letters when the wave of violet-scented water hit the back of her neck and ran down her shirt sleeves. 'What in God's name!' but it was too late; Bess had toppled her pile of books and her basin of shampoo suds and water was lapping across the floor to engulf Mary's precious love letters.

Chapter Nine

The main reason Diana had come to the Hunters' house that Friday evening was supposedly for a committee dinner but truthfully it was to see Gracie. However very shortly after Diana arrived the children were taken off to bed. This happened more and more often now. Diana would arrive to see Mrs Hunter under some pretext – perhaps the accounts of the Spanish Refugee Fund, or the minutes of the Women's Progressive Society – and after a quick hello and a hurried embrace Gracie would be trundled off to the nursery to eat her supper, or to be bathed, or to have her hair brushed and plaited.

It was not intentional on the part of Mrs Hunter or her household – she was not trying to keep Diana away from the child she believed to be Diana's half-sister – it was just the habit of the house: children were indulged on Sundays, but the rest of the week they had their routine with Nanny.

By the time Diana had escaped the factory, changed

her dress at her boarding house, and arrived at the Hunters' home the evening had taken on a very different quality. The Hunters didn't live in rarefied splendour, but their sizeable mansion house on the edge of town was certainly a contrast to the world she had grown up in, and to that of everyone else she knew.

Diana was conscious of the difference in her station and theirs, but she always had a feeling that, as long as she maintained a reserved and dignified air, hiding in plain sight, her position in the family would remain secure and she could continue to see the child who was in reality her secret daughter. Something that night, however, made her feel uneasy; was it the mention of marriage when an alderwoman asked her how long she intended to keep working at Mackintosh's? Or was it the insistence from a stout matriarch that Diana *must* meet her nephew? A fear was creeping in; a fear that some of these society women who flocked to the Hunters' charity soirées would matchmake her out of her daughter's life. Only as a single young woman with time on her hands could Diana make herself indispensable to the adopted mother of her child; only as a secretarial assistant to Mrs Hunter's charity work and her Spanish Refugee fund could Diana drift in and out of the family unnoticed. A wedding was the last thing she wanted.

Diana did not notice being ushered in to dinner, or taking her place beside an elderly matron with pince-nez. A dish of mock turtle soup was placed before her, clear and mocking her for being as artificial as itself. The fish course arrived and a Dover sole was placed before her, baked in sherry and the juice of an orange, with a gratin of breadcrumbs, walnuts, and orange zest. A sharp steam of citrus and strong drink caught her full in the face and her eyes stung. As she fought her watering eyes, the elderly lady with the pince-nez asked, 'Have you ever been to Spain, my dear?'

Diana cleared her throat delicately. 'I can't say that I have.'

'A wonderful country; wonderful people. Such a tragedy all this is happening to them. I do worry, though, about all these child refugees we're bringing here without their mothers. A child shouldn't be separated from its mother, don't you agree?'

Diana did agree, and murmured as much. But she could see that sometimes these things were inescapable, especially if it were for the good of the child. She tried to tell herself it was for the good of the child. But something made her want to fight it.

Diana's heart gave a leap as she saw a tiny hand appear around the door of the dining room, and then two tiny faces she knew well. Mrs Hunter got up quickly to steer the children out into the hallway and Diana excused herself from the candlelit table and followed her.

'No, dears, we're having a very grown-up supper and you wouldn't like it,' Mrs Hunter said to placate Gracie and Lara as they hopped around in their nightgowns and bedsocks, asking to be allowed to stay up late to sit with Diana. 'You've had your supper, and you've had your bath, and now it's time for you to go up to bed and let Nanny Christie tell you your story.'

'But Diana's here and we want to tell her about what our kittens have done.' Lara spoke for both of them. They might only be adopted sisters, but they considered themselves to be one unit now, a kind of twins.

'We have guests to dinner and Diana and I must talk to them very seriously about the refugee charity. How would it look if two little girls in their nightgowns were loitering with intent?'

Gracie looked with pleading eyes into the face of her adoptive mother. 'Could Didi come and tell us our story before we go to bed? Then we won't be in the way and we will be *very* good.'

'Diana has had a long day working at the factory and I'm not sure I like you bothering her so often for bedtime stories. She deserves a rest in the evenings, you know.'

'I don't mind, Mrs Hunter.' Diana was careful not to sound too enthusiastic, she was always careful not to sound too enthusiastic. She was maintaining the pretence that she was Gracie's half-sister, and she knew her continued visits to the secret daughter she'd borne out of wedlock depended on the careful maintenance of that pretence. If the Hunter family found out her true identity, her chances of ever seeing Gracie again would be shattered. 'I can settle them down before Mrs Sutter gives her lecture and it will give Nanny Christie time to listen to the news programme on the wireless; she likes doing that.'

'Diana, dear, you're a treasure. If you're sure you don't mind?'

Diana's dignified poise hovered artfully between indifference and generosity; there was nothing to indicate that she was either put out by the task, or eager to undertake it. For Diana, this was the secret of her place in the Hunter household; she was an apparently passive presence. 'Not at all. I'll be back down when Nanny Christie tells me the news is over.'

Diana was careful to take the hands of both Lara and

Gracie as she walked them up the stairs to bed. Although it would be natural to show an inclination towards her own sister, she didn't want anyone to think too carefully about their connection, so little Lara, and the girl her own age who had been adopted to keep her company, doted on Gracie's big sister 'Didi', and it broke Diana's heart not to be able to dote openly on them.

'Can you tell us the story of the giant who lived at Todmorden?' Gracie was hopping up the stairs which slowed the journey down, but Diana didn't mind, she was savouring every moment of holding her daughter's hand.

'I can't tell you a long story tonight because I've got to go down to the Aldermans' Wives dinner, but if you're very good I'll tell you the one about the Duke of York's regiment.'

Lara looked wide-eyed at Diana's evening gown and said, 'You look very beautiful, Didi.'

'Of course she does.' Lara could never quite get used to Diana's striking looks, but Gracie took it for granted that Diana swept away all before her. 'She's *always* beautiful, that's why it will be so easy for them to find her a good match.'

Diana's ears pricked up at this disclosure, which she hoped no one else in the house had heard as they reached the summit of the Hunters' grand staircase before closing the door of the little girls' bedroom behind them. 'Who's they?' she asked. 'Who's going to find me a good match?'

'Mummy, Daddy, and Aunt Celia,' Lara said as she climbed up onto the bed and wriggled under the snowy white counterpane. 'They talk about it when they're having tea in the drawing room.'

'Auntie Celia said that you have lovely manners for a factory girl, and she said they should put a pea under your mattress and see if you sleep.' Diana was disconcerted to hear Gracie referring to this good lady as 'auntie' but she supposed it was only natural that Gracie would take to her new life so completely.

'Mummy says you're very capable with her committees and she doesn't want to lose you just yet, but Daddy says it's time they found you a match so you can have children of your own.'

This worried Diana. Was it an indication that Mr Hunter felt she spent too much time with Gracie? She had never expected to be able to stay so close to her daughter after she had allowed the court to take her for adoption, but every visit just fed her need for another one, and she tried to find subtle ways of coming back more and more often.

Gracie settled into bed and then held out her hand for Diana to hold. 'If you have babies will you still love me, Didi?'

All Diana's careful restraint broke down at her daughter's words and she clutched the child to her, and whispered into her hair, 'Oh, Gracie. You're all I have in the world.'

Chapter Ten

'I don't want any of you going over to Stebbins' farm these next few weeks – and if any of your friends go round there I want you to stay away from them too.' Mr Calder addressed his brood of children as he entered the family kitchen from the farmyard, but it was their cat Marmalade, Dodger the sheepdog, and the tame goose Brenda who all looked up at him when he entered, giving the impression that the dumb animals were taking note and intended to avoid Stebbins.

'I should be so lucky!' Reenie hurried round the kitchen gathering up a packed supper while trying to disentangle herself from her factory overalls at the same time. 'How much free time do you think I've got? I'm not back from shift five minutes before I'm off out again on the horse to meet Peter. I'm hardly likely to make a detour to Stebbins.'

'It's still worth saying,' Mr Calder called up the stairs after her as she went in search of her going out frock. 'You can't be too careful!'

'It's only scarlet fever, Dad,' John said as he kept his eyes focused on the funny pages he was reading, 'it's not the Black Death. They're all fit and healthy, they'll be reet.'

'That's not the point. It started with septic sore throat and that's very contagious. Just think what would happen if Reenie caught it and took it to work with her? She could take out half the town.'

'Only if you spit in their eye. I'm not stupid, Dad.' John was uncharacteristically stroppy. A fact possibly connected to the boys at Stebbins being his chief source of cast-off reading matter, and the farmer himself being the best source of paid casual labour when John had a free Saturday. Avoiding Stebbins would mean a direct hit to his pocket money and his leisure time. It was all very well for the rest of them to avoid Stebbins, but what was he supposed to do for pocket money in the meantime? Whistle for it?

Kathleen, who it surprised precisely no one to discover had read about scarlet fever in depth already, corrected her elder brother. 'Actually, you can catch it from door handles. Scientists have found the germs under microscopes and they get onto the hands of people who've coughed into a handkerchief, and then they touch a door handle, and then you touch a door handle, and then you go into the milking shed and before you know it, it's in the milk.'

'I *always* wash my hands before I do the milking, *and* all our milk gets pasteurised so it can't get in the milk and that just shows how much you know, Kath*leen*.'

'Yes, but the Stebbins don't pasteurise their milk, do they? They don't believe in it, and *that's* what Dad's worried about. If they've got scarlet fever then they're already going to give it to *everyone* and he doesn't want us helping them.'

Mrs Calder gave her son a pointed look. 'Don't forget, I'm not as strong as I was before I had three kids. Do you know how many teeth I lost while I was expecting you? You took it out of me, my lad, and even if I would survive it, I don't fancy having it, so don't bring it here.' Mrs Calder plonked the half-empty teapot with a slosh onto the ancient family dinner table, pockmarked with hard use, and littered with the detritus of a good tea. 'Just stay at home as much as you can manage for the next couple of weeks and it will all blow over. Don't bring it here, and don't drink any of the milk at school for a bit.'

Kathleen looked around in disgust. 'Does Stebbins supply the milk for my school?' This was new information to her and she couldn't have been more surprised.

'And Stoney Royd!' Mr Calder snorted with derision.

Kathleen shook her head in disappointment. 'This sort of thing wouldn't be allowed to go on if I were on the council.' One of the many difficulties with being thirteen was that Kathleen had grown up enough to develop the capacity to feel grand emotions, but had few opportunities to experience them. She had an appetite for life and for learning and for work, but she was held back in her ambition to take on the world by the very inconvenient fact that she wouldn't legally be an adult with a key to her own front door for another eight years. The offer of a position as a Saturday girl in Hebblewhite's Newsagent and Confectioner might one day seem like a triviality in the story of her life, but at this time it was everything. She decided to announce the news to her family. 'I've got the job of Saturday Girl at Hebblewhite's in town.'

'You've done what?' Mrs Calder had only just sat down to her tea, after feeding all the family first, and as always, was quite put out when her offspring unburdened themselves at the very moment she was about to get a bite to eat. 'You can't get a job, you've got school.'

'Not on Saturdays. Besides, this is perfect for what you want. I can't go to Stebbins' farm if I'm at work in a shop, can I? When war comes and they shut the schools, I'll work there full-time. It's a useful start in business.'

'Since when! Who said you could take a job without our permission?'

John said, 'You can't work at Hebblewhite's, it's a deathtrap. It'll fall down around your ears because it's about a thousand years old and looks twice that.'

'It's eight hundred and forty years old and very solidly built. It's also three shillings a week, which is beautiful money. I thought you'd be pleased; I've only got a year left at Elementary School and I've got to get a move on if I want to get something lined up for when I finish. I'll probably have to leave even earlier if there's a war and the schools are closed down.'

'You're optimistic. They didn't close the schools in the last war.'

'I'm hedging my bets. And Hebblewhite's opens a lot of doors.'

'What doors?' John had a low opinion of his younger sister's employment enterprise, which might have had more than a little to do with jealousy that he hadn't got there first. 'It's a run-down old church no bigger than a telephone kiosk which someone has thought fit to stuff silly with liquorice pipes and a till; it's only a matter of time before the weight of the Sunday papers causes the whole thing to slip into the river for good!'

'The shop is actually an excellent size on the inside.' Kathleen's judicious use of the word 'excellent' fooled no one. 'And it's Mackintosh's only misshapes shop in town. They have a very special relationship with Mackintosh's and it's a good way of getting to know Mackintosh's Sales Department.'

'What's your sister told you about going to work at her factory?' It was a warning more than a question.

'But I won't *be* working for the factory; I'll be working for a shop which sells things *for* the factory. I won't be breaking my promise to Reenie.'

'You're just like your sister; always looking for another way around. You can't go into Mackintosh's by the back door if you've promised her you won't go into Mackintosh's at all.'

'Who's going into Mackintosh's?' Reenie asked as she ran down the stairs and hurried on her riding coat and boots.

Kathleen looked appealingly to her father, always a soft touch. 'Dad, will you tell her she can't stop me going to Mackintosh's?'

'I don't care where any of you go, just stay away from Stebbins!'

Chapter Eleven

'What is all this paper doing in my house?' Mrs Norcliffe did not hold with literacy and the sight of Albert Baum's letters, soaked with Amami shampoo and hung up to dry on a variety of makeshift indoor washing lines made her very annoyed.

'They're for my job, Mother!' Mary's shouts were sharp with panic. She was used to having to bellow at her mother to be heard through the woman's good ear, but these shouts had an unaccustomed urgency. To Mary, the letters were her most precious possessions in all the world, but they were also her most secret. She was loath to let her mother or sister see even that they existed, let alone their contents, but she was also desperate to save any few words she could. The soapy water had caused patches of ink to run, but there were still snatches of sentences here and there which might be saved if they were dried in time.

I miss you even more than I could have believed possible . . .

The bundles of letters had been tied tight and those letters closest to the middle were legible in several places. So long as her mother didn't interfere, she might be able to hang on to some of his words.

You console me when I think I am beyond all consoling . . .

'What job? You've got your factory job. I don't want you throwing up a good job in the factory for some paper job!'

Can I tell you that I love you? Is it too soon, too much?

'It *is* the factory job, Mother. I'm learning sweet making by correspondence!' Mary flitted about the parlour, desperately straightening the sodden leaves of blue and cradling the sheets which had come apart along their folds as the water dissolved them like rice paper.

I feel sorry for the people I pass in the streets each day, knowing that not one of them has ever seen your face.

'What are you doing dripping wet hair on my chair?' Mrs Norcliffe asked Bess accusingly; she was sitting where and how she had been told to sit while rivulets of soapy water ran down the back of her nightdress.

'I'm sitting on my hands.' Bess may have lacked common sense, but she made up for it in amenability. When her sister had told her to stay still and sit on her hands she had taken her at her word. She was not entirely certain what she had done wrong, but she knew that when Mary started getting busy she had to do as she was told. Now she was tilting her head on one side and reading a section of one of the letters which was hanging up close to her. 'Mary's manager is in love with her, but we're not supposed to know.'

'He is not!' Mary was at her wits' end. 'Don't you dare read them! I told you to sit on your hands!'

'I can read them *and* sit on my hands.' Bess had managed to sneak a look at several of the letters which Mary had hidden previously, but the sheet beside her was a particularly good one and she tried to resist her mother's attempts to drag her away so that she could read more of it. 'Don't move me, I've got to a bit where he's missing her eyes. He says, *"There are few sights which could console me today, but the sight of your eyes is one."*'

'You've got soap in your 'air.' Mrs Norcliffe was a blunt woman, and she dealt with one problem at a time. First she would take Bess to the pump at the end of the street and douse her with icy cold water to stop her hair going sticky, then she would come back and dry the seat of her chair with a towel – Mrs Norcliffe slept in that chair every night under an old army coat and she wasn't going to let it stay wet – and then she was going to take down all the nasty bits of soggy paper bunting hanging about the house and put them on the fire. The girls were wittering about something, and she hadn't the least interest in what it was. Mary had a steady job at the factory which would do her, and there was no sense wasting time with writing things or reading things; that sort of nonsense always led to trouble. Mrs Norcliffe led the smaller of her two daughters away by a skinny arm, but grumbled to Mary as she heaved herself out of the front door, 'Take all this mess down. I want it ready for fire-lighting spills when I get back. The place is damp enough as it is without you two doing God knows what.'

Mary would usually have attempted to argue with her mother – she was, after all, twenty years old and an equal wage earner with her surviving parent, perfectly capable of standing her ground. The problem was that her mother won all arguments by default, through being too deaf to hear the other side, and too stubborn to stop what she was doing and attempt a dialogue. Mary's heart raced as she realised that in a matter of minutes her mother would start tearing down Albert's sodden letters and there was no way to save them. If she took them down herself and hurried them away to safety some-where, they would turn to pulp and all his words would be lost; her only chance to save these few snatches of their correspondence was to dry them, and the only way to do that was to keep her mother out.

Mary was not an impetuous or a disobedient girl – she feared displeasing the figures of authority in her life more than anything – which was why it was a testament to the strength of her feelings for Albert Baum that she grabbed the key to the deadlock on their front door and, turning it roughly in her fist, locked her mother out in the cold.

Mary sat with her back to the door clutching the sodden sheaf of her most precious letter, its words barely legible:

I did not think I could love again, I did not think I could feel hope again, but you have brought me both love and hope, Maria, and the promise of so much happiness. The days here are long, and the nights are longer, but the thought that my Maria sleeps under the same heavens is a balm to my aching heart. I think of you hour after hour, day

after day, week after week, but time is cruel
because it does not allow my feelings to gently
fade, but only stokes their flames higher.
If I could just see your face, just for a moment . . .

Mary sobbed as she draped the smeared sheaf of paper as close to the fire as she dared. Now she had nothing to show to Diana, and nothing of Albert until he appeared. *If* he appeared.

Chapter Twelve

One of the highlights of the week for Reenie and Peter was their visit to see their old manager, Major Fergusson. While most courting couples were queuing outside the pictures waiting for the latest offering from Dashiell Hammett on Saturday night, Reenie and Peter waited in the visitors room of the Stoney Royd Cottage Hospital for the visiting hour bell to sound.

St Hilda's was a cosy little place compared to the infirmary the Major had been admitted to at the start of the summer. It had a fresh, clean linen smell, mingled with sweet cut flowers and waxy furniture polish. Oddly enough Reenie took particular comfort from seeing the Major surrounded by homely things again, like the wooden bedside table and the framed picture of Beacon Hill on the wall. She'd visited him in the other hospital ward, the ward which had rattled with the clatter of metal medicine trollies and stung her eyes with the aroma of bleach. It had been the best place for him at the time – it was thanks to the infirmary that he had survived the poisoning at all – but she felt the peace of the cottage hospital was a good sign; he must be getting stronger if he didn't need to be in the 'big' hospital any more.

'Have you thought about what we can safely tell him?' Peter was not a loud lad, but even so he felt the need to lower his voice in the hush of the waiting room.

'We could tell him about Bess's new job in the canteen?' The matter of what they could tell Major Fergusson became more difficult with every passing week. Reenie and Peter had agreed that they wouldn't tell the Major about any of the troubles they were having at the factory while he was recovering in the cottage hospital. The doctor had warned them that the older man must not be agitated, and they thought it likely that if he knew how the land lay in his old department he would be very agitated indeed.

'That's a good one. What about the factory stables? He likes horses. Has Ruffian been up to much or any of the other horses?'

'Not much. Although one of the factory mares is in foal and there'll be hell to pay when they work out whose fault it is, but apart from that it all just ticks along same as always.' Reenie chewed the inside of her cheek in thought. 'Do you think that if we don't tell him quite how bad it is in the factory, but maybe mention one or two of the things very gently, we could get his advice? The Major is very good at advice.'

Peter wished they could. Working in a department where no one fully knew who was in charge was the last thing he wanted. He shook his head. 'I don't think we can risk it. All the troubles stem from his absence and we don't want him trying to hurry back if he needs more rest.'

As it happened, Reenie and Peter fell back on the old, safe topic they always talked to Major Fergusson about on Fridays; it also just so happened to be the topic the two of them least wanted to touch on. It always seemed to be the best way to divert the Major's attention from their real predicament, but it was creating an even greater strain.

'I must say, I'm looking forward to your wedding immensely.' The Major beamed at them happily from his hospital bed. 'Have you set a date yet?'

'Oh, well,' Peter blushed and tried not to seem too keen, 'there's time yet, Major. We've got a bit of saving up to do and Reenie wants to finish off this project she has running an experimental line . . .' Peter trailed off, looking to Reenie to take over the topic of conversation that he wasn't supposed to mention.

'We're in no hurry, Major.' Reenie was torn between the joy she felt at giving the Major something to hope for, and the worry she felt about a wedding in the near future. 'We'll definitely wait until you're back on your feet.'

Reenie saw an opportunity to refill the Major's water jug and seized it, saying she'd be back soon and she'd see if she could find them biscuits. She was clearly more agitated than usual and the Major had noticed.

'I hope I haven't brought up a distressing topic, Peter?'

'No, no, I think we will get married one day, it's just . . .'

'Very early days.' The Major was all understanding and

reassurance, 'You're both still young. Whole lives ahead of you. Don't want to settle down yet.'

'It's not that, Major Fergusson, it's the marriage bar at Mackintosh's. Reenie won't be able to work once we're married.'

'I know your salary isn't quite enough to set up home with, but wouldn't your parents give you an allowance?'

'I think they would but it's not that, Major; it's Reenie. You know how she loves her work – I don't think there's a factory girl in all Halifax that loves factory life as much as she does! If we married she could come back and do seasonal work with the married women when there are jobs to be had, but that would never be enough for her.'

'She would settle down soon enough; I've seen plenty of girls do the same.'

'But I don't want that for my Reenie, Major. I'm so proud of her, so proud of what she can do that no one else can. You set her to a problem and she'll find you a solution you'd never have thought of. I'm sure she'd find a way to make herself useful in the Mother's Union, or the Women's Cooperative Guild, or on some committee somewhere, but it would be a waste and we both know it. I'm proud of how different she is; I love seeing her eyes light up when she's come up with a new plan for a production line and she's talking ten to the dozen because she's just so excited about it. How can I ask her to give that up? How can I ask her to give up one of the things about her that I love best?'

The Major was silent, but sympathetic in his silence. He knew as well as Peter did just what a rarity Reenie was and just how perfectly matched the young couple had always been. There was no easy answer to their situation; the world was not going to change overnight.

'We've got a new project, Major. We're employing some of the married ladies on an experimental line. Reenie got permission to bring back a dozen or so, just temporarily, see if it makes time savings.'

'Excellent news; excellent. You young people have so many fresh ideas, it's wonderful. We must invest in our young people. And speaking of young people, how are your young cousins? Did they make it to Spain?'

'Oh, you heard about that did you?'

'I heard that you tried to go with them.'

Peter looked a little embarrassed, perhaps because he had tried to run away to Spain to fight in their civil war, perhaps because he had been talked out of it.

'I think you made a wise decision to remain here. The factory needs you – and Reenie needs you. We will have war in England soon enough and we'll need you to be ready then.'

'My cousins have been arrested.' Peter didn't like to burden Major Fergusson with his worries, but he was a long way from home, and he knew so few grown-ups in Halifax. 'They were arrested even before they left England.'

'And you're feeling rather cowardly for not being arrested with them?'

Peter nodded and rubbed the back of his head awkwardly with his palm. 'They might have been arrested, but at least they were doing *something*. I'm just kicking my heels here in Halifax making toffees. I should be trying to—'

'You should be keeping an eye on my department for me, and reporting to me on any developments. You could not be doing a more valuable job.'

Now Peter felt even more guilty for not having told the Major any of the things he would have wanted to know.

'Has Mr Sinclair arrived yet to take over as Head of Time and Motion?'

'Not quite yet.'

'But Mr Johns is still holding the fort all right?'

'Oh yes, everything's just fine. Nothing changes, really.' Peter swallowed hard and wished Reenie would come back so that they could talk about the wedding she'd been avoiding.

Chapter Thirteen

'She can't take Reenie's experimental line. It's not right.'
Peter was sitting at the kitchen table with his arms folded
in opposition. It was later that same Saturday night and
neither he, Reenie, nor Diana had to be at work again
until Monday morning, but still they found themselves
turning to the same old topics: who the force was for ill
in their factory and how could they stop them?

Diana preferred a quiet life and was much less inclined
to seek active remedy in these matters. 'She can and she
has. I should stay clear of her if I were you.'

'But the line was given to Reenie by a director!'

'Yes, as an experiment.' Diana reached behind her for
a fresh packet of tea and threw it to Reenie who was
brewing up, despite the fact that she no longer lived in
Diana's boarding house and had invited herself in with
Peter when she'd bumped into Diana on her way home.
'And that experiment failed when Reenie turned the
production line upside down over a tin soldier.'

'Yes, but that was—' Reenie was quick to attempt to explain the intricacies of the mix-up, but Diana didn't give her a chance.

'Only to be expected when you put a seventeen-year-old in charge of a line. I don't care how good you are setting up the machines, Reenie, it takes a different kind of talent to run a production line day-to-day. Say what you like about Mrs Starbeck, she runs an efficient line and we wouldn't keep her on if she wasn't liked by the overlookers.'

Reenie wrinkled her nose as she put the kettle on the range to boil. 'The *horrible* overlookers. None of the *nice* overlookers like her!'

'We don't have any horrible overlookers at Mack's. We have women whose job it is to make sure the girls start work on time, don't leave early, don't run a piece-rate racket for more money, and don't do anything dangerous. You forget that I used to work on the line same as you did, but I did it for a damn sight longer. I know just what chaos we'd have if there were no over-lookers. You think of them all as cruel slave masters but you forget that they're trying to look after their staff same as you are. You're too busy trying to be everyone's friend, letting them go early if they need to pick up their kids, chatting to them about their creaky knees—'

'But it worked!' Reenie wasn't angry, just enthusiastic to expound on her theory of factory governance. 'My line was faster than—'

'It didn't work.' Diana rose to move the cat so that Reenie could put down the cups and saucers. 'You had a shutdown over a tin soldier and called out half the medical staff for a scratched thumb. I know you don't like losing your line to Mrs Starbeck, but sometimes these things happen. People have got better things to worry about just now than Time and Motion. Yours is the smallest department in the factory and the business can run without you. All right, you come along with your stopwatches and clipboards and find ways to make things a bit faster, but in the grand scheme of things it doesn't matter.'

Peter was frustrated by the way that Diana's manager in the employment department allowed Mrs Starbeck to do so many things unchallenged. 'If it doesn't matter in the grand scheme of things, then why can't you stop her just this once?'

'Because she's right,' Diana said. 'Reenie shouldn't have been trying to run a line on her own. Being made a Junior Manager at her age was a stretch, but being put in charge of a line was too much. She needs to wait until she's older and has more experience.'

Peter appeared to feel that this was not the real heart of the matter. 'That's not why Mrs Starbeck did it, though. She's been taking over *everything*. There's not a department where she hasn't tried to interfere and you know it. She had six lines running under her last year, now she's got thirteen.'

'Well, that's unlucky for her. If she wants all that extra work, she's welcome to it. But there are bigger problems for the Employment Department and this isn't one of them.'

'Then what's the Employment Department even for?' Peter demanded.

'It's for the acres of paperwork you generate every time you resign to go to Spain to fight with your cousins, but then change your mind because you've realised you've got no fighting experience; it's for writing up employment contracts and references for Jewish staff at the German factory who want a permit to come here; it's lobbying for higher wages for women staff because they work just as hard as you, but they're only getting paid a third as much, and it's for—' Diana was silenced by a key in the lock of the front door above their heads. 'Shush! That's her. She'll hear you.'

They waited in silence as they heard the front door click shut and quick footsteps disappear upstairs.

Diana slumped back in her chair, relaxing into the gloom of the basement kitchen lit only by the oil lamp on the table and the occasional flash of light when Reenie opened the door of the range. 'She won't hear us now. She's going to change out of her uniform.'

Peter leant forward and asked in a hushed voice, 'What uniform? She's a senior manager, she doesn't have a uniform.'

'It's not work, it's her Blackshirt get-up. She has meetings with the British Union at Crabley Hall and gads about like Unity Mitford.'

Reenie warmed the teapot with a little water and then spooned in the loose tea. 'I thought it was illegal now to wear all that stuff in England?'

'It is in public, but Crabley Hall is a private house, and she sneaks over there with a great raincoat covering her from neck to knee. She's recruited a few more young ones from the factory to join her and she gets them writing to the Home Office to complain every time Mack's employs a foreigner. That's why Mr Baum got sent home early in the summer; she wrote to the Home

Office and told them he was taking a British person's job, despite the fact that there were no British people qualified to do the job.'

Reenie dearly wanted to see the best in everyone, but she had failed to find anything praiseworthy in the Time and Motion Senior Manager. 'Why don't you sack her? Why doesn't your boss sack her?'

Diana held out her hands in a gesture of helplessness. 'Nothing illegal about being in the BUF, and she's entitled to her opinion about us employing foreigners. She's someone who likes order and efficiency and she thinks that's what Germany and Italy and Rumania have all got now they've got fascism, and she wants that here. She thinks the world would be a better place and everyone would be happier if Oswald Mosley took charge and made us like those European countries.'

Peter, who had only recently tried to run away to Spain to fight those very people, struggled to see Mrs Starbeck's point of view. 'How can anyone think that? How can anyone see the newsreels of the fascists in Spain bombing women and children and think that's better?'

'You'd be surprised. This time last year the BUF weren't so popular, but they've doubled their membership since the government started talking about us having air raids here – and that's just the paying members. There's plenty more who think Mosley's ranting bile is all good sense, but they just can't be bothered going to meetings. Mosley says he can prevent war by making us Hitler's allies. People believe him and they join his rotten little party in their tens of thousands.'

Peter shook his head with the hopelessness of it all.

'Why did you let her move in here? How can you stand to be in the same house as her?'

'It seemed like a good idea at the time. And, I don't own the place, do I? Mrs Garner's sons own it and they're still waiting for someone to buy it. Until then I'm just minding it for them and reminding all the lodgers to send them the rent. Besides, it might be worth keeping an eye on her.'

Reenie's ears pricked up. 'I thought you said being in the BUF wasn't illegal?'

'It isn't.' Diana sipped her tea. 'And neither's keeping an eye on her.'

Chapter Fourteen

It was not yet time for the factory whistle to sound the start of the morning shift and Mrs Wilkes was already on her third cup of tea that day. As far as Diana Moore could tell her manager existed exclusively on tea and toast. Where the woman got her energy from was an ongoing mystery; she was a phenomenon. The Head of the Women's Employment Department could be said to hide her light under a bushel; she didn't come to work in expensively cut suits like the other heads of department, or wearing pearl earrings like Mrs Starbeck. Amy Wilkes was ready to do battle on behalf of her employees each day armed only with a tweed suit and her tortoiseshell spectacles. Diana liked her, and she didn't regret moving from the factory floor to be her assistant a year before.

Diana had a reputation for being if not imperious, then at least a little difficult to tame. What Diana liked most about Mrs Wilkes was that she did not try to tame her because she did not want a meek and deferential assistant. Passive acquiescence might be a valuable trait in the Minnows – the fourteen-year-old girls who came straight from school to learn the most menial factory work – but Diana wasn't making Strawberry Creams any more; she and her manager were determined to spend every day making working life better for their women workers, and an accommodating manner wouldn't cut it.

Diana slipped silently into her office with the first clutch of factory memoranda for the day and placed the crisp manilla envelopes on her manager's desk then sat down without waiting to be asked. They had settled into a natural rhythm in the last year of working together and Diana had realised quickly that her manager was irritated by people who waited to be given permission to do things which they ought to do; and that she valued efficiency over antiquated etiquette. They were not quite friends but they had a bond of trust, and they were both glad to be working with the other rather than anyone else.

Amy Wilkes stirred the envelopes on her desk with her fingertips, 'If any of them are about that blasted horse you can return to sender and point out that it's not our problem. There are no women in the factory stables; *Men's* Employment need to deal with it.'

Diana raised an eyebrow at her manager; she had wondered how long it would take that piece of news to reach the senior management. Diana had heard it from Reenie Calder, and it was only a surprise that it had remained secret for so long. 'The mare's female.'

Amy Wilkes pursed her lips; she supposed she should have expected that sort of dry response from Diana. 'I don't want Men's Employment to think of that. It's their problem and I want it to stay that way.'

Diana Moore knew all about the mare in foal down in the factory stables, and she was delighted to work a good distance away in the Women's Employment Department. As far as she had heard – and Diana Moore heard about everything – the factory stables were now a hotbed of suspicion and frayed nerves. The irritability of the staff was feeding an irritability in the horses, and factory work had been disrupted a few times because wagons were not where they needed to be at the time they needed to be there; there had been a toffee spill that morning as the wagons carrying the finished goods to the railway sidings collided with an empty wagon on its way back. There was more at stake than the bills for the vet; this was harming productivity.

However, it was the prerogative of the Men's Employment Department; there were no female staff in the stables, and Diana and Mrs Wilkes counted that as a stroke of luck for their workloads. This would be a rotten headache for someone, but not for Diana or Amy. Men's Employment would have to create a disciplinary policy for the act of allowing a mare to be covered on company property – and decide whether it was a misdemeanour, an oversight, or an act of criminal responsibility – aside from the trouble of investigating, finding the culprit, and putting them through a tribunal. So long as the misdemeanour didn't turn out to be the fault of a female member of staff, Diana and her manager would be safe from the mêlée of nonsense.

Diana thought she could see this landing on their desks all the same, 'And if the Men's Employment Department request our advice on how to manage the general mess they've got themselves into?'

Mrs Wilkes looked up from her correspondence, her interest piqued. 'How have Men's Employment caused it?'

'Mr Davidson in the Men's Employment Department is the one who persuaded the factory stables to buy his mare off him at an inflated price. They'd only had geldings until then.'

'Bloody managers and their bloody kickbacks. I tell you, half the problems in this place are caused by some man who thinks his swollen salary isn't enough, and wants to get a bit more cream off the top. They'd get a short sharp shock if they had to try to live off a woman's wage for a week or two. Now what's on the agenda for today? Any meetings we don't need to have?'

Diana consulted her carefully ordered list, 'You've got an appeal hearing of Tilly Tweddle who had a fling with her Overlooker—'

'She's appealing is she? Good for her! A girl on the production line gets herself in the family way and she's out on her ear and taking all the blame for her Over-looker's indiscretion; but one of their precious horses looks likely to drop and they're all up in arms to find the culprit and see justice done. If God could give them eyes for irony.' Amy Wilkes took a rapid slug of tea while slicing open envelopes with a Mackintosh's embossed letter opener, 'Anything on air raid precautions?'

'Nothing new. The trenches the Estate Department dug are still full of water, so they're looking for a new site.'

'What's Mrs Starbeck up to this week? Do I need to throw salt over my shoulder and carry garlic, or is she still terrorising the Engineering Department?'

'At the moment she's intercepting post from other departments to vet its contents, and she's doing it with the cooperation of Mr Pinkstone in the post room.'

Amy Wilkes took off her spectacles in surprise, 'She's doing what?'

Diana produced an envelope from her pocket which was addressed to Mary Norcliffe. Inside it was a dull memorandum about the ratio of sugar to butter in a toffee recipe, and an exhortation to work with efficiency. It had been typed on an Empire typewriter which – like Diana's own machine – had a slight misalignment of the letter 'e'. Mary had typed it in her office secretly that morning, forged Albert Baum's signature, and then spent a good fifteen minutes apologising to Diana for the whole mess, and worrying about everything from her manager to the state of the nation. Diana decided that Mrs Wilkes didn't need to know any of that and instead said, 'She tried to intercept this one, but it came to me instead. She thinks the volume of correspondence Albert Baum sends to his subordinate in the kitchens in suspicious.'

Amy Wilkes rubbed her temples. 'I have a feeling this is going to be a long day, Diana. A long day.'

Chapter Fifteen

Reenie had woken that Monday morning with a feeling that if she could just get her experimental line back from Mrs Starbeck, then all could be right with the world. Her horse seemed to be thinking the same thing as he clopped down the Bailey Hall road with an imperious tilt to his chin.

Ruffian the horse had settled back into his old routine of taking Reenie from the family farm to her job in the town each day. As Reenie dismounted her horse at the factory gates and beamed a happy grin at the factory watchman she wondered what good thing the day had in store; good things were always happening and she was confident that she could expect another one at any moment.

Perhaps Ruffian would allow himself to be led into his stall in the stables the first time of asking; or maybe he'd volunteer himself for some factory work instead of eating all the hay he could, and then glaring at the other horses when he got bloat.

Ruffian was not a stranger to hard work, but he did object to any work which he appeared to deem to be unnecessary. He was a little less shiftless in the spring and summer, but on dark mornings he had to be coaxed out to work with the twin temptations of sweet hay and fragrant russet apples. Reenie was more understanding with her old friend than some farmers' daughters might be and rather than sending him to the knacker's yard as an impatient owner could have done, she kept him on by insisting that he was cheaper to keep than saving up for a bicycle (which was not true in the slightest) and used him to ride into town on for her shifts at the factory.

Truth be told, it gave Reenie's mother some peace of mind to know that her daughter was being escorted home by the old horse. After that Christmas Eve blizzard the year before when Reenie had been fool enough to try to trudge home to the family farm outside the town Mrs Calder had become convinced that Ruffian had saved her daughter from an icy fate.

Another benefit of owning Ruffian was that his presence provided Reenie and her friends with a kind of clubhouse at the factory. Since Ruffian had acted with heroism in the fire which nearly destroyed the factory, the stable manager had awarded Ruffian the Freedom of the Stables, which he'd said meant 'bed and board whenever he was in town'. Ruffian was no trouble; the workaday horses who pulled wagons of finished goods around the factory yards all bided in the new factory stables while Ruffian bided alone in one of the disused old stable blocks. Bess had been so delighted to discover that Reenie and Ruffian had been assigned a special stable that she had gone to all kinds of lengths to kit it out with posies of flowers, pictures of the king and matinee idols, old blankets, and piles of magazines to while away their dinner-hour breaks when they would sit on hay bales beside the horse and natter. They would even occasionally meet at breakfast time, an hour before their shift, if they had a particular reason.

On that morning, Reenie arrived at the old stables early to find her friends waiting for her with hot bread rolls, salted golden butter, cherry jam, and a cheery welcome. Their lunchtime chit-chat had been cut short the preceding Friday because Reenie had been called away to her experimental line and they'd agreed to resume at breakfast on Monday.

While Reenie led Ruffian in to his stall, Mary and Bess made themselves comfortable on hay bales. Mary had brought not only fluffy white rolls, but also an enamel pot of hot cocoa swaddled in many layers of cotton oven rags. As she laid out her handkerchief like a tablecloth and set to serving up their breakfast, she asked the innocent question which was to bring so much trouble later. 'Are you coming in a different way to work now? You usually come in to the old stables from the other side.'

Reenie gave her friends a confiding smile. 'No, I'm just keeping out the way of the new stables. There's been some brouhaha about one of their mares and no one wants to be around the stable manager just now if they can help it.'

'What's a brouhaha?' Bess liked the sound of the word and hoped it was a kind of party where cocktails flowed like water and handsome young men wanted desperately to find a partner for the dance music which played on through the night.

'It's like a scandal or a fuss. One of their mares is in foal and she shouldn't be. Someone's let her in with a stallion and when the stable manager finds out who it was they'll be for it.'

Bess was frowning in that way she had which told her sister and Reenie that she was trying to fathom the mysteries of the universe, but drawing a blank. Reenie offered the explanation, which was obvious to a farmer's daughter, but which she supposed would be opaque to a town girl like Bess.

'The other horses in the factory stables are geldings, not stallions . . .' Reenie saw that this was not enlightening Bess any further. 'Geldings are boy horses what have had their you-know-whats snipped off by the vet . . .'

Bess's eyebrows shot up in horror; this was clearly new information to her. 'That's awful! Who would do that to a poor horse?'

'It's quite normal.' Reenie shrugged in apology for this veterinary fact of life. 'It happens all the time with work-horses on farms and at factories. It makes them better workers and they do as they're told.' Reenie added for emphasis, 'They're safer round a factory yard if they do as they're told.'

Bess looked pityingly at their old friend Ruffian and whispered, 'Has Ruffian had his . . . you know?'

'No, that's why he never does as he's told. But he's not bad for a stallion.' Reenie patted the flank of her irritable old friend with affectionate pride. 'Ruffian's always been all right if he thinks he's doing a favour for one of the family, but he won't take bossing about. We think he was tret' badly when he was a foal and that's why he's so loyal to m' dad for rescuing him and bringing him to our 'ouse. He's not like most stallions, he's the quiet kind of stubborn, not the lively kind of stubborn.'

Mary's eyes had narrowed in thought as her own pondering of the mysteries of the universe came up anything but blank. She sat on the hay bale with her arms folded and her back leaning against the creaking stable partition and asked carefully, 'Reenie . . .' There was a hesitation as she tried to master her panic that they might be responsible for yet more trouble in the factory. 'If . . . if Ruffian is the only stallion in the factory stables, is it . . . has he . . . has *he* got this mare in the family way?'

Bess gasped in delight at the thought of a 'baby horse' and Ruffian having a sweetheart. 'Oh, yes! Let's hope it's Ruffian's baby horse!'

Reenie rolled her eyes at Bess's all-round noodle-headedness. 'It can't be Ruffian's foal; he's never been in her stable.'

Bess was not to be put off now that she had caught onto such an enjoyable idea. 'But how do you know that he hasn't? You're not with him all the time. He could have gone round to see her while you were in the factory on shift. It might be a secret love affair.' Bess curled a ringlet of golden hair around her finger and sighed dreamily at the thought of an improbable romance of the sort she saw on the cartoons at the cinema between talking cats and dogs.

Mary said nothing, but raised an eyebrow at Reenie which plainly said, *I'd like to know if there's a better explanation.*

'I wouldn't leave him in her stable and I'd notice if he'd been moved from here. I know he's old and lazy, but I still wouldn't risk leaving him in with a mare; I'm not as daft as you are cabbage lookin'!'

But Mary didn't take her eyes off Reenie and a tiny kernel of worry began to take root. Ruffian was the only stallion in the stables, and a mare not a hundred yards away was in foal.

Chapter Sixteen

Dolly Dunkley had plenty of work to be doing, but she was avoiding it by walking up and down some of the factory corridors with a clipboard, attempting to look like she was on her way to a meeting. Dolly's motive for this strategy of avoidance was partly an inveterate laziness on her part, but also a deep-seated knowledge that she was incompetent and that the work she had been given to do was beyond her limited capabilities; even if she had possessed the inclination to do a job of work, she would not have known where to start, or how to ask for help. It wouldn't be so bad if the job had been forced upon her and she had risen to the challenge to do her best in the aid of others, but this was a job which she had demanded as her due and wheedled her way into in the most unpleasant ways. Dolly was in two minds about her job, and this was the problem with being congenitally dishonest: she could not easily be honest with herself and admit that she was not the brilliant junior manager that

90

she had assumed she would be and that it would be better for everyone if she resigned.

Dolly had chosen a corridor which led from the Harrogate Toffee line to the grand staircase at the north gate. This was the place where the VIP parties were led by Mackintosh's tour guides on their way around the factory. The VIPs were rarely especially celebrated people (excepting the visit they had received in the previous summer from His Majesty the King), but they would often include one or two of the Mackintosh family members, or a local politician. Sometimes the guides showed round a radio announcer, or a variety entertainer, but in the main the visitors tended to be dull. This didn't matter to Dolly, who had deluded herself with the fantasy that any day now she would bump into the youngest and most attractive of the Mackintosh family heirs and he would fall immediately in love with her. To this end she had doubled the quantity of ill-applied make-up she usually wore and had begun to resemble nothing so much as a puffin who has recently received surprising news. Dolly thought she looked ravishing; Dolly thought a lot of things.

Dolly had been loitering at the end of the corridor for several minutes – long enough for her too-high heels to make her toes ache – and had been thinking about going to the factory's technical library to complain about the stock when the sound of approaching footsteps made her heart flutter: VIPs were just around the corner.

'We have a staff of ten thousand here in Halifax and another six thousand at our factory in Norwich.' The tour guide sounded unenthusiastic about the success of her employers, but presumably one could only repeat the same information so many times before it lost its magic. 'And still more employees at our factories in Canada, Germany, and South Africa.'

Dolly waited with bated breath for the wave of glamour and importance she expected to appear around the corner, but the sound of the footsteps should have forewarned her that this was a small party; just one tour guide and one visitor. The tour guide was evidently bored, and perhaps a little affronted to be showing someone round who was not important enough to warrant a VIP guide. The visitor recognised Dolly Dunkley immediately. 'Dolly!'

It was an exclamation of surprise, but also of confusion; he clearly found it puzzling to see the girl in this context. The tour guide, on the other hand, gave a very slight roll of her eyes, which Dolly did not understand.

The visitor was a young man in his early twenties; his smartly cut suit was tailored, but not expensively so, and his shoes – which did not look new – squeaked from lack of use. He was not tall, he was not handsome, he did not appear rich or dashing, but perhaps he was influential. All that was important was that he was a VIP visitor and he had stopped to speak to Dolly when she was looking for reasons not to go back to work, so she took her chance and simpered an ingratiating smile.

'You have me at a disadvantage . . .?' Dolly was trying to place the young man's face; it hovered somewhere between blandly unmemorable, and just ugly enough to ring a bell.

'Percy,' he said, turning his back entirely on the tour guide who was no longer disguising her boredom in the slightest. 'Percy Palgrave. You were at the Grammar

School at the same time as my cousin Evaline; I remember you reading an essay on speech day.' He cast a look up and down her, giving the impression that he was remembering the old Dolly in detail. 'Your shoes were white.'

'Oh, well, there were lots of people at speech days so I wouldn't remember everyone.' Dolly tended to be short on charming conversation, but she was aware that she needed to make more of this encounter to justify her extended and unnecessary absence from the office. 'Why are you on a tour? Are you a politician?'

'No, work for Burmah Oil, colonial office. Back on leave. My godfather is a friend of the Mackintoshes; he can't get the time to see me again this visit so he organised a tour of the factory.' This was evidently the first the tour guide had heard of it and she did not look pleased that this long-suffering godfather had palmed his awful godson on to her instead of doing his duty and seeing the little horror for himself.

Dolly's eyes widened. She had heard three things which impressed her: he had a connection with some important people, he worked for an oil company, and he was stationed in a *colonial* office. Percy Palgrave began to take on an immediate appeal. He possessed no personal qualities which she liked, but congenitally dishonest, Dolly did not even register this fact – she was already entranced by the frisson of excitement which came with hints of money, power, and social connection. Dolly did not think to ask herself why someone making a success of a career in the East would be home on leave at the wrong time of year, or why he would be entirely alone.

Chapter Seventeen

'Mrs Skirrow's in quarantine!' Doreen delivered the astonishing news as she burst into the changing room of the Caramel Cup line where her colleagues were putting on their caps, ready for the start of their shift.

'How's that?' Winnifred stopped mid-sentence in alarm. 'Our Mrs Skirrow? You mean Mavis?'

'Yes, Mavis, Mavis Skirrow who works wrapping and packing in our workroom – she's in mandatory quarantine with her whole family.' Doreen squeezed past her colleagues to reach her peg and pull on her white overalls while she explained. 'She lives on our street. One of her lads went to see his cousin out at their farm and came home a bit sickly. By teatime he was sweating buckets and talking drivel so they sent for the doctor. *He* said it was scarlet fever and the whole house has got three weeks quarantine. They can't so much as go to the shop. Not that they could buy 'owt from the shop because they can't go out to collect their wage packets, so they've got nothing.'

'Where did you hear all this?' Pearl was wary of believing scare stories about devastating scourges based purely on hearsay.

'From Mavis hersen'. She came to the window, asked me to tell her overlooker so as they'd know she wasn't swinging the lead, like.' Doreen was quick to reassure the colleagues who were edging away from her, 'Oh, she didn't open the window, she says she's not allowed. She just shouted through the glass. That'll be all right, won't it?'

'We should leave her some basin meals.' Winnifred wasn't going to let one of their colleagues go without food for three weeks, nor her children neither. 'Do you know if her family are doing 'owt? Or your neighbours?'

Doreen blew out her cheeks. 'Her only family are up at the farm and they're under a quarantine order an' all, but I don't think they're keeping to it. I saw one of their kids dropping off some bread and bits this morning when I stopped by.'

'Oh, that's all we need!' Pearl groaned. 'I hope you reported them.'

'I wouldn't dare. It's Stebbins lot – you know the ones who have the motorcycle and the huge dog? – I wouldn't say boo to their goose.'

'But if they're spreading it round . . .' Pearl pulled a face as though she'd smelled something unpalatable. 'Some poor kiddy could easily catch it.'

Doreen tried to move the conversation on from the suggestion that she inform on a well-known and difficult local family. 'There's always a few cases this time of year. They clear up by the Easter holidays when everyone gets a bit more fresh air.'

'That's what they said in Doncaster,' Winnifred said ominously. 'You heard about the outbreak they had there last year; swept through the town and killed—'

'When we're quite ready?' Cynthia Starbeck had thrown open the doors from the production room to the cloakroom and was standing to attention.

'We're so sorry, Mrs Starbeck.' Pearl, being some years older than Cynthia Starbeck, tended to adopt a conversational tone with her, as though she thought they were equals. 'We had just heard the news that one of our colleagues from this line has been put into mandatory quarantine. She's asked us to tell Reenie because—'

'Irene Calder no longer runs this line.' Mrs Starbeck didn't give anyone the chance to ask questions. 'We are now three minutes late for starting and this will be recorded on your timecards. Places, please.'

'But Mrs Starbeck,' Pearl insisted, 'Mavis is in quarantine for three weeks. Shouldn't we inform someone from the Employment Department so that they don't dock her wages?'

'Is Mavis ill?'

'No, but she and her family have to stay in quarantine while her son gets over scarlet fever.'

'If she is not at work she is not entitled to wages. If she is unwell herself then she can apply to the sickness club for insurance. If she is not unwell herself then she is not entitled to sickness insurance and would be well advised to come into work. Now, if you'd be so good as to start work, we are now four minutes late and I will be docking wages accordingly.'

'Yes, Mrs Starbeck.' Pearl swallowed her criticisms of the manager who had the power to make pecuniary sanctions against them all and followed her colleagues to the production line.

The line had changed since the occasion of the phantom spider sighting and subsequent tin soldier discovery. The engineers had been in to rearrange the production line equipment and to shorten the women's workstations so that each woman was now working at far closer quarters with the next, and with far less space to comfortably move. Their wonderful experimental line, which Reenie Calder had set up to test her theory that more space meant more speed, had been transformed on Mrs Starbeck's orders as an experiment to determine the absolute minimum space a production line could operate in, and they were the guinea pigs. The worry over an isolated case of scarlet fever was quickly forgotten in the face of this immediate threat to their working way of life.

Chapter Eighteen

'Mary is having a love affair by correspondence.' Bess offered up her sister's news to Reenie in exchange for a chocolate digestive biscuit which had only melted on one side.

'I am not!'

Bess was unconcerned by her elder sister's protestations and said between mouthfuls of biscuit, 'I saw the letters; they're all from Mr Baum. I saw them when our bedroom got flooded. He says he misses her.'

'He just said that he misses my cheerful face in the morning because I'm always ready to start work on time! Other people *aren't* ready to start work on time.'

Reenie, who was managing to eat a digestive biscuit with one hand, brush down her horse with the other, and carry on a conversation with her friends asked, 'Since when have you had a cheerful face?'

Mary scowled at Reenie. 'I've always had a cheerful face.'

Reenie ducked under Ruffian's neck to brush his other side while Bess and Mary shuffled down the hay bale they were sitting on to give her more room. 'What's he been writing you letters for, then?'

Mary was vague. 'They're just instructions on the work he wants me to do in the kitchens in his absence.'

Bess was gleeful, 'He's sent her *hundreds.*'

Reenie dropped her horse brush; this was exciting. 'But he's only been gone since June!'

'No,' Mary wanted to nip this whole thing in the bud before the news got all round the factory, 'he just sends one each day.'

Reenie raised an eyebrow. 'One a day? Doesn't that feel a bit keen?'

Mary – who offered this information only because she wanted to jump to Albert's defence – said, 'He's only writing so often because he's replying to my letters.' And then protested with even more agitation, 'Diana told me to do it! I'm just sending him a summary of the work I've done each day and questions about my studies. He's just answering questions about my studies!'

Reenie smirked. 'And telling you he misses your cheerful face.'

'It's not like that. *He's* not like that.'

Reenie came and sat down beside her companionably to reach for another biscuit. 'Well, what *is* he like?'

Mary thought carefully, and then said, 'He's just . . . he's just very gentlemanly and he cares about how I'm getting on.'

Bess said, 'He wishes he could take her to Germany one day and show her his city because he thinks she'd like the buildings.'

'There's nothing funny about that! It's just architecture!'

Reenie was enjoying this conversation. 'Is that what they're calling it these days? Oh, but it sounds romantic. Would you really go to Germany if he asked you?'

'Of course not. Going abroad sounds terrifying.'

Reenie thought Mary would find anything and everywhere terrifying. It was a miracle she walked out of her own front door each morning. 'What else do you two write about?'

'Just work and nothing else.'

Bess was remembering more from the fragments of letters she'd seen. 'He talks to her about the news because he wants to reassure her he's not in as much danger as she worries he is.'

'*Is* he in danger?'

'Of course he's in danger!' For once Mary wasn't worrying unnecessarily. 'He's a Jewish man living in Germany! He gets stopped by the police twice a week!'

This put a different complexion on things altogether and Reenie was now very concerned, 'What do the police want with him? What's he done?'

'Nothing.' Mary's eyes welled up a little with anger at the thought of what he was put through by the police, and by local officials, and by anyone else with a little bit of power to wield. 'They've never got a reason. They do it to anyone they think is Jewish and sometimes they take him to the police station and make him sit there for hours while they "check his papers" and he has to miss a day off work.'

'That's awful,' Reenie said, 'he should definitely come back to England. Is he still coming back?'

'We don't know.' Mary kicked at her own heel. 'He's

got to get permission to come indefinitely and they only gave him a three-month permit last time, and they've threatened to stop those. *And* they won't let him bring his sister and his children. Mackintosh's are trying to get him an indefinite permit, and Sir Harold has offered to pay their bond himself, but the Home Office keep telling him his papers are wrong.' Mary didn't dare tell them the latest news – the news which had arrived by airmail on Friday; anything could put the mockers on it and she didn't want to take the risk.

Reenie put her arm through Mary's. 'When he does come back, do you think he'll ask you to walk out with him?'

'Of course not, he's my manager!'

'He's not really, though, is he? Amy Wilkes is your manager, he's just a colleague.'

Bess piped up, 'He says he's counting the days until they can be together again.'

Reenie grinned when she heard this revelation. 'I honestly think he's sweet on you. And he's a nice man and ever so handsome. Are you sweet on him?'

Bess said, 'She is. She's always talking about him.'

'I am not!'

Reenie sighed at the romance of it all. 'Think of all the places he could take you! I bet he'd want to take you abroad for your honeymoon if you got married. Where do you think you'd ask to go?'

Bess squeaked, 'Oh, take me! I've never been abroad.'

Mary pursed her lips, got up, and brushed the hay off her skirt. 'I don't want to talk about this any more.' She said it decisively, but in her heart of hearts she really did want to talk about it. She wanted to pour her worries out to her friend and tell her all her fears and her frail hopes. She wanted to tell her how her heart fluttered in her chest every time a letter arrived from Albert, and how terrified she was at the thought that he would come back soon. Because much though she loved his letters, and much though she wished they could be together, she was terrified of this great unknown. She didn't want to be taken places, or to go abroad for a honeymoon because she feared the unknown. As long as Albert was at a distance, their love affair was just the size she could manage. Truth be told, he had said more in his letters to her than Bess knew about and she had said more to him. When he came back to England it would be impossible to carry on as they had before he had left, and this made a hard lump stick in her throat.

Mary had kept telling herself that it would be a long time yet before he could return and so for the moment she was safe to savour their correspondence – but the nagging worry had remained. There was so much she didn't know about the world and the things she did know she feared: she feared what would happen if he stayed in Germany, and she feared what would happen if he returned.

As time had gone by Albert had revealed more and more of the troubles he and his family were facing at home in Germany, and Mary could not conceal her outrage at the injustice of it. After she'd expressed that the line had been crossed and an intimacy crept into their correspondence which only grew with each delivery of the post. Mary implored him to be careful, not to take risks, not to anger the officials by sticking up for himself or telling them what he thought of their regime. He was too vulnerable, and there was no safety net.

Their correspondence was daily, but not chronological. As their letters flew back and forth across the channel, they often overlapped and jumped ahead of each other, leading to all kinds of confusion and anticipation. They didn't mind; for Albert's part he couldn't believe that a girl in another country, who had never met his children, could be ready to fight like a tiger to save them, and Mary couldn't believe there was anyone in all the world who could cause her so much worry and then, with a word, smooth it all away.

Chapter Nineteen

'I need you to sign an affidavit.' Amy Wilkes was drinking her second cup of tea that morning and, judging by the stack of freshly typed correspondence ready for the post, she had been at her desk for two hours longer than anyone else in the office building. 'It's not here; the Mackintosh's solicitor is drawing it up so you'll need to go over to his chambers with Mr Baum. I've sent for a car to take you both there – there's no time for you to be waiting at bus stops when I've got work for you to do here.'

Diana gave away only a glimmer of surprise 'Mr Baum? Mr Albert Baum?'

'Yes, Mr Baum. Head Confectioner, Mr Baum.'

'But he's in Germany, isn't he?'

'No, he's behind you.'

Diana's head whipped round and she saw a pair of bashful cocoa-coloured eyes look up. Albert Baum had been sitting in a chair behind the door with a crumpled raincoat over his knee. 'Mr Baum,' Diana recovered her composure after her initial surprise. 'I'm sorry, I hadn't realised you were here. Does Mary know . . .?' Diana looked from Albert to her manager.

'Mary?' Amy Wilkes frowned and took off her tortoise-shell spectacles, trying to place the name. 'She's the apprentice confectioner?'

Diana paused very slightly before she answered, 'Yes. She's been holding the fort for Mr Baum.' And then pointedly to the recent arrival, 'She'll be very anxious to know that you've returned safely.'

'Well, he's not safe yet, that's why you need to sign the affidavit. And on that note, you'll find the car waiting outside.'

Diana was a little suspicious of this unannounced arrival of her German colleague. She had always believed that he was a good man and that he had a genuine affection for Mary; indeed, this had been part of her reason for encouraging a long-distance courtship by arranging weekly telephone calls for them and daily letters under the guise of work-related arrangements. But now here he was and he hadn't gone straight to find Mary to tell her that he had arrived. The girl was suffering an agony of worry and waiting and he was riding in a chauffeur-driven car to see a solicitor. But Diana said nothing. It was not her business.

'I will tell her very soon.' Albert Baum was shifting awkwardly in the cream leather seats of the Mackintosh's limousine, clearly he felt conflicted about his situation.

'Tell who about what?' Diana feigned disinterest well; she was so often disinterested that it came naturally to her.

'We both know very well. I want to bring her good news, not more worry.'

They sat in an uncomfortable silence until the car turned off Silver Street and glided up to the door of Equitable Chambers. The ornamented building was as intimidating as the luxurious car; high Edwardian splendour in the fussiest imitation of Renaissance Florentine grandeur. It was not a place which Diana could warm to, but she supposed it had just the right amount of arrogance to deal a blow to the Home Office bureaucrats who were taking them round and round in circles with their applications for permits for more staff.

The polished brass plate on the door gleamed and the name Barstow, Midgley & Lord had a quality which was both worn down through long establishment and consequent long cleaning, and a boldness which made it impossible to misread. The plate appeared to say 'we have always been here, but that does not mean we have ever been ignored'.

Diana attempted to swallow her dislike of solicitors and all things legalese long enough to follow Mr Baum and the solicitor's clerk up to the hallowed hole of Mr Midgley himself.

'Ah, Herr Baum I presume?' He extended his fat-fingered hand to shake and gave it a little twist as he did so. Diana noticed, but Mr Baum did not.

'I hope that you will forgive the short notice of my arrival . . .'

'There is nothing to forgive. We are at the disposal of our clients and Sir Harold is a client of longstanding. He explained your unusual circumstances; so was your errand successful, Herr Baum?'

'Yes, thank you, it was. My colleagues at Mackintosh's have been more than generous in their practical assistance. I travelled with my colleague Mr Johns through the Netherlands and smuggled them out in his luggage rather than my own.' Albert reached into his jacket and pulled out a roll of cloth which he handed over to the solicitor.

Mr Midgley unrolled the fabric, glanced at what it contained, and then stepped aside to allow his clerk to take a seat at his desk and immediately begin writing out an inventory of its contents for a detailed receipt. Diana's eyebrow rose slightly at the sight of rubies red as blood, gleaming gold rings set with sparkling sapphires, solidly ornate silver bangles, and trinkets which were alien to her in their shape but not in their value. She watched and she listened.

'I am sorry, where are my manners?' Albert recollected himself now that the burden of his concealed treasure had been passed to safe hands. 'Mr Midgley, this is Diana Moore of the Mackintosh's Employment Department. She has kindly come to sign the affidavit for the Home Office to confirm my offer of permanent employment, and the fact that I alone am qualified to undertake the work they have for me.'

'Miss Moore, a pleasure.' Mr Midgley shook her hand with that same slight twist: a thumb between two of her knuckles. This perhaps solved the mystery of why one of the partners in the firm was dealing with this matter personally – granted the Mackintosh family were important clients, but Baum was not a Mackintosh. This was perhaps a personal favour; Diana read the newspapers, she knew that Adolf Hitler had inexplicably declared Freemasonry to be one of his many enemies. A Yorkshire Freemason might be more sympathetic than the civil servants in the Home Office, but it didn't explain the jewels; surely Mr Baum wasn't expected to pay in gold for his papers? And even if he were, that amount would far exceed any fees they could bill him for.

Mr Midgley turned to Albert and said, 'Now, we have some papers for you to sign; the lease on the house at Skircoat Green, your new permanent contract of employment at Mackintosh's, your statement of intent. Then we have the written references secured for you by Sir Harold, the affidavit from your employers, and some sundry papers to support your application.'

'And I take all of these to the British Embassy in Berlin?'

'Ah, yes, but not quite yet Mr Baum. We need to have the lease countersigned by the landlord and we need to prepare a statement from the bank confirming the deposit of your family effects,' here he gestured delicately to the sparkling treasures on his desk, 'and include the all-important valuation. The Home Office must know that you have the wherewithal to provide for your children, even beyond the means of your salary.'

'And then I can apply for a permit to return here on an indefinite basis with my children and my sister? It is imperative that the permission is granted for all my family. I cannot leave them behind again.'

'We should have all the papers you need by Tuesday, but I must impress upon you that there are no guarantees. In our experience the Home Office have been making matters unnecessarily complicated for Jews who want to enter Great Britain – especially so for those who have Polish Citizenship to fall back on. I realise that in your case you may never have set foot in Poland, but the Home Office is quite clear; if you have any Polish ancestor you are expected to seek refuge there. Really, Mr Baum, if I may speak frankly, you might consider sending your children and your sister to Poland if all else fails in Britian.'

'I will give it some thought. Thank you, Mr Midgley.'

Mr Midgley sighed. 'I make no promises, mind you. We will have you an excellent application, but even the best applications have been refused. I'd say your chances are 50-50.'

Albert Baum looked brave and hopeful. 'As high as that?'

Chapter Twenty

Mary knew that she needed to get that lock fixed, but it wasn't an easy thing to arrange when your manager was in Düsseldorf. She'd snapped the key in the lock months earlier, but every time the factory locksmiths came out to look at it they did everything except replace the lock itself. Mary wasn't worried, no one really bothered her in the Confectioners' Kitchen, it was her safe haven.

Friday had come around slowly, and the worry for the absent Albert had settled to a background hum in Mary's thoughts. That afternoon she was lost in her work and it was easy work to become lost in. Mary made confectionery by hand in the Mackintosh's experimental kitchens, and it was the privilege of her life that she had been chosen for it. Albert Baum had been brought to England as her instructor, and the Mackintosh's factory had high hopes that they would be able to bring him back permanently once they'd settled a work permit for him.

It was a fairly routine day in the kitchens for Mary.

She had been asked to make a batch of seven hundred Caramel Cups to a new recipe the factory was developing and wanted to try out on their expert chocolate tasters. She had to gently melt heavy slabs of rich brown chocolate in her bain-marie, then temper it on the marble-topped table they kept for the purpose. Then she flicked the liquid chocolate up onto a tin mould, using nothing but her pallet knife and her innate skill, coating the cup-shaped wells with a glossy cocoa liquor. While her rows of chocolate cups cooled, she set about the leisurely task of mixing caramel – not too hastily lest the heat scorch the ingredients and spoil the delicate flavours – and then pouring it carefully into her piping bag while she savoured the aroma of butter, vanilla, and sweetness. It was all just as Albert Baum had taught her in that very kitchen when she was his apprentice, and she wished he could see her now.

The process was just complex enough to be interesting to Mary, but just repetitive enough to be soothing. Mary worked alone contentedly; the kitchens were her domain. She took her time melting the chocolate for the cup moulds, tempering it on her marble-topped table, spreading it onto the decorative indentations and knocking it out. She was so mesmerised by the chocolate that when she finally realised she was being watched she had no idea how long she had been absorbed. But sure enough, there in the doorway with her arms crossed, was the over-made-up face of Dolly Dunkley.

'What do you want, Dolly?' Mary's patience for the girl had been severely limited since she last worked with her in those very kitchens. Dolly's habit of wandering the factory corridors, looking for someone to snitch on instead of getting on with her work, was driving Mary and her friends to distraction. Mrs Starbeck must either be utterly blind, or have had some ulterior motive for keeping her on if she was willing to put up with Dolly's dithering.

'I've come to see—' Dolly's nasal whine was interrupted by a second visitor, who she greeted with a sneering, 'Oh, we're back, are we?'

Albert Baum maintained his composure and replied, 'Miss Dunkley; it's always a pleasure to see you looking so well.' His eyes met Mary's across the room and he could see that she was so surprised to see him there that she couldn't speak. They both wanted to run to one another, but they couldn't move while this unspeakable girl stood between them.

'I am well, as it happens, because I've been promoted to the offices.' Dolly jutted out her chin in a strange, smug, wiggly little gesture which implied she felt she had been promoted in the teeth of Albert Baum's express opposition, but the truth be known he had always been ambivalent towards her.

'Dolly is working for Mrs Starbeck now,' Mary explained wearily.

'Yes, and she'll be *very* interested to hear that you've returned. We thought you'd gone for good.' Dolly Dunkley had an uncontrollable fetish for reporting wrongdoers and she hovered in the kitchen now as though waiting to spot a misdemeanour and then pounce on it in righteous indignation, but nothing untoward was happening.

'By all means,' Albert said with weary patience, 'give Mrs Starbeck my very best regards, and inform her that I am only in the country for a few weeks to arrange some paperwork. I have a dispensation to allow me to visit long enough to make some legal arrangements and then I will be gone.'

Mary's voice caught in her throat. 'A few weeks?'

'Until Easter,' he told her. 'I will be here until Easter at the latest.'

'Well you'll notice that things have changed a lot round here since you left.' Dolly appeared to be in a boastful mood and inclined to leave in a blaze of glory. 'We're getting more and more like Germany every day,' she said with pride, 'and it won't be long now before Oswald Mosley is in power in Britain and then you'll *really* see how a country ought to be run.' Lifting her nose even higher into the air, Dolly marched off in the direction of the door, walked abruptly into the door frame because she wasn't properly looking where she was going, and scowled at Mary and Albert as though they had caused her injury. 'I'll be keeping an eye on you,' she said, although it wasn't much of a threat given that she couldn't even watch where she was going.

When she was finally gone Mary swallowed back a sob and said, 'You're here.'

'I'm here. I promised I would come back.' And Albert took two long strides towards Mary and took her hand in both of his and kissed it, just as he had done in that very room on the day he left her.

'We can't stay here.' Mary looked to the door. 'She'll come back, you know. She'll find a way to make it worse for us. Please, let's meet tomorrow afternoon, away from the factory . . .'

Chapter Twenty-One

'I promise you that this is the one place that Dolly Dunkley would never see us.' Mary clutched their stubby brown bus tickets for dear life as they alighted at Hopwood Lane, strands of her soft, coal-black hair flying loose as she jumped down from the footplate and half ran towards a pair of wrought-iron gates which stood open beside the road ahead of them. 'I doubt she even knows where it is.'

'This is a dangerous place?' Albert Baum did not appear to mind if it was. His cares were visibly lifting from his brow now that he was alone with Mary and he followed her as she marched with determined steps through the gates.

Mary smiled at him, her cheeks flushed pink with the excitement of getting away. 'It's not dangerous. I come here nearly every day after work. It's the only place I can read your letters in peace.' They passed a grand, gothic stone gatehouse and pressed on along a drive flanked with thick old yew trees. Mary looked over her shoulder to make certain that they were far enough into the tree-lined avenue not to be seen from the road and then, with a shiver of nervous excitement, she reached out her hand to Albert. He took it, interlacing their fingers and locking them together. Such a simple thing, which so many couples took for granted, but it made Mary's heart ache to finally be walking hand in hand after all this time apart.

Albert smiled at Mary, and Mary smiled back at him. She couldn't help it, her face ached because she grinned so much; she had never felt so happy before and she thought her heart would burst. There was her Albert in the flesh at last and she could gaze at him, his rich brown hair catching the afternoon light like polished mahogany, his cocoa-coloured eyes twinkling as he smiled down at her. At last, at last, at last.

They walked along in perfect step and Albert lifted the back of Mary's hand to his lips and kissed it. He sighed happily, and then something made him glance ahead of him to watch where he was going and he suddenly stopped short, looked up at the building they were approaching and cried, '*Gott im Himmel!*'

They had broken through the thick wall of trees which had blocked their view from the drive and now he could see that an immaculately kept lawn stretched for two acres ahead of them, divided by a neat gravel path which wound round a fountain and led to a palace.

'But this is French; this is like the chateaux of Louis XIII, we cannot be in Halifax.' Albert's eyes were wide with astonishment and Mary couldn't help feeling a little proud of her town for owning something that could make a well-travelled foreigner stop in his tracks.

'We're in Halifax, I promise you. One of the big carpet mill owners wanted to live in a French palace, so he built one. I've never been to France so I don't know if it looks the part or not.'

'It is *very* French!' Albert was looking over his shoulder and around in concern as Mary strolled contentedly through the grounds. 'But are we permitted to be here? Will the owners not . . .?'

'Oh, no, it's all quite all right, the owners are long since dead. This is the public library, now. Why did you think I came here? It's where I read the newspapers to see the news in Germany. They even have a wireless in the music room.'

'You are reading about my country?'

'Of course. I'm afraid for you every day. I read about all the things which are happening to your people and I check for your name in case something has happened to you.'

Albert tucked a lock of hair over Mary's ear which had come loose from her tight bun and asked earnestly, 'Does reading the newspaper each day make you feel less worried about me?'

'No, it makes me feel worse. But I do it anyway. I've got the worry habit.' Mary looked over at the lights glowing in the windows of the grand old palace and tugged Albert's hand to draw him onward. 'How long do you think it will take you to settle your affairs in Germany before you can come back to Halifax? You *are* coming back, aren't you? That's what the papers are for?'

'Yes, yes, that's what the papers are for. Sir Harold Mackintosh has requested his family solicitor to draw up all the applications for the permit this time. We must present them with many different documents and it is complex work; when I sent the documents previously, the Home Office say that they are not correct, but this solicitor is an excellent legal man and they will not argue with him, I think. We will have the application dealt with very quickly now.' Albert Baum stopped to look more carefully at the outside of the library building. 'Do you know of what this building reminds me? It is like the Remplin Palace; I knew it felt familiar to me. It is a grand palace near the town where my grandmother lived. Now *they* have a library. It is full of great works of German art; they have letters written by Goethe and paintings by Winterhalter. I will take you there one day and show you the observatory; you would like it I think. Would you like to come to Germany one day?'

Mary did not have the opportunity to answer because at that moment she turned her ankle on a Victorian drain cover and the heel snapped off her shoe with an audible crack which threw her forward into Albert's arms and nearly toppled them both onto the manicured lawn.

'*Mein Gott*, are you hurt? Did you injure your foot?' Albert caught Mary up in his arms and she was able to feel that although he was lean he was strong.

She recovered herself and managed to stammer out, 'No, no, I'm quite unharmed, I've only broken my shoe.' Mary had nothing but trouble from shoes, and she thought it typical that it would be a shoe that would spoil everything. She hobbled towards the door of the library where there was an empty bench to sit on. With help from Albert, who gave her one hand to lean on, and put the other around her waist to support her, she was able to reach it and lower herself gently down. 'I'm sorry to give you so much bother.'

Albert came and sat beside her once he had made certain that she was comfortable and not in any distress, looking confused by her choice of words. 'Bother?'

'Yes, you know, trouble, problems?'

He smiled to himself as though he knew a secret. 'You are not the source of my problems, Maria.'

'Sometimes I feel like I might be.' Mary leant closer to Albert and tried to ignore the harassed-looking mill workers who trudged past them toward the library door. 'I bother you with an awful lot in my letters; all I do is send you a list of things I'm worried about. I worry that the letters I send you aren't as lovely as the letters you send to me.'

Albert held her closer and looked around him for somewhere they could go where they would not be over-heard, but Mary could not walk far. He spoke hurriedly, in a low voice, 'But you must know how I feel about you, Maria?' He had wanted to conduct their interview in the same kitchen where they had met and had spent so many happy hours in one another's company before they were separated; but in the end he sensed that this was the only place he could secure them anything close to privacy. 'Your letters to me are a light in a very great darkness because they come from you. I do not care if you list laundry soap labels and tell me that the weather is bad, I only want words you have written because all the words you have written to me will never be enough. It is you; it is your brave soul, your compassionate heart, your quick temper, your inquiring mind – all of it has captured me. And you are so beautiful, Maria; you think that you are plainer than those other factory girls, but you are like a swan among ducklings.' Albert looked deep into her eyes and said earnestly, 'I know that I bring a great deal of trouble with me, but I also bring love. I want to look after you and to protect you from all the world. There will be much uncertainty in our lives, but my love is not an uncertainty. I can barely dare to ask it, but tell me, Maria, even with all that holds us apart, if we're given the chance,' he paused, summoning up a new kind of courage now that they were together in person and he couldn't hide behind the written word, he finally asked, 'could you love me?'

Mary, pale with nerves, tried to catch her breath, 'But what if you get to know me and change your mind about me?'

'I already know you, and I won't.'

'But where would we go? What would we do?'

'We will go to many places and do many things; that is the nature of being alive. We cannot predict all of them now, but we can choose who we want to share them with.'

Mary, feeling the seriousness of his question took a deep breath and asked, 'What if you can't work in England?'

'Then I'll take you somewhere else. I do not pretend that our lives together will be easy, or free from distress, but I love you Maria. I want to spend time with you for the rest of my days. If I'm willing to wait for you, could you be willing to wait for me?'

Mary opened her mouth to speak just as the exodus started. Suddenly readers were pouring out of the library hurriedly, looking around them and making their way to the gates. There was an air of excited panic about the people who were bustling past the young couple on their bench and both Mary and Albert knew at once that something was very wrong.

Albert stepped forward and stopped one of the more frantic-looking men. 'Excuse me, sir. Can you tell me what is the matter?'

The man only partially took Albert in, so intent was he on getting away to the nearest bus stop. 'It's been on the wireless. Didn't you hear the wireless inside?' He waved his arm toward the library which was even now disgorging more of its visitors. 'I have to get home. I have to see a newspaper.' He hurried away, anxiety writ large across his features.

Albert tried a lady who was not walking quite so quickly, and she looked up at him with a kind of sad disgust. 'You German?' she asked, hearing his accent.

'Why, yes I am.'

'Well,' she ground her teeth, 'your lot have taken Austria. It's all Germany now. The Austrians didn't even put up a fight when *your* army rolled in. Hitler's on his way to make victory speeches. You've broken the Treaty of Versailles, you know that, don't you? How soon will we need those gas masks, that's what I want to know?'

Albert staggered backward and found himself once again beside Mary. He was clearly in shock. 'This cannot be! They were to have a referendum tomorrow, it was all planned. Hitler agreed it with the Austrians, this was publicly announced, this was not to be forced upon the Austrians, they were to keep their sovereignty.'

Mary was ashamed to be more worried for Albert than she was for the nation of Austria which had just been invaded and occupied by a hostile force. 'What does this mean for us? Does this mean you can stay? Will the Home Office see how dangerous it is now?'

Albert shook his head sadly. 'They've always known how dangerous it is, that is not the trouble. I think this will make things very much worse for us, I am afraid. I am no longer a Jew from Germany, I'm a Jew from a country which has broken its peace treaty with the British, and with everyone else. I am the enemy.'

And Mary looked around her at the yew trees which surrounded them on all sides and in that moment remembered that they were symbols of death. She shivered. It had suddenly turned very cold.

Chapter Twenty-Two

One of the things which irked Cynthia Starbeck about the Crabley Hall fete was that it was held far too early in the year to be anything like summer weather which would have attracted more crowds but Lord Mayhew could not be found at home from the start of the Cheltenham Festival in March to the end of Cowes Week in August and then he dashed off to the Bavarian Alps to hobnob with prominent German politicians at their mountain retreats. This year would be slightly different; he'd squeezed in the annual fete for his estate workers, but intended to be on the boat train to the Continent before they'd packed away the coconut shy to help celebrate the great triumph of the Anschluss in Germany. Membership of the British Union had been dwindling a few years previously, but the very real threat of war had sent membership soaring again, and those who had kept faith all that time were reaping the rewards of their loyalty.

Perhaps what had irked Cynthia most was that she had previously been among Lord Mayhew's set, spending her two weeks annual holiday in Berchtesgaden, enjoying the air and the local culture. However, funds had been in short supply over recent months and her summer holiday was just one of the sacrifices she had been forced to conceal that she was making.

The Crabley Hall fete was a nuisance in her social calendar. It always fell on the third Saturday in March when it was as likely to be cold and wet as it was to be changeable. Dressing for it was a chore now that they weren't permitted to wear their BUF uniforms, and so was attending. However, attend she must. Mayhew was an important member of the local branch of the British Union and a prominent fascist. She had to be seen to attend. The only problem was that all the other members of their local branch would likely be in attendance, and this included Dolly Dunkley.

Cynthia had first met Dolly at a fascist meeting at Crabley Hall, not ten months earlier. If she'd known that her best chance of ridding herself of the Dunkley problem would cross her path at the fete, she might have shown more enthusiasm for it.

A chill wind shivered through stalls and tents and caused a brief flurry of flapping canvas, then died down again. Cynthia had tried to find somewhere to stand in the weak warmth of the sun without looking too much as though she was biding her time until she could leave. She had chosen a spot close to the tea tent because she could at least nurse a warm piece of china. It was here that an acquaintance – eager to palm him off onto someone else – introduced Percy Palgrave.

'Miss Starbeck knows all about Mackintosh's.' The acquaintance, a steward of some sort on one of the local estates, hailed her with the enthusiasm of a drowning man. 'Miss Starbeck, may I introduce you to Percy Palgrave? He was just telling me how much he enjoyed a recent tour of your factory. Mackintosh's is still your factory, isn't it?'

'Well, I don't own it personally, but I flatter myself that I have a hand in keeping it ticking along.' Cynthia attempted to warm herself with her own charm, but it wasn't enough to keep the acquaintance from pleading an appointment and leaving her with the young man who had been treated to a day at her place of work, as if it was a zoo and she a caged beast.

'Jolly interesting place.' Palgrave gave the words an odd emphasis, suggestive of having seen something secret or illicit. 'Met an old school pal of my cousin's while I was there.'

Cynthia's cold teacup was beginning to give her fingers a chill, but the shiver which seized her then was caused by the way this young man looked at her. His eyes seemed almost permanently on the verge of closing, but somehow they leered at her beneath their red, watery lids. He had pale hair which had thinned prematurely at the temples, a fact which he had tried to disguise by very brazenly combing as much of his hair as possible from the very back of his neck over his crown, and then up in a wave of white fluff over his brow. He looked as though a seagull had flung itself on him and died prostrate, and he didn't even have the good grace to look embarrassed by it. He reminded her of Dolly with her surprised-puffin maquillage, and it was with a jolt of surprise that she heard him mention her name.

'Dolly Dunkley – from Stump Cross?'

'Yes, do you know her?'

Starbeck decided to keep her cards close to her chest. 'I know most people at Mackintosh's factory. Tell me, what brought you on a tour? Do you have a particular interest in manufacture?'

'Oh, well, manufacture.' He spluttered out some platitudes about the empire, but to Starbeck's relief it was clear that he had no real interest in her place of work. 'In oil, myself; Burmah Oil. Out in the Rangoon office. Home leave to check on my mother. She's not been well.' Palgrave nodded in the direction of a bilious-looking woman with distinctly red cheeks who was even then trying her hand at the Test Your Strength stall, where her swing of the mallet was not far off ringing the bell to indicate virility. Cynthia thought she recognised her; if she wasn't mistaken, this woman was on the board of trustees of the Bankfield Museum.

The ghost of an idea was forming in Starbeck's mind. 'And have you brought your wife back with you, Mr Palgrave, or has she stayed on in Rangoon with the children?' Cynthia Starbeck judged herself to be a good fifteen years his senior and thought she could get away with asking the question without seeming coquettish.

'Ah, no; not married. Bachelor. I'd had some hopes, but . . .' He gave her a tragic, self-pitying look from beneath his sneaking, hooded eyes.

'"But", Mr Palgrave?'

'Dashed, Miss Starbeck, dashed.'

Cynthia Starbeck thought she knew something about these 'hopes' he hinted at. If his strong-arm mother was the woman she thought she was, then she had heard rumours. She'd heard about the woman's son who was stationed abroad and who had been writing to three different girls to hedge his bets and had arranged to come home to 'get himself a wife'. Whether they had all turned him down because they couldn't stomach the reality of him she didn't know, but she did remember that money had come into it. His family had none and he'd chosen girls who – while not being heiresses of the grand sort – would certainly bring him some solid, short-term comfort in the form of immediate ready cash. Starbeck thought she could use this weakness to her advantage.

'Not dashed by Dolly?'

'The vicar's daughter? No, no, I hadn't seen Dolly in years until the other week. Happened to bump into her by chance at the factory.'

'Well, if you'll allow me to give you some friendly advice, don't let her hear you calling her father a vicar. He's a Rector, and she doesn't like anyone to think he's just a lowly parson.' Mrs Starbeck made it sound very grand indeed.

'Is there a difference? My lot are nonconformist, so I can't say I ever paid much attention to these ecclesiastical distinctions.'

'Money.' Cynthia conveyed the information in a whisper to make certain that the young man would pay attention. 'Vicars have a stipend, but Rectors get a living from the land their church owns and rents to farmers.' Here Cynthia Starbeck told the very precise lie which she felt would be necessary to nudge the whole thing along. 'Her father's put it all into stocks – or so my uncle tells me. They've invested in some similar companies. I expect her father will settle the lot on her. I shouldn't mention it, though; so many young men have taken an interest in her when they've found out how much the father's got tucked away. Someone will snap her up before long and I do so hope it's someone who appreciates her for her personal qualities rather than just the pecuniary assets . . . well, here I am wittering on.'

Chapter Twenty-Three

Dolly Dunkley liked to seek the approval of her manager through easy tasks which she hadn't been asked to complete, rather than difficult ones which she had. This led to a surprising amount of disappointment on both sides. On Dolly's desk that day waited a pile of ledgers full of numbers which she had been told to do something with, but she hadn't listened fully to the instructions, and asking to have them repeated seemed too hard, so once again she was wandering the corridors looking for something easier to do.

It was with a pleasant feeling of surprise that Dolly discovered the noticeboards all over the factory had been covered with a dire warning from Nurse Munton about a small local outbreak of Scarlet Fever and Septic Sore Throat. The posters, which claimed to have been printed by the District Medical Officer, extolled workers to be vigilant and report symptoms and then quarantine until they could be tested. Bold black and red type told the toffee workers that this latest scourge was a second wave of scarlatinal infections caused by the new strain of the disease first seen in Doncaster the preceding year. The Medical Officer emphasised that this strain was more contagious, more dangerous, and more deadly than anything they were used to, and that it was imperative the people of Halifax played their part in containing it before it could do the same damage it had done in Doncaster – or worse.

Dolly was delighted; there were scores of posters and if she took them all down she'd have a whole pile to give to her manager and that should distract her from the unfinished work for quite some time. Dolly set about her task with gusto, imagining how her manager would praise her for stamping out this nonsense and by the time Dolly arrived back at the Time and Motion office she had worked up quite a glow. Her manager was waiting for her.

'Dolly, I have just had a telephone call from the gatehouse. There's a young man here to see you from the Burmah Oil company – in a motor car. I understand he was here at the factory recently as a VIP visitor. He asked if he might call on you this afternoon and I told him that I'd allow it as he's only going to be in England for a short time.' Mrs Starbeck's benevolent smile was convincing.

Dolly Dunkley had a visitor at the factory gates, and he was driving a *motor car*. The news of this would spread around the factory for days to come and Dolly would revel in the celebrity of it for all it was worth. The bundle of posters in her arms were quite forgotten and she was ready to chase out of the door, but before that she had an obstacle to overcome: she couldn't just leave her job for the afternoon to go and chinwag with a visitor. Dolly had anticipated that if she asked to be excused she would be belittled, but Mrs Starbeck took her by surprise:

'You may take the rest of the afternoon off on condition you begin work half an hour earlier in the morning.'

It was an unexpected boon and Dolly didn't question the easy price, nor did she stop to show her manager the bundle of posters she had brought her as an offering. She was still wearing the cotton overall she'd put on to visit the production line earlier and she didn't think to take it off before she ran out of the brass and glass doors at the bottom of the office tower.

Down in the old canal basin, where all the girls in Albion Mills could see, was the unmistakable white mop of hair which belonged to Percy Palgrave. But to whom did the car belong? The idea that the well-connected young man with the exotic line of work should also come with a car was too thrilling to imagine. Dolly hurried over to the gleaming metal monster and breathlessly greeted its driver.

'Hullo. Remember me? I came on a tour of the factory.'

'Yes, yes!' Dolly's puffin face was alive with excitement. 'My manager told me you wanted to call on me and she's given me the afternoon off.'

He gave an awkward sort of chuckle and pointed to her overalls. 'I've got the loan of a Ford for a couple of hours. Just trying it out. See if I want to buy one.' He did not explain how he would get a car to Burma if he did buy one, but that wasn't the sort of thing Dolly would notice. 'I thought we could take the car out for a drive. I know all girls like cars.'

'Rather! If I run and go and change my overalls, will you wait? I'll run fast.'

'Run your fastest!' And Percy Palgrave followed her with his hooded, lascivious eyes.

The drive was a bumpy one over the roads out of Halifax. Industrial towns attracted industrial traffic, and the heavy goods vehicles showed the tarmac the corporation had lavished upon them no mercy. Palgrave was keen to take the car up to the top of Beacon Hill 'to see what it was made of'. It was the purest of coincidences that the view of Halifax was breathtaking from that spot and that the sun was over in the sky in the afternoon, tinting the clouds with pretty colours by five o'clock when they arrived at the lip of the Devil's Cauldron.

Percy did not ask Dolly many questions, but he paid her an almost implausible number of compliments. Her dress sense was 'up-to-the-minute', her hair was 'jolly chic', her decision to give the factory a bit of her time was 'very patriotic', and her knowledge of the locale was like that of Ariadne to his Theseus.

The car performed its job well, but the view from Beacon Hill performed its job even better. Dolly was keen to point out the spire of her father's church at this great vantage point that looked out across half the Calder valley and which didn't look to her like it was suffering under a great plague of scarlet fever.

'And where's his rectory? Nearby, is it?'

'Oh yes, it's just the other side of that wall. It's ever so big, and we've got walled gardens to keep the parishioners from wandering in at all hours.'

'Must be an occupational hazard if you've got a large parish, what?' Palgrave managed to sound both concerned and casual.

131

'Oh, it's ever so much work. The parish stretches from all the way down there at Clough Mills and covers the two farms on the other side of that ridge. His parish is one of the biggest for miles around.'

This was all lies; Dolly hadn't the faintest idea where the boundaries of her father's parish were, but she had cottoned on to the idea that big things made her visitor happy and so she had decided to make everything gargantuan in order to win his approval. She liked his approval.

'Your father, he's a Rector, isn't he?' That practised, casual note held just long enough. 'Where is his rectory land? Got much of that these days?'

'Oh, all of this you can see is his rectory land.' Dolly had no idea what she was saying, but she enjoyed impressing Percy – and he did look very impressed.

Chapter Twenty-Four

'That's bad news for Herr Baum.' Amy Wilkes put down the telephone receiver and took the cup of tea her assistant Diana was offering her.

'A problem with the Home Office?' Diana had put the call through herself and she knew it was the solicitor, but she didn't like to give the impression that she eavesdropped on her manager's telephone calls.

'No, a problem with a landlord. Won't sign the lease.' Amy Wilkes took a thoughtful sip of her tea. 'People can be such beasts.'

'I thought the lease had already been signed. Isn't that what Herr Baum was doing at the solicitor's office when you sent me there with him?'

'No, it wasn't as simple as that. The solicitor had arranged the lease and the landlord was going to counter-sign the contract once Herr Baum had signed it, but when they saw his name – and realised that it was a Jewish name – they refused to sign and said they won't lease him the property.'

'But whatever for? What do they think he's going to do to the place? Fill it to the rafters with bagels?'

'The landlord happens to be a member of the British Union and so he won't lease property to Jewish tenants.'

Diana said nothing, but closed her eyes and squeezed the bridge of her nose.

'Which leaves us with a very immediate problem: Herr Baum cannot apply for a permit to work here without a signed lease on a full house to prove he has a permanent home here for himself, his children, and his sister.'

Diana nodded. 'We need to find him another house.'

'How long did it take us to find the last one?'

'Five months.'

Amy Wilkes blew out her cheeks and took off her tortoiseshell spectacles. 'All right, well let's be less fussy this time. We don't need to find the perfect house, just four walls and a roof.'

'With respect, those were our criteria last time. With the current housing shortage in Halifax we are competing against scores of other families who are just as quick to put in offers on homes they haven't even seen; this could take some time. How long can he stay in the country to sign a lease?'

Mrs Wilkes consulted her notes. 'His current permit allows him to stay until he has signed all the papers relating to his application and his lease – he has until the Tuesday after Easter, so approximately four weeks.'

'I'll see what I can do.' Diana turned to leave her manager's office.

'Pull out all the stops, Diana. It's not just about the

job – although God knows we can't get another trained confectioner of his calibre in England – it's the thought of sending him back. You've seen the newspapers, it's . . .' Mrs Wilkes shuddered. 'We can't let it happen.'

Chapter Twenty-Five

'He's a good lad, is your Peter.' It wasn't a throwaway remark. Reenie's father was shuffling from one foot to the other, turning his cap in his hands in front of him. He exchanged a glance with Mrs Calder which plainly said *why don't you tell her, you're her mother?*

Reenie did not notice the silent battle of wills which was going on over her head between her parents because she was elbows deep in the cupboard underneath the Welsh dresser, rummaging for a length of string.

'You could do a lot worse than your Peter,' her father persisted with hesitant steps.

'Did you ever doubt it?' Reenie emerged triumphant with a shank of good cotton string and then caught a look between her parents. Something was afoot. 'Am I missing something, Mother?'

Mrs Calder pursed her lips at her husband in the universal signal of displeasure and then said to her daughter, 'It's just that we want to know if you're thinking of setting a date right soon, you and Peter.'

Reenie couldn't imagine what had got into her parents, but she hoped that *it* passed right soon. 'What? For announcing an engagement? I've said I don't mind us having an understanding, but it's a bit soon to be talking about properly announced engagements.'

'Your mother didn't want to ask you about engagements, she wanted to ask you about a date for a wedding.' Mr Calder's eyes were wide and earnest. This was a topic neither of her parents took lightly, and the realisation that they had planned to speak to her about it together – and without her siblings present – was now dawning on her.

Reenie put down her string. 'What do you want to go thinking about weddings for? There's no hurry and neither of us are thinking of doing anything hasty. Peter said he didn't mind us having a long engagement so's I could stop on at Mack's a while longer and make the most of my time in my job, and—' Reenie stopped short and narrowed her eyes at her parents. 'This isn't because you think I'm in trouble, is it?' She looked down at the fit of her dress, a little more irritated than self-conscious. 'I'm not in trouble, I've just got a very healthy appetite!'

'I know, love,' Reenie's mother was consoling, but at the same time casting accusing looks at her husband which plainly suggested that she thought this misunderstanding could have been avoided if he'd done a better job of saying the things which they had both agreed he ought to say. 'It's not that we think you've done anything wrong – quite the reverse – we think you've found yourself a lovely young man. It's just that we think it would be a good idea if you set a date, perhaps early in the summer.'

Reenie pulled back a chair and slowly lowered herself to the kitchen table, keeping her eyes all the while on both her parents. 'Early in the summer? It's spring now! You were the ones who said you wanted me at home and not in a boarding house in town—'

'We're not trying to get shot of you!' Mr Calder was quick to interject. 'We just don't want you left with nothing, like my sisters!'

'There's war coming.' Mrs Calder was nothing if not pragmatic. 'We read the papers same as everyone else. They're making munitions and the government's talking about stockpiling food.'

'When the war comes,' Mr Calder said with obvious reluctance, 'we don't want you working in a factory. There were air raids with bombs during the last war, and now that aeroplanes are bigger they'll only be worse this time. It was in the paper only last Christmas that they'd made it law that all factories have to have shelters in case they're bombed with gas. Gas, Reenie! We think it would be safer if you weren't at the factory. Perhaps now's the time to think about setting a date for a wedding and giving up work at Mack's.'

A silence hung heavy in the air before Reenie asked, 'What did you mean about my being left with nothing like your sisters? Neither of them worked in a factory, they were both on the farm.'

'You know they both had young men who went off to fight and they were both dead set on long engagements. Wanted nothing hasty; wanted to wait until the war was over. Thought it would be over by Christmas. Both lads were killed and there was not a widow's pension for either of them. Your Peter is a young man so he'll be one of the first to be called up. Marry him now, lass, because you don't know what tomorrow will bring. Your mother says have a summer wedding, but I remember the last war; I remember couples who clamoured at the register office and the parish church wanting to be wed, but who couldn't get their names down for the queues. When war's declared you might not be able to get anyone to marry you in time. I say do it *now*. We'll pay for the licence and any bit o' clothes you want, just don't wait. There's none of us know if there'll be anything left to wait for.'

Reenie felt tears sting her eyes. She had been blithely going on with her work and her busy social calendar and had never thought that she would be faced with a decision like this one. Of course she knew the sad story of her maiden aunts who had never married, and who would never marry, but she'd always thought of them as so different from herself. They were powerless spinsters to whom things happened, whereas Reenie would always have her get-up-and-go; Life didn't happen to Reenie, Reenie happened to Life. The thought that a future like theirs was waiting for her, that she might be about to stumble into it, terrified her. But so did the thought of having her job taken away. She had never planned to go and have a career at Mack's, the job had been an unexpected birthday present. But once she had it she realised she never wanted to be anywhere else or do anything else. The sense of belonging she felt, the sense that she has a talent that no one else had, and that it was being put to good use – it was too precious to explain.

'There might not be a war.' Reenie said it weakly, almost

pleading with providence. She knew in her heart of hearts that the chances of peace were shrinking by the day.

'If there's no war, what have you lost?' Her father was keen to emphasise that what they were suggesting was a good and happy thing. 'Either way you gain a cracking good husband and they're not easily come by. All right, you're a bit on the young side, but only a year younger than your mother was when she married me.' Mr Calder hesitated, then asked, 'You do love him, don't you, Reenie?'

Reenie didn't answer. It wasn't an easy question for a seventeen-year-old.

Chapter Twenty-Six

'Broadsheets are better for catching ball bearings; there's more for them to stick to.' Peter's intriguing statement might have proved fertile ground for a conversation with Reenie about the romance of bicycle maintenance and repair, if it were not for Reenie's failure to find enthusiasm for the mechanics of bicycles. It was uncharacteristic, in her case, because machines had always fascinated her, and bicycles were a kind of machine, but there was no teamwork about a bicycle and perhaps that was why, when faced with an evening of keeping Peter company while he poked cone-shaped tools at his wheels, Reenie chose to read a library book and eat a scone.

'Mother's baked Moggy for you.' Reenie produced a sticky dark loaf sliced into thick, moist slabs, all wrapped up in cheesecloth. Her mother like to bake Moggy because she still thought it was funny that Peter had believed – when he first heard about it – that they were somehow baking the cat, not a wonderful sticky ginger cake. Reenie sat down on the edge of the wall for a long evening's vigil while Peter covered the yard behind his boarding house in the greasy parts of his bicycle. She was staring intently at the open pages of her library book, but she was thinking seriously about the question her father had asked her.

'How's your mother?' Peter asked, absentmindedly biting into the slice of Moggy he held in one hand, while rooting through his collection of tools with the other. He didn't notice that Reenie hadn't answered his question. She hadn't been paying attention.

One of the particular comforts of their early courtship had been the way their routines had slotted together. They were both in the privileged position of having their own modes of transportation – Reenie her horse and Peter his Raleigh bike – and the upkeep of both had rubbed along together. Peter's Raleigh was new when he first met Reenie – an investment in his future by his parents when they sent him to Halifax to take up his career at Mackintosh's – and because it was new it did not need quite so much maintenance as a well-used machine. Other girls frequently failed to understand the time that boys needed to invest in their cycles, but Reenie had her horse to tend to and it was companionable to brush Ruffian down in the stable while Peter cleaned his bicycle chain and they chatted away to one another. The shift in their relationship had been subtle at first, but now it was becoming more pronounced. Peter would need to cycle over to Reenie's farm if he wanted to see her in the evenings, but he couldn't if the bicycle needed a repair. Then there were the times he could come to her, but he wanted to do some unnecessary but enjoyable alteration to the bike, like swap out the gear set for a better one, or try a lighter set of pedals he had on approval, or check all the ball bearings in the wheel for wear before re-greasing them. On those evenings Reenie could ride out to him and sit in the back yard of his boarding house while he worked, but she'd have to bring her own sandwiches because Peter's landlady wasn't going to allow a female visitor to cross the threshold, let alone join them for dinner.

In those early days, when they were fresh back from their Norwich factory adventure, they had been eager to criss-cross the valley for one another, with packed tea and a thermos to warm themselves. But time had wrought its changes; Peter needed to spend more time taking the bicycle apart at his boarding house and Reenie was more and more reluctant to ride into Halifax in the dark every evening (after she'd been home to change) just to sit in a cold yard, eating cold sandwiches. Like an old couple who don't remember when they drifted into separate beds, or separate rooms, Reenie and Peter hadn't noticed that they weren't saying goodnight to each other any more.

'My parents were asking after you.' Peter sounded tentative; there was something he was holding back.

'Oh, really? When did they write?'

'They didn't write this time, they asked me in their last letter to go down to the post office and have a telephone call with them. They've got a telephone at home now.'

'How did it sound? Have they got a good line?'

'Not bad. They're sharing it with a neighbour who's quite close by, so it's a convenient one.'

There was a silence. In the old days their silences had

been comfortable, easy, contented. Now these silences were hard work sometimes.

'Reenie, my mother would like me to think about making some plans for if there's a war.'

Reenie bristled: had her parents written to his? 'Do you mean about what you'd do in an air raid?'

'No.' The silence was long until Peter himself broke it. 'They want me to go to Sandhurst; they want me to go for an officer.'

'Do you want to go?'

'No. But I don't want there to be a war either and we've got to make the best of what is. They think if I go for an officer now I'll be well into a career when war starts and I'll be in less danger.'

'What do you mean "now"? You don't mean soon, do you?'

'When do you think you would like to be married, Reenie?' It was a tentative question, heavy with the fear of rejection, but heavy too with that sense that they had lost the closeness they once had; he couldn't read her thoughts any more.

'We talked about this not long since.'

'We talked about it six months ago and you said you wanted a long engagement. Six months is long.'

'We're not engaged yet, though. We've got an under-standing, but—'

'If this isn't an engagement – if this isn't the waiting part – then when does the waiting start? How long will it be?'

'What's put this in your head all of a sudden?'

'It's always in my head – isn't it in yours?'

'We're very young, Peter. Are you saying all this because

144

you think that if we marry your parents won't make you go for a soldier? You're old enough to tell them yourself—'

'No, Reenie, I want to take you with me! If we marry now we won't have to be separated, but if we don't marry before I go, then . . .'

'First you want to go off to Spain to fight the fascists and face near-certain death, and now you want to be an officer so's you don't have to fight. Make up your mind, Peter, do you want to fight or not?'

'Not with you, but it does feel a lot like *we're* fighting! If you must know, my parents made me realise how selfish I was being by not making provision for you now, so I'm doing this for you. If the worst happens and we're not married—'

'Have you been talking to my parents about this?'

'No, of course not, I just—'

'You might not have to fight! You're making all kinds of assumptions about what might happen, but you don't know anything at all! If it's anything like the last war they'll have reserved occupations and you'll probably spend the whole time in the factory as a fire marshal. Throwing up your job at Mack's and going for a soldier is—'

'It's Mack's, isn't it? You don't want to leave Mack's and you know you'd be out on your ear if we married. *That's* why you're hanging on for a long engagement. You're choosing the job over me!'

Reenie wanted to argue with him – but she knew in her heart of hearts he was right.

145

Chapter Twenty-Seven

When Dolly Dunkley next saw Percy Palgrave it was in the visitor's reception of the Mackintosh's toffee factory. Percy had arranged himself another VIP tour of the factory and this time Mrs Starbeck had encouraged Dolly to show him around.

'This is where we make the Caramel Cups,' Dolly said proudly as they stood on the viewing balcony above the Mint Cracknel line, the menthol from the vats of hot melted sugar stinging the eyes of the tour guide who accompanied them, and who had long since stopped giving any commentary.

'My goodness me,' Palgrave chuckled, 'what a lot of funny little people! They look miniature from all the way up here. And what are those ones up to?' Percy pointed towards some men who were cutting fingers of soft, glistening, minty sugar with rotating blades, ready to separate the pieces and slide them along a conveyer under an enrobing curtain of hazelnut-brown liquid chocolate.

'Oh,' Dolly shrugged noncommittally, 'they're just on some cleaning duty or other, you can ignore them. The next room is the best.' Dolly led him on to the experimental line where she'd heard rumours of an exotic spider on the loose. 'This is the most dangerous room to work in at the entire Mackintosh's factory. They handle nuts and fruits and things from tropical countries and sometimes there are dangerous animals in them. They had a scorpion attack a worker recently.'

At this the tour guide had to intervene. 'I think you'll find it was a child's toy which someone mistook for a—'

'Oh no, miss, I'm quite sure your colleague here knows what she's talking about.' Percy's patronising tones silenced the tour guide immediately. 'Miss Dunkley, like myself, has a wider experience of the world than just Halifax. We both know scorpions when we see them.'

Percy Palgrave had given Dolly the impression of sophistication and wealth from the very first. He'd talked dismissively about Halifax and had said he was only there with his mother on sufferance because his London club was closed for cleaning.

To Dolly, a native of nurturing Halifax, this was proof of good breeding: someone who scorned the rest of the nation in favour of the capital. 'I expect you see a lot of scorpions when you're away in Burma,' she said now.

Percy leant close enough to Dolly to whisper in her ear, 'Bit rum having this guide girly tailing us everywhere. It's like being followed around by a footman!'

'Well, you'd know about having footmen,' Dolly sniggered.

Percy had talked about the cheapness of servants in

Burma and the luxuries colonial life could afford for an enterprising young man, had spoken also of his own distaste for a career in his own land. In short, he boasted and whinged constantly and Dolly found it intoxicating. Percy Palgrave was not a man of very much charm, but he had just enough of it to make his griping sound like the boastfulness of the better off and this was Dolly's language.

They moved on to the tin-making section, where men and women with calloused hands flicked gigantic sheets of painted metal into cutting and shaping machines as if they were no more trouble than the centre pages of a tabloid. The sound of billowing tin was terrific and an outsider could have been forgiven for thinking they were hearing thunder. A man on the shop floor, with age-weathered cheeks and creased brow, pulled a length of shining tin towards him which was at least eight feet long and made a singing noise like a musical saw as he ran an oiled rag down its edge.

'Plum-looking job, that.' Percy waved in the direction of the man who had mastered metal in his youth. 'Money for nothing, moving around scraps of tin all day. He ought to try my job for a spell, then he'd know what hard work really was, I can tell you.'

A brighter girl than Dolly might have noted that Percy had not mentioned any servants of his own when he talked about their cheapness where he lived; he didn't mention experiencing any of the luxuries of colonial life himself; and – crucially – he didn't mention the name of this London club which was so conspicuously 'closed for cleaning' at a time when it would be in much use. Dolly had always been a girl who could avoid facts which were inconvenient to her immediate desires, and in Percy she had found a wealth of inconveniences to ignore.

'You know, I've always been terribly, terribly interested in Burma.' Dolly had little experience of successful flirting, so she attempted the only topic she could think of as they moved from the racket of the tin-making room to the relative peace of the factory corridor beyond.

'Oh, really?' Palgrave had no enthusiasm for his posting, because he had no poetry in him, and so this opener prompted no enthusiastic eulogy from him. 'What bit of it?'

Dolly looked flustered and blurted out, 'The *southern* bit, of course.' Making the assumption that just as all well-bred people are prejudiced against the north of England, the same snobbish prejudice would transfer to any country.

There was a long lull in conversation as Dolly had now run out of things to say about the country she had never showed any interest in until that moment, and Percy wondered how he could turn the conversation around to her father's money and finding out how much of it there was.

'So . . . your father is a Rector and not a vicar. Does it make much of a difference?'

'Oh, yes!' Dolly was keen to emphasise that she was almost on a par – socially – with Percy Palgrave and his people. 'We get a much bigger house. Vicarages can be quite small.' Dolly was worried that she wasn't sufficiently emphasising her social superiority so she blurted out, 'And we have servants.' The fact that they were dailies and not live-in, and that they were only there to char for her poor stepmother who was busy enough with her brood of small children was by the by. They passed through the Strawberry Cream corridor without stopping to notice the exquisite delicacy of the strawberry scent.

'I read something in the papers a while back about Rectors and rectories.' Palgrave threw the information around casually lest it be too obvious that he'd looked it up in the library and read it in depth and been electrified with excitement by it. 'They get to claim monies from people living thereabouts – tithes and chancel funds and whatnot. Must be pretty handy whenever you're short of a few quid to just tap the locals. Queer thing, English law. Best in the world, mind you, best in the world.'

Dolly flashed her grimace-like smile and tried to pretend that her father did have those rights, and that he hadn't told her to get a job because she was spending more on make-up than he could afford to provide. Dolly was trying to find a way to draw the conversation round to shopping, because she wanted to see if she could get this young man to buy her things.

'I suppose you must find it difficult, living so far from civilisation.' Dolly meant Burma, but Palgrave thought she meant Halifax. 'Do you need to go on a little shopping outing for some new things to take back with you?' Poor man must have money burning a hole in his pocket, Dolly thought to herself.

Palgrave's eyes lit up at this invitation following on so quickly from his hint that she could tap into limitless funds. Was she suggesting she buy him something? He tried his luck. 'I could do with a new set of luggage,' he ventured as casually as he could.

Dolly smirked to herself – they were getting on so well

so quickly. They were obviously the same sort. 'Let's go and choose you some,' she said, and they left the tour guide beside an empty noticeboard which had once warned employees about the dangers of scarlet fever.

Chapter Twenty-Eight

There is a long list of people that a journalist doesn't want to see walking purposefully into their newsroom at midnight, but top of that list must surely be the District Officer for Health, flanked by the Chief Veterinary Officer for the West Riding County Council.

Chester 'Sleepless' Parvin was typing up the last few lines of the *Halifax Courier*'s lead story before he sent it down to the presses, but by and large the paper had been put to bed, and so had its staff. His editor – Mr Pickles – had left only moments before, and he suspected that whatever this unannounced visit was about, it was about to fall on his shoulders.

'Gentlemen, can I help you?' Sleepless rose from his desk, picking up a notebook and pencil, ready to start taking notes immediately.

'We're here to make an announcement.' The Medical Officer thrust a typed memorandum toward Sleepless. 'How fast can you print this as an extra?'

Sleepless was not so foolish that he would suggest adding whatever it was to the morning edition without reading it and, as his eyes scanned the type, they widened. 'I'll call down to the presses; we can have the first ones ready in under thirty minutes if we hold the morning edition. How many men do you have to distribute these door-to-door?'

'Not enough,' the Medical Officer said gravely.

'That's all right,' Sleepless checked his wristwatch, 'I think I can call the army.'

A hasty series of telephone calls, including more than one to the newspaper's editor who took it upon himself to wake 'God' – the newspaper's owner – resulted in the agreement that the *Courier* would print an extra edition as a single bulletin, to be distributed for free to local householders on the assumption that it would push up sales of the morning edition as everyone scrambled to hear the latest news.

The first copies of the bulletin were run up to the pressroom by one of the print-room boys a little after half-past midnight, and the waiting company found the paper hot against their cold fingers when the neatly stacked sheets arrived. The arrival of the bulletins coincided with the arrival of Sleepless's reinforcements and at the sound of military boots marching up the stairs to the pressroom, Sleepless announced, 'The army's here.'

The Medical Officer looked startled. 'I thought you were joking! You haven't called in the Duke of Wellington's Own Regiment, have you?'

'No chance.' Sleepless walked over to the newsroom door and held it open in anticipation. 'This is a regiment much better suited to the work we have at hand.'

And there, marching up the stairs in battle-ready dress uniforms of midnight blue and warm burgundy, was a regiment created not to threaten but to reassure: Lieutenant Armitage, Captain Honeywood, and a dozen more officers of the Halifax Salvation Army, armed with social work training and the confidence to wake people at night to give them a message they couldn't ignore.

The night was long and the reception the news bearers received was mixed. As they went door-to-door, waking householders and handing over the urgent bulletin and the potentially life-saving advice from the Medical Officers, they were met with everything from hostile threats to tearful thanks.

At a doorway in Back Ripon Street they met an older woman standing in her doorway smoking a white clay pipe and looking up at the stars; Mrs Grimshaw had been kept awake by the coughing which echoed through the walls from her neighbours in the house which backed onto her own. The sight of men and women in suits and smart coats, carrying bundles of newspaper and marching alongside the uniformed Salvation Army, did not appear to trouble her, but she watched them all the same.

It was Sleepless who approached Mrs Grimshaw and said, 'An emergency notice from the District Medical Officers, ma'am. If you've got any milk or cream in the house you're to boil it immediately. At first sign of scarlet fever or septic throat in your household, call for the doctor and he'll have the patient removed to the isolation hospital. Anyone who has been in contact with a case of infection, or with a child from Stoney Royd school, is ordered to quarantine. The number of days is listed on the bulletin.'

Mrs Grimshaw's face fell as she looked at the extra and then at Sleepless. 'How bad is it? How many cases?'

'A lot more than usual. Enough to qualify as an epidemic. But the Ministry of Health people are confident that we can contain the spread if we prevent anyone else from drinking the infected milk, or mixing with infected persons. If you would be so good as to share the bulletin with the rest of your household, we will continue to spread the word to your neighbours.'

Mrs Grimshaw craned her neck to look up and down the street at the ragtag group of officials, civilians, and holy rollers who were knocking on doors. 'Is it just you lot to cover the whole town?'

Sleepless blew out his cheeks in assent.

'I'll get my big coat.' Mrs Grimshaw tapped out her pipe and left it on the window ledge. 'Winnifred an' Pearl are in the next street so let's knock them up an' all; strength in numbers. Way I see it, we could save a life if we're quick.'

But they weren't quick enough for the Norcliffe family.

Chapter Twenty-Nine

'Well, we'll have to close down the factory crèche.' Amy Wilkes didn't like to do it because she herself had been the champion of the enterprise, but it was too risky with an epidemic of scarlet fever tearing its way through the town. 'How many staff will that lose us?'

Diana Moore leant a clipboard on the edge of her manager's desk while she consulted a list. 'Only three from what was Reenie Calder's experimental line, but we've still got twenty married women on hand-making in Coffee Fudge. I think we'll have to get the factory manager to suspend that line altogether.'

'Very well. Are there any more precautions we can take on the lines themselves? Give them more space to work or something?' Amy Wilkes knew her factory well, but she often said to her assistant that her senior position left her at a disadvantage when it came to seeing the smaller details of the running of the factory.

Diana shook her head. 'The space available at present

is excellent thanks to the work we've already done for the latest Factory Act, but we might consider laundering all employees' overalls here to reduce the chance of contamination at home.'

'Yes, but what would that cost us?' The question was rhetorical, but Diana Moore was ready with the calculation of the precise cost per department and handed it to her manager. 'That's not as much as I thought. And if it reduces our chances of having to shut down a line for an outbreak then it's definitely worth it.'

'We might also consider closing the cafeteria.'

Amy Wilkes hadn't expected this. 'You can't be serious? There'd be a riot. Workers have to eat.'

'They already eat and drink at their posts during the morning and afternoon breaks. If they bring in their own, they can eat their lunch at their posts too. The District Medical Officer has advised local people not to go to crowded places like cinemas and dance halls. How much more crowded is our factory canteen?'

Amy Wilkes knew that Diana was right, but she also knew that there would be a riot from the craftsmen if they made them eat cold food. The men at the factory expected a fully cooked breakfast before they started their shift, and a slap-up dinner at midday; an outbreak of potentially lethal infection would not and probably *could not* deter them from covering everything they ate in steaming hot gravy. Diana had a tendency to take pragmatism and individual sacrifice to extremes which Amy Wilkes thought impossible for the average worker. 'Have a notice posted in each workroom to announce that all staff will be permitted to eat in their workroom during the dinner hour, and all staff are encouraged to bring cold food from home, rather than overcrowd the canteen.'

Diana took a note. 'I will need the keys to the noticeboards in Mrs Starbeck's sections.'

'Keys?'

'She's had the joiners department put up glazed doors on all the noticeboards in her sections to prevent unauthorised posting of notices.'

'By whom?'

'By us. She has taken down all of the notices from the District Medical Officer.'

Amy Wilkes put her head in her hands. 'Why?'

'She does not believe the precautions are necessary.'

'Did she give any reason for this unorthodox point of view?'

'She claims that most factory staff have already had scarlet fever at some point in their childhood and won't catch it again.'

'That's not how it works! You only develop the rash the first time you contract the infection, but you could be infected every year for the rest of your life if you don't take care. There is no immunity. This isn't the measles. Good grief, that woman will be the death of me one of these days. Draft a memorandum from me to the head of the joiners department telling him that I need to approve any work of this nature in future – and tell him I want the locks changed! If I didn't know better I'd think that woman had a perverse desire to shut down the factory and blame the workforce.'

Chapter Thirty

'I need to know if I can still come to work.' Siobhan Grimshaw waited at a safe distance from the factory gate and shouted across to Diana Moore on the other side.

Diana advanced towards her, but Siobhan stepped backwards at the same rate, maintaining a gulf between them. 'Do you have a scarlatinal infection?' Diana called.

'No. And no one in my family does either. But they've transferred my husband to the isolation hospital.'

'Is he very ill?'

'No, he's fine. He's a hospital porter at the maternity home, but the corporation transferred him because they're short of staff with the epidemic.'

Diana nodded in understanding; she wished all of her employees showed this presence of mind; the man might not be infectious himself, but he could spread infection on his clothes and hands and shoes. 'Does he have any symptoms?'

'None.'

'All right. Wait here and I'll call the factory doctor.' Diana ducked into the watchman's cabin and made a call through the switchboard, then returned to Siobhan, gesturing to her that it was safe to talk up close. 'He says you can come in so long as no one at home shows any symptoms, and you're to get a medical thermometer from the chemist and check all your temperatures in the household – morning and night. So long as you all stay healthy you can come into the factory.'

Siobhan breathed a sigh of relief, but there was no gladness with it. She needed to work because they needed the money, but this didn't mean that she had the hours in the day necessary to work in.

'Make sure to leave your overalls here to change into before your shift and I'll give you a chit to present at the factory laundry so you can have them all cleaned here.' Diana pulled out her notebook and pencil to make a memorandum. 'You will be sure to show extra vigilance watching for signs of infection?'

'Yes. Yes, of course.' Siobhan felt guilty for bringing this problem to her employers; she felt guilty for working when there was so much to be done at home, and she felt guilty that all her troubles at home were coming with her to work. She felt that she was somehow responsible for the inconvenience she was putting everyone to. Siobhan was still standing by the factory gate five minutes later, looking at the chit Diana gave her when a gaggle of her colleagues arrived, all having dismounted the same tram.

'Oh, lord, Siobhan, what's happened?' Winnifred asked with concern. 'You look shattered.'

'Ach, it's nothing,' Siobhan picked up her heels and

followed her colleagues as they walked towards the wide welcoming doors of the factory building, 'just more on me plate. At least my kids aren't at Stoney Royd school – I hear they've been closed down.'

'Not completely.' Winnifred gave a meaningful look at Doreen Fairclough. 'They had three cases on Friday and they've sent home any kids who were at the school on the same day in case they caught it off them. But the school's not closed . . .'

Siobhan raised an eyebrow. 'They're keeping it open with no kids in? I bet the teachers are having a high old time.'

'They've got two kids,' Winnifred said. 'They've got the two kids who were off last week because they'd got head lice and were being kept home while they had their hair soaked in coal tar soap.'

Doreen Fairclough looked mortified. 'I honestly keep them very clean! We go to the public baths twice weekly and I wash them at home twice daily. I keep a very clean house!'

'You don't have to tell us, we know you keep everything clean as a whistle. These things happen to the best of us.' Siobhan looked sympathetic. 'It sounds like you were lucky in the circumstances. If they're all right and there's no harm done, then just make the most of them being at school and be glad for it.'

'But they're only opening for my two. The whole school is being put out for my kids.'

'That's not *your* fault. They're getting paid to teach them and your taxes are paying for it. You just come to work and enjoy yourself.'

'Have we lost anyone else from our shift?' Pearl was

conscious that she and Winnifred were the only women among their line with grown-up children. Chances were there'd be a lot of women stuck at home now that Stoney Royd was as good as closed.

'We've lost three, but I think we can keep the line running.'

It was at that moment that Beverly Keillor came running to meet them from within the factory. Breathless and urgent, she said, 'Our line is suspended until further notice.'

'What? They can't do that! We've moved heaven and earth to come in!'

'No, no, we're still working, but the line is gone. We're being sent out to prop up everywhere else. They're sending home the minnows. Any of them with siblings of school age, whether they're at Stoney Royd or not, are being sent home. We're back in the factory proper – oh, I wish they'd make up their minds!'

Chapter Thirty-One

'This is Mr Baum, Mother.' Mary had explained to Albert in advance that they would need to shout, but she was still cripplingly embarrassed by the whole situation. She knew that the neighbours would be able to hear every word at this volume. 'He's got something he wants to ask you.'

Mary had done her best to make the parlour of their dark one-up one-down look as presentable as it ever could be, but it was an impossible task. There was no disguising that they were struggling to make ends meet in some of the worst slum conditions in Halifax.

'We're not buying anything!' Mrs Norcliffe had taken an immediate dislike to Albert Baum, evidently assuming that he was a purveyor of encyclopaedias, or some such other corrupting influence.

'He's not a salesman, Mother!' Mary filled her lungs, ready to holler at full volume, but Albert placed a gentle hand on her arm and gave her a reassuring smile.

'You do not have to take the burden of communication on yourself alone, Maria. I am here now, I will explain to your mother; there is nothing for you to worry about.'

'But she'll not hear you . . .'

Albert took Mary's hand and kissed it, then looked to Mrs Norcliffe to understand.

'What's all this?' Mrs Norcliffe sat up. 'You're not that letter-writer are you?' It was more of an accusation than a question. 'I don't hold with letter-writing!'

'She doesn't go in for reading or writing,' Bess tried to explain to their visitor. 'It's a rotten shame because it would be a lot easier to tell her what we're on about if she could read it off a slate or summat.'

Mrs Norcliffe was preparing to shoo Albert Baum from the house. 'What use is letter-writing? You won't get work writing letters. You'll be on the dole and expecting to live here; well, I'll not have it.'

Mary reverted to bellowing. 'No, Mother, he's at the factory! He's at Mack's.'

'Not in those clothes, you're not.' Mrs Norcliffe looked appraisingly at Albert Baum, who was not dressed for factory work. 'You're not from round here, are you?'

'No, Mrs Norcliffe.' Albert remained bright and cheerful. 'I am German.'

Mrs Norcliffe frowned. 'You're who?'

Albert raised his voice a little louder. 'I am *German*.'

'Well, Mr Herman, I think you've got a foreign look about you, and I don't trust foreigners.'

Albert Baum did not take offence; he was used to far worse treatment at home. 'I am a foreigner. I am German, and I am Jewish, and I am proud of this.'

'You're what?'

'I am German and Jewish.'

'Welsh? I knew it! Black hair! Celtic look about you! I've never trusted the Welsh; nor the Cornish, neither. Well, you'll not walk out with our Mary, and I'll not have you under my roof, so don't you think about coming calling here.' Mrs Norcliffe went shuffling off in search of her broom, the better to sweep away the dangerous Celtic stranger.

Albert Baum's polite smile did not falter, but he did betray a certain confusion when he asked Mary and Bess quietly, 'What is Welsh? Is this a profession?'

Bess did not appear surprised that the conversation had taken this turn, nor was she attempting to disabuse her mother of the idea. 'No, Wales is a country. It's British – you know, England, Ireland, Scotland, Wales?'

'Oh, Welsh is a person from Wales? I see . . . no, I don't see, why does your mother become angry at the thought I might be Welsh?'

Bess shrugged. 'She's never liked the Welsh, so don't mind her, we never do.'

'But is the German accent very similar to Welsh?'

Mary sighed in resigned exasperation. 'It is if you're deaf.'

'I see. Mrs Norcliffe, I am here to ask if I may walk out with your daughter; I wish to court her.' Albert said this so loudly and clearly that there could be no mistaking him. 'I can provide excellent character references.'

Bess pointed out, 'She can't read 'em. You could try giving her flowers. Or oranges – she likes oranges – she ate all mine when I were poorly.'

'If you think there is a chance then I will try it. For Mary, I will try anything!' Albert Baum wasted no time in dashing up to the shop on the corner of the next street, purchasing a crate of oranges, and returning with them to present to the mother of his intended.

'Mrs Norcliffe,' he cried, 'I propose an exchange!'

But he was too late. By the time he returned Mrs Norcliffe had stomped off to her job at the Sunlight Laundry where she washed the linens from the Isolation Hospital. She had left Mary and Bess sitting on the front step to await Albert's return.

'We don't need her permission,' Mary told him, with the sadness of a daughter who had never shaken the need for her mother's approval but had also never got it, 'we're only going to the People's Park.'

'Don't worry, Mary,' Bess piped up, 'I'll talk her round. She listens to me.' But even if her mother had been capable of hearing Bess, there was much less time than Bess thought.

Chapter Thirty-Two

Reenie had never thought that there would come a day when she would find herself sick of the sight of Peter's bicycle. She was convinced he'd changed the ball bearings in the wheels three times that month alone, and she couldn't understand why he needed new pedals when there was already a pair attached which fitted his feet. Reenie began to suspect that Peter was playing for time alone when they could talk but Reenie didn't want to talk – not about the same things Peter did, anyway.

Reenie had left Ruffian at the stable behind the factory and walked round to Peter's boarding house where his easily irritated landlady gave her 'one of her looks'. The yard at the back of the boarding house was not inviting, not like the yard up at her parents' farm where her mother would bring out a hot cup of cocoa and a toasted scone, and the warm light of the kitchen would flood the flag-stones from the window where her sister always sat. At one time Peter had tried to plan his bicycle jobs around

Sunday afternoons at her parents' farm; he would ride up for lunch with them and then he'd get on with whatever he needed to do while Reenie chatted away to him, or brushed Ruffian down, or did some mending while she sat on a kitchen chair. If it was a cold afternoon, her father would throw some rubbish from the farm into a brazier and she'd keep warm beside it while Peter worked as quickly as he could. But he rarely came up to the farm any more and she realised now that this was deliberate; he was doing things this way so that he could talk to her away from her parents. He asked again about the wedding.

'Are you sure it's marriage that you want?' Reenie found it contrary to her nature to be resisting a new experience and a new opportunity, but this felt so much like that threatened future in domestic service which she had thought the factory job was saving her from forever. There was a suffocating quality to the feeling and she wanted to put it off for a while longer because she was sure she'd come around. 'Couldn't you go for a soldier while we have a long engagement?'

'But don't you want our lives to start? Don't you want to get on with being whoever you're going to be?'

'I'm already who I'm going to be, my life's already started, it started when I was born. Getting married is just one of the things I'll do and I'm not kicking my heels until we can set up house, are you?'

'Yes, Reenie! That's what I've been telling you! This feels like treading water until I can get to dry land. I don't understand how you can bear it. Everything we do now is temporary; we don't get to choose what our home looks like, or who crosses the threshold to eat dinner at our table – we can't even choose our own furniture. We're living like children in a nursery when we're old enough to make our own decisions.'

'If you think that will all change by making me an army wife, then you're more fool than I thought, Peter Mackenzie.'

'That's just until the war is out of the way – and if it starts by Easter it will be over by Christmas.'

'Where have I heard that before?'

'It's true this time. Things are different this time.'

'And if we get married you'll be impatient for your army commission to be served before our lives can start; and then you'll be impatient for us to have a baby so that our lives can start; and then a bigger house so that our lives can start; and then get the children off to school so that our lives can start. If your life hasn't started yet it never will and you'll always be reaching for something. Marrying me isn't going to start your life off in a new world.'

'But I love you, Reenie! Why shouldn't I want to marry someone who I'm in love with? Why shouldn't I want to start a life *with them*?'

'You've already started it. I'm here. And if you really want to go for a soldier, I'll wait for you and I'll write to you. If the war's really over by Christmas then you'll be back long before I turn nineteen. Still on the young side for a bride, if you ask me, but significantly less hasty than marrying at seventeen.'

'Are you saying that if we wait a year we can be wed?'

Reenie didn't answer.

That damn bicycle. She had felt a strange fondness for it when they'd first started walking out. She'd thought of it as his loyal steed, as reliable as Ruffian. It had been invaluable that night of the factory fire when they needed to go in search of Bess, it had made the search for the poisoned chocolates over the summer so much quicker, and it had given them a means of seeing each other when they weren't at the factory. She used to be glad at the sight of his blue racer, but now it felt like one more thing trapping her. She realised that if they married she would spend the rest of her days watching him take it apart on the kitchen table, before slowly, messily putting it back together again.

Chapter Thirty-Three

'I'm so exhausted I can't see what I'm doing.' Siobhan Grimshaw turned the sweet carton over in her hands and squinted at it. 'Is this the right way up?'

'Don't ask me.' Pearl folded up another carton and passed it to her colleague. 'I haven't been able to see anything without my glasses since 1922.'

'Change places with me.' Doreen Fairclough rose from her stool at the wrapping table. 'You can foil-wrap for a bit and I'll pack.'

'I can't touch the sweets, look at me hands!' Siobhan proffered her hands for inspection, and sure enough they were red raw and deeply cracked around the knuckles and fingertips.

'What have you been doing to yourself!'

'It's all the washing. Stuart's been transferred to work at the isolation hospital while they're rammed, but they make him change his porter's uniform at every break in case he's picked up some contagion. That's four uniforms

171

a day, and they've all got to be clean on! But he's only got five uniforms, so there I am every night after work, waiting with a sack for these uniforms which have got God knows what on them, and I've got to have the hot water at the ready to begin washing immediately, because they need to be dry by morning, and the only way that's happening is if I stay up all night and keep ironing them until they're crisp. Then we both go out to work for the day so that the whole bally palaver can start again. I'm run ragged, *he's* run ragged, my fingers are run ragged – and I don't know how long his uniforms will stand up to this sort of treatment; they'll be fit for nothing.'

Pearl was incredulous. 'Don't the hospital have their own laundry?'

'Yes, but they're busy with all the extra sheets and masks. They've even had to start sending loads out to the old Sunlight on Hebble Street, so it's mayhem.'

'Well, let's just hope none of your kids get sent home from school, because then you're really in trouble.' Pearl remembered only too well the difficulties of having children of school age; it was a privilege, but it was a job of hard work.

'Are you worried about your Stuart?' Doreen was of an age with Siobhan and she worried daily about her own husband's dangerous work.

'I'm not worried, I just . . . it's like a field hospital up there. The things he's seeing just break your heart. And I feel rotten guilty for being sick of the laundry and the drudgery when we're the lucky ones. All our kids are at school, I've kept my job, and we're all healthy. The worst I've got to complain of is Washer Woman's Knuckle and bad eyes.'

'Yes, but it's not a competition, love.' Pearl was known for her pearls of wisdom. 'You don't have to be having a worse time of things than anyone else in Halifax to be allowed to have a moan. A good moan now and then's not so terrible a vice. Besides, we're all in it together, aren't we? Your troubles are our troubles. Look, how about I take your load of washing off you on Wednesdays? Wednesday nights are my nights for the washing when we're all working in the week. So there you are, one less wash night for you.'

'And I can do Friday nights,' Doreen volunteered eagerly. 'I get mine done Fridays and hung up round the parlour to dry through Saturday when I do me baking, so I'll take Fridays.'

Winnifred, who had heard most of their conversation as she busied round them with sweet wrappers, called, 'I can move mine to Monday if it's in a good cause.'

'Crumbs, do you remember when we weren't working and we used to get a whole day to do the washing in and a whole night of sleep? Halcyon days!'

But they didn't realise that *now* was the time of the halcyon days; very soon something far worse would be taking their sleep.

Chapter Thirty-Four

'This is not an acceptable standard.' Cynthia Starbeck had returned to her office and she was brandishing a sheaf of papers at her waiting assistant. 'I expected better of you, Dunkley; you told me that you were a grammar school girl.'

Dolly said nothing. Dolly's sense of disillusionment with her manager and her office job were now complete. When they had first met at the glamorous meeting of the British Union of Fascists in Crabley Hall she had thought they were kindred spirits, destined to form an alliance that would last a thousand years; then Mrs Starbeck had recruited her to do 'special work for the fascist cause' and she had seemed so charming and had lavished her with praise and cake – Dolly's two great weaknesses. But since then Dolly had failed again and again and she knew it. She was not the success that she had felt certain she was going to be and it hurt her every time she saw it.

Mrs Starbeck's nose twitched in irritation. 'I left you

to type my memorandum for the Harrogate Toffee line and I find *this* waiting for me on my desk.'

Dolly shrugged sulkily. 'I don't know what you want. I typed up the thing you told me to type. It's all there.'

'You've smudged some of the lines and you haven't used the guillotine to cut the paper; you've torn them down the sides and given them a ragged edge. Do you honestly expect me to put my signature to these and have them distributed?'

'I did my best, but I'm not a secretary,' Dolly whined. 'You said I was here to learn how to be a junior manager, not do paper cutting.' A part of Dolly sometimes hoped she would be dismissed so she could pack in this stupid job and go back to terrorising her stepmother and stepsiblings in the rectory.

'I want you to do these again and have them finished by noon. I want them perfect – and I want you to use the guillotine to cut the paper so it doesn't look like I've had my memoranda typed on old fish-and-chip wrappings.'

'But then I'll get paper cuts! The guillotine always cuts the paper too sharp and I get paper cuts from it. If I just tear it neatly with a ruler—'

'No one ever died from a paper cut, Dunkley. Please be more careful.'

Cynthia Starbeck swept up her notes for her next meeting and strode out into the hall where she proceeded several paces before she noticed that there was blood on her clipboard. By an unfortunate coincidence Starbeck had sliced her own hand on the notes she was carrying because the guillotined paper was so sharp. The paper cut had made a slice through that fleshy join between her right thumb and forefinger and it had gone surprisingly deep. Cynthia Starbeck dabbed at the wound with her handkerchief to soak up the blood before it could spoil her notes, but had no intention of bandaging it; Cynthia believed in treating these things with good fresh air and no nonsense.

Dolly Dunkley was growing increasingly irritated by the amount of work she was expected to do both at Mackintosh's and at home. At home she had grown up with the expectation that she would always be waited on by servants, but in recent years their numbers at home had dwindled. The diocese continued to pay for a gardener to maintain the rectory gardens alongside the churchyard, and her father could still stretch to a char and a daily, but the cost of educating his brood of stepchildren was beginning to loom, and the Reverend Dunkley was making economies. The first thing had been to suggest to Dolly that she got herself a little job earning the money for her 'lotions and potions', then there had been the suggestion that she offer 'little bits of help' to her stepmother when she needed someone to help with the children. Now Dolly found herself being given regular jobs around the house which she was expected to perform daily as her designated duty. This, she thought, was beyond the pale. She was slaving away at the factory all day only to be given skivvying jobs at home which her stepmother ought to be doing for herself. Her stepmother was still young, and if she didn't want the work of so many children, she shouldn't have had them.

Dolly's latest job was boiling the children's milk in the morning before she went to the factory. It was a ridiculous exercise as far as Dolly was concerned. The Salvation Army – of all people! – had hammered on their door at two o'clock in the morning to warn them that their milk was from a tainted batch and that they must boil it to save themselves and their children. But the Salvation Army were notorious for their hyperbole; you only had to look at their chapels (which they called Citadels) to see how far they took things, having the words 'Blood and Fire' carved in the lintel stone above every door. If the Salvation Army were claiming that Dolly needed to do something, then Dolly doubted she really needed to do it. She'd been in a hurry that morning because the Sally Army had disrupted her sleep and then she'd had trouble getting herself up in time to make the tram, or even the late tram. She had put the children's milk into a saucepan and put it onto the hot plate while she fetched their beakers, but it had only really warmed it. She was confident that they wouldn't catch anything, and if they did they wouldn't die of it; they were healthy children and they'd certainly survive a bout of scarlet fever. The month or so of suffering might even do the household some good because they'd all be forced to be quiet and keep to their beds. Dolly was not afraid of suffering: it was something she delegated to other people on an almost hourly basis.

Chapter Thirty-Five

'You have wonderfully clear eyes.' It was the sort of compliment veterinary surgeons paid to lame dogs when they wanted to look on the bright side, but in this instance it was the best thing Percy Palgrave could manage to say to the girl he was attempting to pay court to. Fortunately, Dolly had received few compliments in her life and was ready to gobble up any which were offered.

'Do you like my new dress?' She shrugged her shoulders in an odd sort of twitch which made the ruffled sleeves sparkle. It was an unusual choice of garment for a trip to the pictures and although a small ruffled sleeve had been fashionable a year or so ago, it had never been the done thing to attach eight ruffled sleeves one on top of the other. Dolly had obtained a length of gold lamé and the services of a seamstress who had no pity for her. The glitzy gold sleeves, which had been added to the already ugly blue knee-length frock, created an effect reminiscent of poultry preparing for a fight. The ruffles came up so high above Dolly's ears that she would spoil the view of at least three of the people in the row behind her, if not more, but Dolly was clearly delighted with the effect, and Percy said: 'Spectacular.' He was absolutely convincing, but then he wasn't really thinking about her dress; his mind was in the building behind her. Percy had given back the car, but he'd still said he'd walk round to her house and collect her because, truth be known, he wanted to get an appraising look at her father's place.

Percy Palgrave was not disappointed by the Stump Cross rectory. Whatever he had been expecting, he hadn't, even in his wildest dreams, expected anything as magnificent as this. There was nothing fashionable about it – how could something so solidly, ornately, rudely Victorian be fashionable? – but it had clearly been expensive when it was built, and if there had been the money to build it, there must still be money somewhere. The grand front garden was professionally kept, the great bow windows, piled on more bow windows, and topped with gables were clean and bright, and the flagpole which competed for space on the roof with the weather vane, had evidently had a fresh coat of paint within the year. Some artistic soul had even made a spring garland the size of a motor car tyre to hang upon the broad front door, like a sort of Christmas wreath, but in celebration of spring. The garland comprised a tasteful mix of foliage and blooms in greens, whites, and the contrasting shades of bold pippin apples tied all around. Anyone who could afford to use good food to decorate their front door must have more money than they knew what to do with, so Percy Palgrave meant it when he said, 'Spectacular.'

'I like to put time into my appearance because it's so

important to make an effort. And tonight's a special night because it's exactly two weeks since we met.' Dolly gave Percy an adoring grimace as they walked side by side down the hill in the direction of the tram stop.

'Is it, by Jove?' Percy was evidently pleased that she'd remembered and that she wished to mark the date. And well he would be; thoughts of Dolly's father's money ran through his mind all day long. Even when they weren't together, Percy Palgrave was thinking about the smell of it, the weight of it, what it would feel like to the touch. There was no doubt in his mind that he wanted it, but he was mindful of Cynthia Starbeck's words: *so many young men have taken an interest in her when they've found out how much the father's got tucked away.* Percy did not want to appear too keen, nor fail to mark his territory clearly enough and risk her falling into the hands of another. He walked a tightrope and to tilt too far in either direction could result in a fall from her favour. He had decided to shower her with flattery on their way to the cinema, and then – if she was amenable – try for a squeeze of the knee in the darkness.

'You know, Dolly, I do admire the way you manage these cobbles on your natty heels. You totter one way and then another and every time you lose your balance I think you're going to take a tumble, but you always manage to right yourself again. Can't be many girls who can do that.'

'Well, I had deportment lessons at the grammar school, so that does make a difference.' Dolly stumbled into Percy and he caught her by the elbow before she could land face down on the clog-polished granite.

'Would you do me the honour of taking my arm?'

When Percy offered it he was not looking at her arms, but into her eyes – which were still as clear as a healthy collie dog. There followed an awkward tussle between Percy and one of the gold lamé sleeves which he would be forced to bury his face in for the duration of the journey to the cinema, but once Dolly had the offer of walking arm in arm she wasn't going to allow him to let go. Between Dolly's inappropriately high heels, and Percy's obscured vision, they hit three lamp-posts, two dogs, and a policeman on their way to the new Odeon, but when they finally arrived a certain bond had definitely been cemented, and they were both glad of it.

'I want to see you always dressed in gold, Dolly. You look like a film star.' Percy settled into his seat while the slide advertising Rowntree's Dairy Box was still casting its pale cream light over the big screen. He had to wrestle for a few moments with Dolly's wing-like ruffle sleeves so that the scratchy lamé wedged behind his shoulder didn't obscure his view of the picture which he had paid good money to see. Several people in the rows behind them did not appreciate his efforts, or the film-star quality of Dolly's Frankenstein fashion creation. They complained loudly about the 'bloody awful stuff sticking out everywhere. What do you want to go bringing a thing like that in here for?'

'How dare you, sir!' Percy was delighted to have the opportunity to play the knight in shining armour to Dolly and was on his feet immediately.

'Sit down!' someone called from higher up.

'Usherette!'

'Call the manager!'

'Get 'em out!'

It was inevitable that Dolly and Percy would attempt to stand their ground, despite the fact that Dolly was entirely in the wrong for wearing what could best be described as a strange fancy-dress angel costume to a cinema. It was also inevitable that the patrons of the Oscar Deutsch Picture Palace would begin pelting the obstructive couple with bread rolls and their rolled-up sweet wrappers.

Dolly was visibly shaken by the experience and, as the usherette saw them pointedly out of the side exit, Percy took the opportunity to take Dolly consolingly in his arms – as best he practically could with the obstacle of the sleeves to contend with.

'I hate this town!' Dolly wailed into Percy's starched shirt collar. 'I want to go far, far away!'

'This town doesn't deserve a girl like you.'

Dolly looked up earnestly, her thick, puffin make-up smeared into vampish streaks. 'Do you really think so?'

'Oh Dolly, I do! You must know how much I admire you.'

Dolly croaked with delight and the pair prepared to deceive one another some more.

Chapter Thirty-Six

'I brought you back a paper from town because there was an extra edition about some people in the 'ospital.' Kathleen threw down her satchel, school coat, a newspaper, two bags of sweets, and two armfuls of books bound together with her father's borrowed belts.

'And where have you been?' Mrs Calder was wielding a wooden spoon dripping with batter the way a magistrate might wave his gavel at an accused man. 'I expected you home from school over two hours ago. I've been worried half to death! And what's all this you've brought home? Is this more things to take up space on my dinner table?'

'I went to the public library. I *told* you I was stopping at the library. I've got the loan of another couple o' library tickets, so's I can borrow more books.' Kathleen hung up her school coat and then went to warm herself by the fire while she warmed to her subject. 'Did you know,' she began, ignoring entirely her mother's annoyance, 'that Halifax's first public library was in the crypt under the parish church? The priest who was there in the 1430s wanted a book room, so he went down into the crypt, gathered up all the bones, took 'em outside, dug two pits his'self, and bunged 'em all in. Hey presto! – he had somewhere to keep his books. That was the only public library we had round these parts until the eighteenth century. They've still got all his books from the fourteen hundreds. The Librarian at Belle Vue showed 'em me and they smell *awful.'*

Mrs Calder put down her wooden spoon and the mixing bowl of batter while she cleaned her hands ready to look at the latest news from the *Halifax Courier*. 'You've got an obsession with library cards and churches and I don't think I like it,' Mrs Calder said.

'I dispute that. I've got a passion for learning and an enthusiasm for 'avin' a job. It just so 'appens that right now my best means of learning is getting the loan of a couple of extra library tickets, and my best chance of further employment is to show my employer that I appreciate his mouldy old premises, which happen to be a chapel. It could be the Park Road Baths for all I care; I'm going to look lively and make sure he takes me on full-time in the holidays.'

Mrs Calder picked up the newspaper without looking at it; her eyes and her thoughts were still on her youngest daughter. 'I'm pleased for you that you've found a job you like, but I'm really not sure about you keeping it on after the summer. Your father had talked about getting you some shorthand lessons at the college, wouldn't you like a chance to—' Mrs Calder didn't finish her sentence. Her eyes had caught the headline of the extra edition of the *Halifax Courier* and she was motionless with shock.

The paper carried a stark and urgent warning to all local people that they were now in the midst of a true epidemic: the cinemas, theatres, music halls, and mission halls would all have to close their doors. Children were being kept home from school wherever there had been contact with infection, whole families were being asked to quarantine, and the District Medical Officer advised people to avoid crowded places, like the market or the pub. 'Kathleen! Why didn't you tell me you'd brought this home! This is important!'

'I *did* tell you I'd brought it home. I said to you there was an extra, so I'd got you one.'

'But you didn't tell me it was an urgent warning from the authorities!'

'Well, I wouldn't have got you one if it wasn't important, would I? I keep telling you, if you want your news straight away you need to get a wireless. You're living in the past up here.'

Mrs Calder sat down at the kitchen table with a thud, only narrowly avoiding the marmalade cat who leapt out from under her in the nick of time. 'It says 'ere that the isolation hospital is nearly full up and the doctors and nurses have run out of masks!' Mrs Calder became increasingly agitated as she read more of the growing tragedy. 'There's a quarantine order! My God, there's a quarantine order!' Mrs Calder threw off her apron and ran out into the farmyard, calling for her husband. 'Arthur! Arthur! There's an epidemic!'

Mr Calder dashed out from the milking shed and followed his wife into the house the better to see the news for himself. '"The public is advised that any households in which a member is suffering from scarlet fever

185

or severe tonsillitis, or shows any of the symptoms of the same must quarantine for a minimum of three weeks from the date of onset. Mild tonsillitis or sore throat: two weeks minimum quarantine. Persons with throat swabs which test positive for—" I can't read that, what does it say?' Mr Calder held the paper out to his younger daughter.

'Haemolytic streptococci,' Kathleen said easily.

'What does that mean when it's at home?' Mrs Calder's fear had turned to affronted anger that this illness which threatened her children should throw up technical terms and complicated ideas when it had no right to.

Kathleen sighed. 'It's just the name of the bacterium everyone's spreading between themselves, which gives you the scarlet fever. They can do tests nowadays to find out which kind of bacterium you've got. This one's the same strain as they had in Doncaster last Christmas. It's quite interesting really.'

'Do you mean the one in Doncaster where people died?'

Kathleen could see that answering in the affirmative wasn't going to help matters, so she changed the subject. 'They've said that if you think you've got it, or you've been near someone who's got it, you can go and get a test done which means taking a swab from your throat. If the result of the test is negative you don't have to quarantine. It's a marvel of modern science, really, when you think about it.'

'Well, where do you go to get this test?'

Kathleen was reluctant to admit that the situation wasn't as straightforward as she wished it was. 'They don't say. I looked through all the papers in the library reading room and none of them said.'

'Right, that's it!' Mrs Calder began clearing the kitchen table ready to scrub away any trace of exotically-named bugs which might have crept into their home uninvited. 'You're not allowed to go back to that library until further notice!'

'Oh, Mother! What's wrong with learning about things? If I hadn't learnt about it at the library I wouldn't have known about it to buy you a newspaper, would I?'

'I'm not worried about you learning about it, I'm worried about you catching it! If pubs and mission halls are dangerous, then so are libraries! And you're not going back to that shop either. You tell her, Arthur, we're not risking it.'

'But this isn't fair! I'm the one who warned you it was happening!'

'Your mother's right, Kathleen. You've never been strong and we can't take any risks. If this is the bad one they had in Doncaster where those people died, then there's no question of you going to the library, your shop, or your school. You're stopping here, my lass.'

'What?' Kathleen's casual confidence was all gone now and she was on her feet with indignation. 'But you know I love my job!'

'Not as much as we love you!' her mother burst out, and then ran from the room. It was all too much for the generation that remembered the Spanish flu, and who still found the masks they'd worn in the pockets of old coats and saw names they knew in the churchyard.

Chapter Thirty-Seven

Dolly Dunkley knew all about Hebblewhite's Misshapes shop. She didn't know that it had been built in 1490, she didn't know that it boasted architectural embellishments unique in all England, and she didn't know that it had been sold to the De Whyte family, who had gradually come to be called the Hebblewhite's, because they owned that little disused chapel on the bank of the Hebble Brook. Dolly would not have shown any interest in these facts whatsoever – even if she had known how important they would later be to her – but would have dismissed them as 'school stuff'. No, when Dolly talked about knowing all about it she meant she knew that they sold large quantities of sweets for very low prices and that old Mr Hebblewhite had barred her from entry after most unfairly accusing her of the triumvirate of crimes of theft, littering, and rudeness. Dolly had attempted to brazenly re-enter the shop a year or two later, but Mr Hebblewhite had remembered her, and turfed her out with cries of 'Greedy little snaffler!'

When Percy Palgrave took Dolly on a walk down to the river for 'a surprise' she thought – inexplicably, given the rowdy working nature of the Hebble Brook and the coldness of the morning – that he was going to take her on a romantic boat ride to some remote nook with a hot picnic. It came as an abrupt shock to find herself at the door of the place she had avoided for so long, and to be there with the young man who she wished to impress enough to make him marry her.

Dolly had to think quickly of an excuse not to go in – and quick thinking had never been something she excelled at. 'I can't go in,' was all she said shortly.

'Why ever not? It's a sweetshop, you love a good sweetshop.'

'Not that one, it's . . . it's sacrilegious!'

'Sacrilegious? Surely not. What are they doing, selling toffees in the shape of Moses?'

'No, it's the building. They've turned a good Christian chapel into a place where you buy things and I'm boycotting it. They should turn it back into a church.'

'But surely it was never really a church? That's a bridge chantry and they've got them all over Europe. They were never churches proper.'

'But it could be used as one. They could *make* it a church. It could be used for funerals where there's hardly any mourners and it's not worth putting the heating on in the big parish church. Or for weddings under a quick licence.'

'Ah, *that's* it! You have your heart set on being married

in this little place one day, that's why you want the shop-keeper turned out.'

Dolly thought this sounded like an excellent excuse for steering Percy clear of the shop, while also putting thoughts of marriage in his head. She seized on it immediately. 'I want to be the first bride to be married in the place after it's been turned back into a church and I can't go in because if I see it all decked up as a shop I'll get upset.'

Palgrave was inspecting the worn gargoyles, apparently lost in thought. 'That's not a bad idea, being the first couple to be married there. You'd certainly have your photo in the local paper, maybe even the regionals. Be a good story to tell, and the news clipping would look fine in a frame on the office wall. Something to talk about, make one memorable among the colonial set. Not a bad idea at all.' Percy snapped his attention back to Dolly. 'What would it take to get it done? The change back to a church for a wedding, I mean. Get up a petition for the Halifax Town Council, I suppose? Ask them to turf out their tenant and hand the keys over to your father?'

'You'd just need a special licence from the archbishop – and that's easy for me because he's my godfather and I can ask him to grant me one.'

'Truly? Is your godfather really an archbishop? Who *is* the chappy round here? Archbishop of York, is it?'

'No, the Archbishop of Wakefield. He was at theological college with my father before they were both ordained. He doesn't remember my birthday any more, but he'd certainly draw up a special licence for me if I asked him to.'

'Godfather an archbishop, eh? You *do* have some

connections.' Percy Palgrave tried to hide his growing anticipation of all the money he was about to marry. Where some good souls dreamed of the day when they would meet their beloved, and in a summer haze of romance be wed with memories to treasure, Percy, had no interest in romantic love beyond the feelings of total adoration he felt for gold sovereigns. Percy loved money and the idea that this source of wealth might slip through his fingers if he didn't act fast made him impatient to secure it. Dolly Dunkley was – as the American pictures might describe her – a cash cow, and Percy Palgrave didn't like the thought that his gravy train might be derailed before he could secure her money for himself.

To Percy it did not seem odd that a churchman should have a comfortable wealth; in Percy's experience the Church of England was always a useful way in to society circles. He'd never known a Rector to sit on any sort of vast fortune – he did not assume the Dunkleys' was in the league of the Rothschilds, but he had no difficulty imagining a nice, solid sum of money coming their way. Maybe the price of a motor car, or the membership fees of a good London club.

Chapter Thirty-Eight

A letter from the Home Office lay on a sampling table in the centre of the Confectioners' Kitchen. It lay open, and Albert and Mary sat quietly looking past it, holding hands. The letter was a reminder: Albert Baum could not bring his children or his sister to England because he was not given leave to remain in England at all. His latest permit would expire on Easter Monday, and he was expected to be on the boat train bound for Paris the following day.

'Why do they need to send you these horrible letters anyway?' Mary scowled tearfully at the typed communication. 'They *know* you're trying to get a house to lease. Don't they realise how difficult it is? It's bad enough without them sending threatening reminders.'

'They hope that I will give up, I think. They hope that I will admit defeat and leave.'

'Why does it need to be a house? Why can't we find

192

a family who will let you lodge with them and then just get them to sign an affidavit, and then—'

'Because the Home Office don't want to make this easy. It has to be a house on a lease, somewhere settled.' Albert reached up and tucked the loose strands of Mary's hair back over her ears and then leant forward to kiss her forehead. 'Don't worry about it today, we have time. Don't let them steal the time we have together.'

'But time is running out. And who knows if they'll give you a permit to come back again and sign another lease if you don't get one this time,' Mary said anxiously, 'that's if they even let you stay this time and don't cut your permit short like they did last summer.'

Albert looked around him sadly. 'We could do such great things here, you and I, Maria. We could do great things for Mackintosh's.'

Tears ran silently down Mary's cheeks and Albert gently rubbed her back with his free hand. It was an odd feature of their situation that all the usual stages of courtship had been hastened over and they had found themselves talking about a future life together before they had had a chance to go to even a dance. Perhaps if there had been no sense of urgency, no sense that they could be separated forever at any moment, they might have spent years tiptoeing around each other, trying to find the courage for a kiss, but as it was, they had been bound by the conviction that their futures lay together and that once Albert had brought his family to safety they might find the time for slow courtship.

'I've been reading in the newspapers about other Germans who have come to England, other Jewish

Germans.' Mary looked as though she were trying to find the courage to suggest something which Albert would not want to hear.

'I know that some people stay after their permits have expired, Maria. But they get caught, and they are sent to prison. And then there's the children. I can't abandon the children in Germany.'

'No, I didn't mean that. I'd never suggest that! I know that you're a good father to them – the best father – you'd never abandon them like that.' Mary struggled to find the words to explain what she wanted to say to him. It was possibly the hardest thing she had ever had to say in her life. 'No, I read that there's a way around the permits, a legal way. It wouldn't solve all our problems, but it would buy time.' Mary steeled herself to ask the question she'd been burning to ask since Albert had returned to England. She wiped the tears from her cheeks, pulled herself upright on her stool, and took a deep breath. 'Albert, I'll be twenty-one the day before your permit says you have to leave.'

Albert squeezed her hand a little tighter and nodded a weak apology. 'I'm sorry, it's not much of a birthday present for you, my dear.'

'No, no, I mean I'll be twenty-one. I mean that I can marry you; that you can marry me.'

Albert Baum was silent for a moment. He adored Mary, but he loved her too much to let her give away her life to save his. 'Maria, you don't know what you're saying. You have so much of the world still to see, you are so young to decide such a thing. To decide—'

'I have so much of the world to see and I don't want to see any of it without you! I've read the newspapers and I know that the only way for you to get a permit to stay here is to marry an Englishwoman before you leave. I'd have liked to let you court me a while,' Mary said, pondering for a moment this other life that they might have had if things had been different, 'but I don't think I'd have liked leading you a merry dance like other girls do with their young men. I'd have liked to spend months on end pointing at things in shop windows and telling everyone I'd have them at my wedding, and I'd have liked to have met your children before they greeted me as their new mother, but some things just have to be as they are, not as we want them to be. I'll love your children because I love their father – and perhaps one day I'll get to plan them the weddings I wish we'd had – but for the moment I'll just be glad to have you safe and sound, here at my side with them and your sister, and forget all the worry we've had this year, start next year as a family in peace.'

'Are you sure that you want to do this, Maria? You know that I am not your responsibility, you do not have to save me.'

'No, but I *want* to.'

Albert did not look at Mary; he looked around the kitchen in desperation, rummaged through his pockets, and then began throwing open drawers and cupboards while Mary sat still in the middle of the room, watching in bemused curiosity.

'Albert, I've just asked you a very serious question. I don't think you've realised that you haven't given me an answer.'

'I cannot allow you to ask it. There is something I need to find!' He tipped out cartons and threw open cupboard doors until finally he found what he was looking for: a golden toffee wrapper. He peeled the toffee away from the foil and cellophane, leaving the sweet on the marble-topped table, and folding the wrapper over into a band as he returned to Mary. Albert Baum took a deep breath, looked at Mary's tear-streaked face, looked at the sweet wrapper, and looked at Mary again saying, 'You know this is not what I wanted for you, but you are everything I could have wanted for me. You are kind and clever and you will make a wonderful mother to my children. Mary Norcliffe, my darling Maria,' here he knelt before her and offered up the band of golden toffee wrapper which he had folded to form a ring, 'will you do me the honour of becoming my wife?'

Mary's tears began again, but this time they were of joy and of relief. 'Yes,' she said, 'it's all I want in the world.'

But through her happiness Mary felt that little shiver of cold again, that odd foreboding she'd had in the grounds of the library. It was like someone, somewhere, had walked over her grave . . . and she couldn't shake off the feeling.

Chapter Thirty-Nine

It had started as she was walking home from work the preceding evening. Siobhan Grimshaw had complained about the smell of the tannery, but Doreen couldn't smell it. Doreen couldn't smell anything at all. It was odd when she noticed it; it was a chilly spring evening, and she'd have expected the smell of coal burners to be strong, but there was nothing. She hadn't felt as though she had lost her sense of smell, she just couldn't smell anything. That night at tea she'd lost her appetite, but she picked at a bit of bread and beef dripping. She thought the savoury tang of the meat fat might nourish her and give her an appetite, but she found the fat coating her tongue tasteless and strange; the bread a cotton-wool wad she couldn't swallow.

It wasn't like Doreen Fairclough to waste good food and her husband worried that she was working too hard, but he made a mental note to talk about it with her once this rush at his own workplace was over and they could get a day off together.

The shooting, burning pain in her throat was there when she woke up, but she told herself she had probably been snoring and that had made her throat dry. She knew she snored sometimes when she slept on her right side. She told herself not to make a fuss; she always made such a fuss.

Her walk to work was an agony of indecision. She knew that if what she had was the septic throat infection, she must stay at home to prevent it spreading to her colleagues and her fellow travellers on the daily tram, and all the people in the corner shop. But what if she was making a fuss about nothing? What if she was crying wolf? What if she went home on the sick but then was all right again by teatime, and then was really, truly ill next week and had to go off properly, and everyone thought she was malingering?

It didn't help that she was always late and always having to take a day here and there for her children's various sniffles and mishaps. And why was that? Why were her children so much more trouble than everyone else's? She took them to Sunday School, she kept them clean, she fed them healthy food and she kept a healthy discipline in the running of the house; she tried her damnedest. But it didn't change the fact that her kids were the only kids she'd ever heard of who had shaved their dog and then eaten a bee.

Doreen was at the factory gate and she turned to leave and then turned back to go in half a dozen times. If she told them she was quite well she would be putting everyone at risk, but if she cried off she risked extending her reputation as a nuisance. And she felt such a nuisance. She wished she was a different person entirely, but it was too late for all that now; the factory watchman was coming out of his cabin at the gate and she'd have to decide whether she was going in or giving a message.

'I'm sure I don't need to remind you, Doreen, that I am extremely busy at present and that coming out to the gatehouse cabin costs me more than a little time.' Mrs Starbeck said it sweetly enough, but there was an implicit threat: this better be worth my while, or you will pay.

'I'm s-sorry.' Doreen's stammer was partly nerves, but also the awful foggy feeling the cold air had brought with it. She shivered and stammered and felt more ashamed than ever – and then was even more determined to put a brave face on it and work until she dropped.

'Come along, quickly now, I haven't got all day, have I, Doreen?'

'I-I have a sore throat, Mrs Starbeck.'

'And I suppose you want to take the day, do you?'

'No, no, I-I just thought that I should tell you in case – in case it was . . . you know . . .'

'No, I don't know, Doreen. In case it was what?'

'Well, the scarlet fever. I don't want to spread the fever.'

'And do you have a fever, Doreen?'

Doreen sweated with the chill of the morning and her foggy mind told her that meant that she did not. 'No, I just—'

'And do you have a scarlatinal rash?'

'No . . .' Doreen felt humiliated and foolish, and very, very ashamed.

'Then, if we've quite finished here, I'd be glad of your presence on the production line which is already short-handed.'

Doreen mumbled her apologies and followed Mrs Starbeck through the winding factory corridors to her workroom, where the adjacent changing room was already empty but for one or two stragglers like herself. Mrs Starbeck must have been in a particularly foul mood, because she took the time to give the remaining workers a perfunctory lecture on the necessity of 'working through' some ailments, inconveniences and challenges.

'We're all under strain and we're all feeling run-down. I'm sure half the women in the factory woke up with a scratch in their throat, but fortunately most of them realise that it's their patriotic duty to press on.' Mrs Starbeck noticed that Doreen was struggling to remove her coat and dress herself in her overalls. 'When you're quite ready?'

Doreen followed Mrs Starbeck into her workroom where her colleagues were jammed into their high chairs at close quarters. The air felt dry and she coughed into her hand and then pulled herself up into a seat. She was dimly aware of kind faces closing in on her and helping her down, moving her round to the far end of the work-room past all her colleagues, and then came a rising warm fog which took the workroom with it.

It was at that moment that Doreen fainted into unconsciousness.

'Nurse Munton says we've got to keep all the women at their places on the line and not allow them to move. She's sending for the District Medical Officer.' Diana kept to the edge of the production room, careful not to get too close to the waiting employees.

'This is ridiculous,' Cynthia Starbeck was irritated

200

enough that she'd lost time to a shutdown while ambu-
lancemen removed one of her quickest workers, but to
have to tolerate a further disruption while the Women's
Employment Department made a song and dance about
it was really too much. 'Doreen Fairclough was in this
workroom for but a moment; it's highly unlikely that
anyone has caught scarlatina from her – and even if they
had it's no worse than a mild case of influenza. I must
insist that you vacate my workrooms.'

'The shutdown stands, Cynthia.' Diana's voice rang
clearly through the production hall and all eyes were
upon her. No one could have failed to notice that she
used Mrs Starbeck's first name. 'This is an Employment
Department matter and my authority comes straight
from the head of that department. Doreen has been
working on this line all week and if she caught the
infection here there might be other infectious cases.'
Diana addressed the assembled women who were
waiting anxiously at their workstations in grim silence.
'The District Medical Officer will be coming here with
his staff to take medical swabs of the throat. If you're
found to have a scarlatinal infection you'll be quarantined at home—'

'Miss!' One of the minnows who had been brought in
to work on pallet filling put up her hand as though
she were still at the school she had clearly only recently
left. 'If we don't want to do it, can we go now?'

'If you don't want to do what?' Diana asked.

'If we don't want to do the medical thing and the
quarantine. We've got to be on the bus at four thirty, and
then we need to be back here on shift tomorrow.' Some
of the other minnows muttered agreement; they didn't

mind a shutdown, but they didn't want to lose wages or miss the bus home to their tea.

'This is compulsory.' Diana answered clearly enough for all the room to hear. 'Someone came into this workroom with scarlet fever, and by law that's a reportable illness. You all have a legal requirement to stop here until you've had your test and seen the Medical Officer.'

'Yeah, but hardly anyone ever dies of scarlet fever, do they? It's up to us if we want to take the risk, isn't it?'

Cynthia Starbeck smirked at Diana. She'd chosen these girls for the line herself and they were just her sort.

Chapter Forty

'Can't we send them away until morning? There's nothing to be done tonight, surely?' Director Hitchens was already pulling on his overcoat and readying to leave his office. It was after office hours and he didn't like being held up on his way out the door, even if it was by the Head of Women's Employment.

'I'm afraid we don't have the luxury of sending them away.' Amy Wilkes was wary of being too direct with her director, but beating about the bush at that time of the evening would only irritate him more. 'They've sent a telegram on ahead to say they're on the 4.20 from King's Cross. Someone has to be here to meet them and it can't be an office junior.' Amy Wilkes was surprised that the director wasn't more alarmed at the news that the Ministry of Health were sending officials to their factory to deal with a potentially fatal illness. 'If we're employing women and young people then we have to be ready to accept orders to make changes. The new Factories Act is very clear: if we want the cheap labour they provide, we have to invest in the means of making them safe.'

'What time do they get here?'

Mrs Wilkes handed over the telegram for inspection. 'I think it's unlikely they'll shut us down completely, but we do need to be ready to make substantial changes to working arrangements for the duration of the outbreak.'

The director rubbed the tips of his fingers across his weary brow as he reread the telegram. 'I'm supposed to be in Norwich tonight; they're planning air-raid precautions. We've got the Ministry of War Preparedness at Norwich testing a gas shelter, and the Ministry of Health in Halifax. Why can't we have one panic at a time?'

This made more sense to Amy Wilkes; war preparations were an unknown quantity, but to the director she supposed that scarlet fever felt like the sort of thing which the factory ought to know enough about to manage without him. 'I can telephone your secretary in Norwich with developments as and when they occur, but at present they haven't asked to see you, which is a good sign. If they only want to see the Head of Women's Employment then they clearly don't intend to shut us down.'

'What have we done so far that we can tell them about? We must have made some changes of our own?'

'I stopped all deliveries of milk to the factory canteen, but that's only cut off one route of contagion – we need to prevent it spreading between the girls themselves and they're their own worst enemies on that front. A restructuring of the lines might help?'

Mr Hitchens heaved an almighty sigh. 'All right, give them my apologies for absence and telephone me with developments. Bring in Time and Motion, Engineering, and Production to make any changes you think useful. I want us to do everything we can to head off a factory shutdown before it's forced on us by circumstance. We've got enough to worry about without that, believe me. They want us making gas masks here for the national stockpile – and we can't very well do that if half our staff go down with plague.'

Chapter Forty-One

'There's a question that I've always wanted to ask you.' Amy Wilkes didn't take her eyes off the main factory door. It was late in the evening and the rest of the office staff had gone home for the night, leaving the commissionaire's desk and the visitor's entrance empty. Amy and Diana remained for the emergency visit of the District Medical Officer, the Borough Factory Inspector, and the man from the Ministry of Health. It must be bad if they were getting a visit of this sort, but could it really be as bad as all that? As they sat in the empty stillness of the deco ground-floor entranceway they had a sense that something awful was coming and they wanted to make the most of the last few moments of normality.

'Out with it, then.' Diana was very respectful of her manager – especially when they were in company – but they had built up an easy rapport when they were alone together and they spoke their minds.

'I heard that you once refused to speak for a month

on the production line. I've seen the written warning in your employment file.'

'Is that a question?'

'Why did you do it?'

There was a long silence, but not because Diana was deciding how to answer; she just enjoyed the slowness and the silences she had with Amy Wilkes.

'My father had died. I lost my voice.'

'It wasn't stubbornness, then?'

'Would it matter if it had been? There are plenty of managers at Mackintosh's who would prefer it if all the girls stopped talking tomorrow; most of them don't listen either way.'

'You put a lot of people's back's up at the time; I remember it.' Amy Wilkes pondered the effect Diana's silence had made on the overlookers. 'It's funny how some people can ignore what you say, no matter how loudly you say it, but are threatened by persistent silence when they see that they have no control over it, and you do.' A gust of wind made the glass front door clatter in its brass frame, but there was still no sign of the officials. 'Why did you ask to come and work for me?'

Diana thought about the question, and then asked, 'Why did you agree to take me on?'

'Curiosity. I'd heard a lot of things about you; I wanted to know which of them was true.'

Diana kept her cards close to her chest, but she thought her manager was a greater mystery. She appeared to be well-educated and she suspected she was not from a factory background, but something had driven her to not just join Mackintosh's, but to become head of Women's Employment. 'Why did you choose this work? You could have worked somewhere better. Like a law office, or a bank; why a factory, why Women's Employment?'

Amy Wilkes gave a light shrug, 'I suppose it's because I knew that in any other position I'd have been voiceless; another underpaid, overworked woman ignored by her so-called betters. Here I can make a difference to the lives of voiceless women and girls. When people like Starbeck try to wring them out, I can stop them. This is one of the largest employers of women in the town and I'm here to protect their interests. Not only that, but we set the standard for neighbouring employers. There is no better use of my time than this. I could have taken up secretarial work in a nice, straightforward bank which never required me to sit up at night waiting for a medical officer, but what a waste of a life that would have been.' Amy Wilkes frowned and then narrowed her eyes at her assistant. 'You haven't answered my question.'

Diana was saved from having to do so by the arrival of the Medical Officer.

'It's a good job this didn't happen three years ago; the old fever hospital only had room for fifty-odd patients; this one's got nearer two hundred beds and the way this outbreak is looking we could need all of them.' The District Medical Officer had burst in like a hurricane in full force, throwing off his overcoat and beginning a tirade of information before his party had even finished walking through Mackintosh's front door.

'Surely not so many as that!' the Borough Factory Inspector was already trying to underestimate the extent of the problem in the hope that he wouldn't have to recommend too many alterations to the factory-floor plans. The new Factories Act had given him enough trouble.

'Gentlemen,' Amy Wilkes rose to meet her visitors and tried not to look as though her eyes were closing with fatigue and the lateness of the hour, 'I am Mrs Wilkes the Head of Women's Employment, and this is my assistant—'

'Have you stopped the milk yet?' the Medical Officer barked, perhaps being used to talking to the hard of hearing. His colleagues, presumably, were now somewhat deafer than when they first encountered him.

'I heard about the outbreak of scarlet fever in the town and I had the deliveries of fresh milk to our canteens stopped two days ago. Our staff have been making do with tinned milk since then.'

The civil servant from the Ministry of Health spoke timidly, 'I'm afraid we have traced the source of the outbreak and the dairy in question, in addition to supplying two local schools, they do . . . err . . . in point of fact . . .'

'They supply your factory!' The Medical Officer couldn't abide beating about the bush.

'The incubation period is anything from . . . er . . . a week to perhaps . . . a fortnight?'

'In short, madam, you should expect your staff to start showing signs of fever. Possibly even you yourself.'

'Well, erm . . . we hope that you will all stay quite well, but as a precaution we have arranged for some testing to be done. Nothing to worry about unduly . . . The government are allocating capacity at a testing laboratory in Reading to deal with the extra testing which will need to be done . . . a lot to do in Halifax . . . erm . . . not just this factory.'

'It's a bad one!' the Medical Officer was evidently not trying to maintain confidentiality. 'Seen it before.'

'Erm, yes, this is the same strain which caused the epidemic in Doncaster, you know? Very interesting case, er . . . did you read about it over the summer?'

'Terrible thing, the Doncaster outbreak! Turned into the largest outbreak of scarlet fever in this country for twenty years. Not only that, but it's a particularly dangerous strain; damages joints, causes pain for months afterwards. We need to contain it as best we can so that it doesn't move to other towns!'

The Factory Inspector, who was expected to follow along with this travelling circus of doom, was still trying to argue that he might not need to recommend any changes to the factories they would inevitably visit. 'But scarlet fever isn't so very dangerous, is it? Fatalities are only one in a hundred?'

'That's bad enough! If we carried that across the whole nation we'd lose more of the populace to scarlet fever than we did to the last war! Besides, it's not just the fatalities we need to worry about, it's the effect it will have on *industry* while the workers are quarantined and the transport network if the tram drivers are too ill to work. The influenza epidemic in London this winter took out two-thirds of the operators on the London telephone exchange and all hell broke loose; we cannot let this spread and cause the same level of disruption!'

Amy Wilkes wished she'd ushered them up to her office first so that this discussion could be conducted in comfort, but it was too late now, she supposed. 'I'm pleased to report that we've only had a few cases here at the factory.'

The District Medical Officer towered over Amy Wilkes.

'We can only hope that it stays that way, but we cannot hope idly. There will be quarantine orders on families of school-age children.'

Amy had not expected this. 'Oh, but that's hundreds of parents! We can't lose that many workers.'

'That's only the start of it! We want you all wearing masks! We want you to increase the allocated floor space for each employee from twenty-two inches to twice that and we want you to close the communal areas where staff might usually eat together – and tell any pregnant women to stay away from work indefinitely!' The District Medical Officer did not notice the Factory Inspector shudder as he made his demands.

Amy was glad now that they had taken some action early. 'We've already closed the staff canteen, but I really was hoping that we could avoid all the rest of this sort of thing until we saw just how serious the outbreak was.'

'Hope is an excellent thing, Mrs Wilkes, and I always encourage it. But hope must never be idle! We can hope for the best, but it would be unconscionable laziness in the circumstances not to prepare for other outcomes!'

Chapter Forty-Two

'Mother, you need to take care!' Mary was bellowing at the top of her voice and she felt certain that her mother could hear her, but was choosing to ignore something that she thought overwhelmingly inconvenient.

'Don't bother me while I'm at the supper.' She was frying up mutton chops and had a particular dislike of interference while she was handling a pan of hot fat.

'Have you been told the news? Has anyone told you what's happening in the town?' Mary brandished a copy of the *Halifax Courier* with a headline she knew her mother likely would not have read. She had never established whether her mother couldn't read, or refused to read, but it didn't matter; she needed to be told.

'Yes, yes, you're gettin' married; you told me. I've got my dress down for you, it's on the back of the wardrobe and I've taken it in. You'll want a shawl with it.'

This stopped Mary short – a matter which in any other household would be a cause for shared joy conveyed in the same irritable manner her mother told her they'd run out of coal. She had come to impress one item of news on her mother, but found that she had taken in another. She wondered when it had happened, when her mother had finally come around to it; had Bess worked that strange magic of hers and explained to their mother without raising her voice? Mary suddenly felt a desperate need to protect her mother from everything and shouted very much louder, 'There's scarlet fever, Mother! You have to take especial care!'

'Scarlet fever?' Her mother wrinkled her nose and brow in a show of disgust and disapproval together.

Mary's shoulders sagged in relief as she made her first step of progress towards getting her message home. 'Yes, Mother, scarlet fever.'

'You've already had it.' She said it as though the whole epidemic was swept away and powerless through the sheer force of her own will to ignore it.

Mary took a deep breath and threw herself once more into the breach of her mother's determined ignorance. 'It's you, Mother! I'm worried about *you*!'

'I haven't got scarlet fever and I don't care either way. It's nothing. You were all right. People make such a fuss.' Mrs Norcliffe flicked the mutton chops onto a cracked willow pattern dish and didn't flinch as the hot fat splattered on her calloused red hands.

With her mother there was always going to be stubbornness. She was a dying breed, sleeping in the chair in the corner of the parlour under an old army coat through the coldest night. Mary had come to expect that when everyone around her was making compromises, her mother would refuse.

'It's everywhere, Mother. It's a bad one. They've had it in Doncaster. Folks have died.'

'I want to eat my chop in peace. Go and put the dress on, it wants fitting. I didn't sew all those beads on for nothing.'

If it were any other day Mary might have run straight to the dress, one of the few examples of her mother's sporadic care. She'd have luxuriated in the opportunity to feel like any other excited bride-to-be, would have rehearsed her progress down the stairs on her wedding day. But the weight of the responsibility she had to her mother outweighed any anticipation she felt for herself. She wondered how she'd ever leave her, if she really could leave her to be wed.

To an outsider looking in on their family it might have looked like a loveless and uncaring household, but their situation was not as simple as that. Mary could remember life before her father and brothers died and she knew that her mother had got worse since then. Vera Norcliffe had cut off emotionally from her last surviving children so that she needn't feel any more loss if they too succumbed to the tuberculosis which had ravaged the men in the family, but seemed to be biding its time with the women. Mary's father had told her that the change had started when Mary was born. He had been away fighting and the worry of keeping a new baby and two boys safe on her own during wartime had broken her. Perhaps that was why Mary worried so very much, or perhaps it was because her sister didn't worry at all and she needed to provide the counterbalance.

There was a variety of love and care in the Norcliffe household, and while it might not be understandable to outsiders, it ran deep and it bound them tightly together. Mary accepted that she had to supply what her mother and sister were lacking – and they in turn did the same for her: Bess supplied affection and Mrs Norcliffe pragmatism.

Mary knew that she wasn't going to get her mother to listen while she ate; a fried chop was one of her few pleasures in life and Mary supposed she would be safe to leave her to it for a few minutes. There was a dress waiting to be seen, and something about the thought of it upstairs made Mary's spine shiver. She took off her coat and hung it over the bannister where their coats had been polishing the wood smooth for the best part of a decade and made her way up the stairs whose every creak she could have mapped in her sleep.

It was odd to think that in the house she knew so intimately, her mother could still produce items she'd never seen. There were tea chests up in the eaves of the roof which they raided every so often for shoe leather, but by and large they went untouched, filled as they were with the effects of the dead.

Mary reached the doorway of her bedroom and stopped. It occurred to her that she'd never seen the dress that her mother was married in and she felt an odd reluctance to be reminded of her father and the hope her mother must have felt on her wedding day and the way in which all that hope was dashed by consumption.

And there it was, immediately recognisable. It was near identical in cut and design to the black silk dress Mary had borrowed from the tea chest last May, a twin of the very same dress her mother had worn to her father's funeral, and she knew that it was just her size. Obviously the black funeral dress had been copied from the white wedding dress, but why? Perhaps her mother only had one dress pattern and couldn't afford to buy another on top of the cost of the black silk and her husband's funeral. Perhaps it was a farewell, a message to him that she would never let go.

Mrs Norcliffe had sewed pearlised beads around the neckline of the old-fashioned gown, and Mary didn't know what to think of her mother, who could still surprise her by producing from nowhere things that Mary had never seen.

Chapter Forty-Three

Percy Palgrave believed the little chapel under the bridge was a gift from the gods. Ordinarily, he thought, he might have struggled to bring Dolly's mind around to the topic of marriage only a few weeks after meeting her, and to persuade her to hurry along and marry him before his leave was ended, but as it was, he had the sweetshop.

Dolly had clearly always wanted her own wedding to be in that crazy old pile one day, and if he could champion the cause to have the shop owner chucked out and some religious types chucked in, he'd not only win her favour, but he'd also be able to point out that if Dolly really did want to be the first bride to be wed in the chapel, she'd have to hurry before some other blushing bride beat her to it. What better way for him to propose marriage than to present her with the fait accompli of her dream wedding chapel? And Percy Palgrave *did* intend to propose marriage. He had returned from Burma with the express intention of picking up a wife to cook, clean and iron for him and he wasn't going to return to colonial life without one. Dolly would get the little wedding she wanted and he would get both the house-keeper he needed and a nice little pot of money as a sweetener. If he could just get the use of the chapel changed, everything would fall into place.

Starting his campaign was easy; a letter to the Halifax Town Council, another to the editor of the *Halifax Courier*, and a third to the member of parliament. Palgrave had them all signed by his mother – a pillar of local philanthropic society – and given weight by her headed notepaper which listed her various trusteeships. For the trifling price of three stamps he could now, quite naturally, turn Dolly's thoughts towards a quick marriage.

It was while reading the letters to the editor in the *Halifax Courier* that Kathleen Calder discovered her shop – and by extension, her job – had been threatened. She had never previously known of any objection to the commer-cial use of the premises, but now, all of a sudden, some old buffer called Mrs Palgrave was writing to the paper to complain.

'*The chapel must be returned to its original use!*' the letter writer had demanded. '*Too many young Halifax couples have been deprived the chance of a Christian wedding in this hallowed ground. Trading must not be tolerated in the temple of the Lord.*'

The reasons given in the letter were patently ridiculous and, as far as Kathleen was concerned, this old Mrs Palgrave didn't have the first idea what the chapel had been built for. Putting it back to its original use would mean undoing the Reformation, abolishing the Church of England, and bringing back cash for prayers. Kathleen was always exasperated by people who presumed to know what something's original use had been but hadn't bothered to read up on it. And all this nonsense about couples deprived of weddings on hallowed ground! It had never been hallowed ground and it had never been intended for weddings. Kathleen was fuming with anger when Reenie came home from work and the kitchen table was piled high with books and handwritten notes which were being condensed into a very strongly worded reply, which Kathleen would be sending to the editor by the first post.

'The De Whyte's got it lawfully at the dissolution,' she declared, scowling, 'and if this Mrs Palgrave don't like it she can go back in time and take it up with Henry VIII, because not liking an owner is completely different to an owner not being well within their rights!'

Percy Palgrave was pleased with the Town Council's response to his mother's letter. It had hit the right note. They were concerned about the safety of the old building which sat so precariously over the bank; they were frustrated by the litter which built up around it; and they were alert to rumours that illicit Sunday trading was going on. The suggestion of a compulsory purchase order was mooted and the police were requested to watch for any sign of commercial life on the Sabbath, so it was a hopeful time for Percy. The more time he spent with Dolly, the more he fell in love with the idea of never having to do his own domestic chores again. Percy knew that Dolly wasn't a rich heiress, not in the style of the Mackintosh family, or any of the big industrialists in the town, but when he looked deep into her clear eyes, he saw all the ease and comfort of a second-class ticket on the boat back to Burma, instead of a third. Dolly represented a few more luxuries – and a lot less hardship – and his heart ached lest he should lose her after he'd got this far.

A wedding in that little hole in the wall would be perfect. Barely room for a handful of guests, so nice and cheap. Plenty of money left over for a nice family car, or a few really good lounge suits.

Kathleen might have been stuck at home, but she was still keeping abreast of the various letters now circulating about her shop. The Palgrave woman who had written to the local paper had also written to the Town Council and they had sent Mr Hebblewhite a carbon copy of their reply. Kathleen was incensed. She would not be beaten by someone who did not know the difference between a chantry, a chapel, a church, and a temple. Not only that but she wasn't going to take the Town Council's accusations of 'a litter nuisance' lying down. She'd have them know that since she'd started working there it was cleaned thoroughly every Saturday and Wednesday – Mr Hebblewhite had soon given her an extra shift after school on a Wednesday – with special attention paid to gathering litter which had blown down to the other end of the road.

Kathleen was being kept home from school, from the library, from her friends, from her foes, and from her job; this left her ample time to launch her own campaign of letters in defence of Hebblewhite's.

Kathleen's mother knew that the girl was just angry at

being cooped up at home, but all that frustration was spilling over into the shop business. It was like Reenie and the flower pots all over again; when Reenie had got her first job she'd paced up and down the farmyard holding two flower pots in each hand to build up strength in her fingers so she'd be better at working quickly on the sweet-wrapping line. Her girls had determination and it was a mixed blessing. At least Kathleen's letters couldn't get her into any real trouble – or could they? Mrs Calder worried so much about her children and these days there was plenty to choose from. The fire at the factory Reenie had been caught up in, the poisoned Mackintosh's sweets which had been frighteningly close to Reenie, and now an epidemic in the town. If that wasn't enough, the talk of a coming war in the newspapers increased by the day. The government were still talking about stockpiling food and they'd already made it law that the local councils had to have plans for aerial gas attacks. She worried most about the gas attacks. How would they know if there was one? Kathleen was right about one thing: they needed to get a wireless.

Chapter Forty-Four

Amy Wilkes outranked Cynthia Starbeck, but still she found the woman disagreeing with her again and again. It was almost pathological. When *she* argued about the work of the Women's Employment Department, it was usually to insist that employees were made to work harder, for longer hours, and less money. Starbeck's overriding obsession was that the people who ran the factory machinery should become machines themselves.

'I can't make any changes to my lines at present.' Cynthia Starbeck did not look up from her desk where she was fully and conspicuously occupied with putting her many typed memos into envelopes ready to send out and disrupt the various departments for whom she was a bane. 'We're conducting studies which require absolute continuity.'

'Might I remind you, Cynthia, that this direction does not come from me, but from the chief of the District Medical Officers? We have an outbreak of scarlet fever and it could tear through our workforce like a hurricane if we don't make the necessary undertakings.'

'The District Medical Officers are notorious Liberals. They come up with a scare story like this every so often to disrupt business and keep themselves in work. I remember the Spanish flu and I can assure you that no one fussed this much in those days.' Cynthia herself was suffering, but was managing to make the best of it. The very deep paper cut in the web of her hand would not close and was throbbing horribly, but she didn't allow it to prevent her from doing her duty.

'If you've apprised yourself of the details of the changes then you'll have seen that all of them will improve productivity on your line, not lessen it. The staff canteen is closed with immediate effect, and the girls can only eat food which they have brought with them and no one else has touched; they will eat at the edge of the work-room and not leave it. They must all wear gauze masks – which will prevent them from slowing the line by chat-ting – and we will take over the laundering of overalls and distribute them at the start of each shift and they will be required to change in silence. Every single one of these changes gives you what you've been lobbying for for years, so what, precisely, is your problem now?'

'It's an unnecessary disruption to routine and the results of this study are reliant on nothing being altered.'

'I would have thought the results of your study are reliant on none of your staff dropping dead from contagious disease!'

'It's septic sore throat, not the bubonic plague; I think we can keep a little perspective.'

'I think you can spare the time to stop what you're

doing and give me your undivided attention for five minutes. What could possibly be so important that you need to send out this much internal correspondence?'

'Yours is not the only department which seeks to interfere with the smooth running of the important work of Time and Motion. A great deal of work is involved in defending the climate in which we work.'

Amy Wilkes had heard about her colleague's 'defence of her climate'. She must get up before dawn to type all the things she did. Some were as innocuous as demands to the head porter that he have his bogies' wheels oiled because they all squeaked, to the more sinister letters she wrote to the Home Office complaining about staff from overseas. Their very own Albert Baum had found his three-month work permit revoked earlier in the previous summer after a tip-off that a local woman could easily do his job and he wasn't really needed. Amy Wilkes believed that all Mr Baum's present difficulties were as a result of Cynthia's continued efforts to keep foreign workers out of the country. Well, she'd very quickly have to get used to foreign workers if she killed off all the British ones by giving them contaminated milk and refusing to let them wear masks.

'Mrs Starbeck, my instructions in this matter come from the board of directors. Where do yours come from? I'm curious to know?'

There was a knock at the door and a messenger girl tentatively poked her face around the office door, wary of germs. 'Mrs Starbeck? There's someone asking for you at the gatehouse, Mrs Starbeck.'

Chapter Forty-Five

Dolly Dunkley enjoyed the feeling of riding around on her high horse. In Dolly's case this was figurative rather than literal. She was not lucky enough to have a horse of her own like Reenie did, and even if she had owned a horse it was unlikely that she would have had the necessary dedication to take care of it. However, she liked feeling a combination of moral superiority, righteous indignation and having something to complain about. This new project to evict the Mackintosh's misshapes shop from their old premises was just her cup of tea.

'I've always said that it should be put back to how it was,' she told her young man as they walked out of step through People's Park. The moment Dolly had heard about Percy and his mother's campaign of letters to convert the old sweetshop chapel she became convinced that she had been lobbying for it all her life. Dolly was not alone in this; there were one or two genuine anti- quarians who had spent decades writing letters to the corporation and the diocese to request that 'something be done' to preserve the history of the building, but it was only when Percy started making discreet suggestions in strategic places that scores of people suddenly realised that they had always been in favour of converting the chapel back to its original function and that they were appalled at the immorality of its existing tenant. How the sale of wonky Caramel Cups was immoral was never specified, but it was certainly a running theme.

'It should be put back to its proper purpose; it should have a congregation again.'

Percy, feeling more secure in his courtship with the Dunkley daughter, was beginning to challenge her mistakes a little now. 'But wasn't it a Roman Catholic chantry? It wouldn't have had a congregation, would it?'

'It might have had a Catholic one,' Dolly said defensively.

Since beginning his campaign of letters Percy had been directed to an accurate history of the building and was now not so sure he wanted to wait as long as it would take for a full restoration of the building; he just wanted a quick wedding in a sweetshop, then back to Burma with his housewife and his new set of luggage. Starting the campaign at all was going to give him the entrée into the topic of marriage, and that was all he really needed and he said, 'It would have just been one monk on his own, praying for lost souls and eating people's forgotten sandwiches. What's the use of restoring that? I thought you were Protestant?'

Dolly didn't like it when Percy corrected her with such bluntness, but she had failed to notice that he was correcting her with bluntness almost all the time; he appeared to enjoy feeling superior just as much as she did. It did

not occur to Dolly that this might not be the ideal basis
for a lasting marriage, especially if theirs was going to
involve living in so-called 'primitive conditions' and with
no social company but one another for months at a time.
Dolly flustered to defend her position, but shifted her
ground. 'Well, yes, obviously I know that, but it's not
what I meant at all. I meant that it should be restored
to the purpose it would have had if there had been some
Protestants back in the days when it was built.'

'Like what?'

'Well, a little church congregation for people who live
along that side of North Bridge. It could be run like a
sort of mission in the town – maybe we could get some
of the railway men to go along between their shifts in
the railway yard?'

Percy Palgrave opened his mouth to ridicule the idea,
but just as the words were forming in his mouth, his
stomach rumbled, which reminded him that if he didn't
want to cook his own dinners and iron his own shirts
when he went back to Burma, he needed to get a move
on and do the deed. With this prosaic thought in mind,
he said, 'What if we were the first couple to be married
in it?'

'Be married? In the chapel on the bridge?' Dolly was
breathless with excitement. She hadn't noticed that this
was not a romantic proposal because it didn't matter.
All that mattered was that it was a real proposal and
that she was going to be married.

'Yes.' Percy was optimistic, but not enthusiastically so.
'It'd be all right, I'd have thought. Tart it up a bit, take
down the sign with the cigarettes on it and it ought to
be rather jolly. Bit on the small side, but we could get

our pictures in the paper if we were the first couple to be wed there. What do you say? Shall I ask your father? Do you think you could be ready to come back to Burma with me before Easter?'

Dolly was over the moon. She did not notice that there were no professions of love, or even a suggestion of devotion. All Dolly heard was that someone wanted to marry her and this would be a way out of Mackintosh's, Halifax, housework in her father's rectory, and all the trouble of paying her own way in the world. Palgrave might not be handsome, but he offered a life of ease with servants to wait on her in glamorous, colonial Burma. If her newly acquired fiancé had a yen to be married in the chapel under the bridge then she would make damn sure that the Hebblewhites were chucked out before they'd had time to so much as pack. Dolly Dunkley was getting her wedding.

Chapter Forty-Six

'Are we allowed to meet here?' Mary hovered at the door of the old stable, nervous about doing the wrong thing.

'What do you mean, "are we allowed"? We've always been allowed; this is Ruffian's stable.'

'Yes, but if we're not allowed into the staff canteen because it's too crowded, isn't this just as bad? There's never been much room in here.'

Reenie cast her eyes around the stables which had always been their safe haven, a kind of clubhouse and refuge, now – like all innocent pursuits – potentially deadly. 'Well, you always sit on that side with Bess and I always sit on this side, so if we just stick to our own sides . . .' Reenie didn't finish her sentence; she had lost heart. There was something so very sad about having to treat everyone as a possible threat. Reenie could put an optimistic light on any topic, but not this one.

They sat in silence for a minute or more, unwrapping sandwiches and unscrewing thermos tops. Their breaktimes in the stables were usually abuzz with eager chatter from the moment they were within hailing distance across the cobbles, but life these days seemed to have knocked the wind out of their sails.

Bess chirped up, 'Mary's got a wedding dress.'

Reenie's eyes brightened at this news. 'Has she? When did you choose it? Where's it from? Why didn't you tell me you were—'

'It's not one I've picked out.' Mary was careful not to get too enthusiastic on the subject. Perhaps it was the fear of putting the mockers on it, or perhaps it was that feeling of hallowed ground which accompanied anything to do with her parents' life before her father died. Either way, she was careful to keep a matter-of-fact tone. 'It was my mother's wedding dress, so it's already the right fit and she's sewn some new pearlite buttons on it to brighten it up.'

Reenie sensed that this was not the time for over-enthusiasm, and in a moment of Herculean restraint she managed to dampen her own excitement enough to say, 'Oh, well, that's good. You just need something borrowed and something blue now.'

'And a wedding licence.' Mary rolled her sleeves up, unconsciously preparing for the battle she was anticipating with another official body. 'I have to go to the register office in Halifax to make appointments for us both to go in and declare our intention to wed.'

'Wouldn't Albert do that for you? Save you the worry?' Reenie knew that Mary's capacity for worry was beyond that of most mortals.

'He's got residency permits to apply for. Sometimes I think the solicitor's clerk sees more of him than I do. He's there now. And none of it does any good.'

Reenie tried to bring her thoughts back to the one bright ray of hope on their horizon: the wedding. 'What happens once you've both declared your intention to wed? Will it be plain sailing after that?'

'Then they put a notice up in the register office to give folks a chance to object.'

'Do you think folks might object?' The idea shocked Reenie, but then she remembered that when Mr Baum had applied for his last work permit he had been refused because Mrs Starbeck had taken the time and trouble to write to the Home Office and tell them that he didn't deserve it. Reenie had never thought there could be such strong personal feeling towards a stranger, but as she got older she was beginning to realise more and more that you never knew what went on in other people's heads.

'We'll just have to wait and see. Neither of us are married and I'll be of age, so the only objection anyone could make is that we're marrying for the permit.'

'Surely the register office will be able to see that you love each other and that it's not anything like that?'

'Yes, but we'd have to prove it – and how do you prove something like that?'

'You can prove it.' Bess chirped, 'You can show them all your lovely letters from him.' Bess appeared to have forgotten that the letters had almost all been all completely destroyed and that she had been the instrument of their destruction.

'How would anyone find out that you'd been to the register office and put your name down? It doesn't go in the paper, does it?' Reenie asked.

'It's only posted on the wall in the register office. If

you-know-who doesn't go in the register office then maybe we're plain sailing.' Mary patted Ruffian's flank absentmindedly and he snorted his support of her plan. 'I've got to go to the register office this week to get an appointment. Would you get off work early and come with me, Reenie?'

Reenie was honoured. This was the kind of thing friends were for and she was confident that Mrs Starbeck wouldn't think to watch the register office for notices. This was – at long last – the happy ending that Mary, Mr Baum, and his family deserved.

'Don't put the mockers on it. She might have a friend at the register office. We'll just go and fill in the forms – and we'll wait again, because it's the only thing we can do.'

A tense silence filled the air in the stable as Reenie wrestled with all of the hopeful, cheerful things she wanted to say, but knew she shouldn't. Bess turned the pages of her magazine and gazed at the pictures of foreign radio stars who lived apparently charmed lives in the capital.

Ruffian's ears were the first to prick up. The tread on the cobbles out in the stable yard was a familiar one to him. Peter was approaching and he was doing it quickly.

'Have you heard the news?' Peter was a little breathless; he'd obviously hurried to find them. 'The Sunlight Laundry on Hebble Lane's been shut down. They've sent all the workers home to quarantine. They've had an outbreak of scarlatina.'

Bess's face lit up at the name of the business, clearly not registering what this truly meant. 'That's where our mother works. She's a laundress. Do you think she'll be in the paper?'

Chapter Forty-Seven

Kathleen Calder had a particular liking for Sherbet Fountains. She didn't like them for herself, but she liked the ease with which they could be sold in secret at her Sunday School, the last remaining opportunity she had to go out and see her friends. The Sherbet Fountain might have been made for illicit sale on ecclesiastical premises because unlike chocolate and toffees, it contained no fat so it wouldn't melt in her pockets, or in her school satchel if she were forced to leave it beside the old Victorian heating pipes. It came wrapped in a card and paper tube so it didn't rustle, and, best of all, it was one of the shop's cheapest lines, so she was in a much better position to buy them in bulk from Mr Hebblewhite and sell them on at a tidy profit under the pews at All Saints Stump Cross. The other Sunday School scholars liked them too. They could get into terrible trouble if they were caught munching a sweet or a piece of chocolate bar during the sermon, but Sherbet Fountains were easy to conceal. One only had to take the liquorice strip out and loosen the collar of the paper sleeve, so that it was then an easy matter to discreetly put a hand into one's pocket, get a dip of sherbet on an index finger, and then put it to one's lips as though in a pose of thought on some great theological question which had just been raised by the vicar. The number of children who now appeared to be pondering deep eschatological conundrums in Stump Cross Sunday School was increasing every week, and so were Kathleen's profits.

'Can you get us some Mint Cracknel next week?' a tough-looking lad asked Kathleen as he crossed her palm with three grubby farthings outside the Sunday School hall in exchange for his sherbet. 'And a quarter of chocolate eclairs for me mam; she says she could do with something to pass the time when the curate's preaching.'

'No can do.' Kathleen pocketed the money while casting a glance around her with the automatic caution of a practised fence. 'Not allowed to work there right now, but in any event they're too high value, too likely to melt, and too conspicuous in the packaging – those twist wraps don't half rustle. Tell her she'll have to come into the shop in the week once this fever is over and we'll do her a good price.'

'She can't come in the week, she's got work at Mack's in the day and she's taking in laundry on a night; Sunday's the only day she could visit . . .' The lad exchanged a look of knowing with Kathleen; they were both only too aware that the Sunday trading laws barred commercial premises from opening on a Sunday at all, and that shop owners caught operating then were regularly fined by the police. It still happened, though; you heard about some places selling things out the back door on the quiet. And after all, wasn't that what Kathleen was already doing? Running a mobile shop from her pew in the back corner of the Sunday School hall? The rough-looking lad asked, 'Do you have a set of keys to the shop, like?'

Kathleen had been considering this potential new business avenue for some time and it just so happened that the lad's query coincided with her own musing on the subject. 'You're a Grimshaw, aren't you? Back Ripon Street. What's your mother's name?'

'Siobhan. She's from Dublin, Irish Free State. She'll not split on you to the English police, no fear. She just wants a quarter of a pound of chocolate eclairs and the same again of coffee caramels whenever you get them in.'

'Dublin? What's she doing in low Church of England? Shouldn't you all be at St Eilfred's with the papists?'

'Aye, but me mam wants me to get a place at the grammar school like my sister, so she's biting her tongue until we've all matriculated.'

This had a ring of truth for Kathleen; she knew that people would do a lot for sweets and school places. She would trust the Grimshaws, but she'd have to be careful.

The covert Sunday opening hours at Hebblewhite's began as Kathleen intended to keep them: discreetly. Kathleen read the papers, she'd seen plenty of reports of police waiting outside shop premises ready to pounce on illegal traders, and she had no intention of being caught and marring her reputation – that would put back her plans for her elevation to the peerage. No, Kathleen was clever and she had already planned her lawful excuse for entering the shop premises on the Sabbath: history. She was recording the history of the old building and she was there to sketch some of the gargoyles while the shop was empty. She even had her sketchbook prepared with a selection of well-executed drawings which she had paid a lad to do for her in exchange for a half-pound bag of Toffee Pat. Kathleen was ready with her excuses if she was caught. The only difficulty would come if she were seen handing over goods at the back door, and for that she had made up a box marked 'Lost Property' in large black letters into which she would place any pre-ordered produce for a doubly concealed exchange.

Kathleen was enjoying the extra pocket money, but this was not why she did it: Kathleen was flushed with excitement by the idea that she was making a success of some real grown-up work. Old Mr Hebblewhite could never have done the things she had; he didn't have her initiative, her astute judgement of character, her capability. Kathleen had always known that she would make a good businesswoman; even when she was very small and she'd play at being grown-ups with the other girls in the playground. They were always mothers with pretend babies, and she was always the shopkeeper they came to visit for make-believe toys. For Kathleen there was no innate appeal in playing at being mothers – why make-believe something that was going to take away all your playtime one day? – *she* idolised a different kind of existence. She daydreamed fabulous stories in which desperate businessmen met her in a Lyon's Corner House and were so impressed by her very presence that they begged her to save their businesses. Kathleen planned to learn from Mackintosh's and then beat them at their own game. She just had to wait until they weren't in the midst of an epidemic, then she could really get to work.

Chapter Forty-Eight

'I know it's my fault.' Siobhan Grimshaw was holding her head in her hands as she sat, slumped forwards on the bench in the factory changing rooms. 'I gave her my Stuart's uniforms to wash; they'd been in the hospital picking up God-knows what.'

'You weren't to know,' Pearl reassured her, 'they were just uniforms, you couldn't have known the uniforms were dangerous in themselves.'

'And who says it was the uniforms, anyway?' Winnifred was putting on her own uniform ready to go back onto the Toffee Penny line and start up her twist-wrapping machine. 'She could've picked it up anywhere, any of us could. She might have caught it on the bus or queueing at the gates. There is no telling where it was.'

'But it was so soon after . . .' Siobhan shook her head. 'It was so soon after I gave her that basket to wash and I just can't stop thinking about it. I feel awful.'

'This will sound hard,' Pearl said, 'but feeling awful

won't help her. Working like stink to earn double piece-rates so we can all chip in for her doctor's bills, *that'll* help her. And working twice as hard to keep the line running so that it's here for her to come back to will help her all the more.'

'Is she under the doctor yet?' Winnifred asked.

'Yes,' Pearl said. 'She was sent home from the isolation hospital last night after her fever broke. They needed the bed in the hospital, apparently. Her husband's not caught it so he's nursing her while they all quarantine.'

'You know she lost her sense of smell?' Siobhan's suspicions had first been raised when she noticed that her friend didn't recoil as they passed the tannery. 'They say that's the first thing to happen when you get scarlet fever; you can't smell anything and you can't taste anything. That's when I should've known. I should've said something.'

'You know Doreen has always loved the smell of the Mint Cracknel room – and myself, I've always thought it was very therapeutic.' Winnifred produced a tattered toffee tin from the shelf above her coat hook. 'Why don't we fill up a tin with Mint Cracknel wrappers for her to smell when she's better? I'm sure she'd like that.'

Pearl was not convinced. 'Wouldn't she be a bit disappointed not to be given the Cracknel to eat? I'd have thought the smell without the sweets themselves might be considered mean.'

'Oh no, dear.' Winnifred knew about these things. 'She's slimming. And it's the thought that counts.'

Pearl shook her head. 'I don't think her whole family are slimming, so how about we collect them a tin of Mint Cracknel – not just the wrappers – and a tin of Quality

Street fresh from the line? We can leave them on her doorstep and she can smell them or eat them, or share them as she likes.'

'Are we allowed to leave things on her doorstep while they're in quarantine?' Siobhan asked.

'Well, the milkman does it, so I don't see why we shouldn't if they don't open the door.'

Siobhan thought for a moment. 'Do you think I should leave her a note? You know, something to say that I'm sorry.'

'No, love,' Winnifred reassured her, 'there's nothing to be sorry about. She wanted to help you. She wanted to take some of the burden that your family were feeling; we all did. It's a frightening time for everyone and we all wanted to find a way to do our bit to make it better for someone. Just send her a note to thank her and tell her she's missed; she'd like that.'

Chapter Forty-Nine

Halifax had a reputation for manufacturing the most hardwearing workers clogs and Mary had always hated them. It was an odd thing to hate – a plain wooden sole with a leather upper affixed by metal rivets – but even the sound of them clattering over cobbled streets sent a chill down her spine. Hatred of clogs was a family trait bred into her by her mother who had told Mary, in her own blunt way, that clogs meant death. Years before Mary's birth, when Mrs Norcliffe was just a child herself, her father had been killed in a mining accident. The mine had collapsed on several men and when their bodies were finally recovered they could only be identified by the clogs they wore. Mrs Norcliffe remembered being taken as a seven-year-old to a Sunday School hall somewhere where the bodies were laid out on trestle tables beneath sheets. Wooden-soled clogs weren't like leather shoes, they were meant to last the owner a lifetime, and each set of clogs had been worn down in varying places by the owners varying idiosyncrasies of gait, or attack by over-friendly dogs, or accidents of the home; each set, too, had been mended over and over in ways the families of the dead men would have known even at a distance. Mary's own grandfather had been identified by his wife and daughter through the patches he'd hammered over his heels.

Mary had not worn a pair of clogs for a long time and she would rather go barefoot than wear clogs again. She would need new shoes for her wedding day and the horrible thing was, in order to be married at the register office, she would need to pass the place where the clogs had always come from. Mary knew it was a ridiculous thing to fret over, but she couldn't help herself; she just didn't want to go alone.

Mary asked Reenie to go with her to the Register Office. It was only a preliminary visit to request an appointment, but it still put Mary on edge. At first Reenie had assumed her friend's anxiety over the visit was the natural nervousness of a bride who was having to undertake arrangements which the groom – being a foreign national – was not well-placed to undertake, but there was something more, and Reenie could have kicked herself when she realised what it was.

The Halifax Register Office was not a familiar place to Reenie, but then she had never been in need of any of the additional services which Carlton Street offered.

The pair took early shifts in the factory so they could arrive at the place at four thirty. Mary had not needed to look up the address in the directory, or how to get there, and that should have raised Reenie's suspicions immediately.

'Should we ask directions when we get off the tram

just in case it's not where you think it is?' Reenie asked as they shuffled their way towards the back of the moving vehicle which was approaching the stop.

'No. I know where it is.'

'But we're cutting it very fine for time and if we go the wrong way for a bit we might not get there before they close. But if we take a quick half a minute to double check by asking someone the way—'

Mary cut Reenie off mid-flow in her torrent of helpfulness just as they were alighting from the tram. 'I know *exactly* where it is; I used to go there often.'

'Why did you go there often? You're only just of age – you can't have needed to go to the register office often.'

Mary looked around to see that they were not within clear earshot of any passersby and then hissed, 'It's the same address as the Relieving Office.'

This information silenced Reenie, who realised she had put her foot in it. She had always known that Mary's father had died and that they lived in poor circumstances, but she had never thought about what it must have meant in practical terms. Reenie's family had never been forced to seek help from the Relieving Officer, but her heart went out to Mary.

The Halifax Register Office was squatting in two old Georgian townhouses which had been knocked together to form a nest of civil servants and was located, for convenience, just a few doors from the police court and the big borough police station. One could register a death and then be tried for causing it, all within a few hundred yards.

Mary stood stock-still in the doorway, unwilling to cross the threshold. The place looked smaller than she remembered, but then she had grown since her last visit. The classical stone columns which formed a decorative portico looked a trifle ridiculous now that they had shrunk down to their true size and were not looming over her childish self like biblical totems. Seeing how reduced the old place was gave Mary a measure of solace.

'Who have you come to see?' a receptionist with a pinched look about her demanded of them barely before they'd stepped through the door.

'We're here about a wedding,' Mary mumbled, trying to put from her mind the memories of being asked the same question in the same place, while she waited for the handouts from the relieving officers – parcels of clothes and two pairs of clogs made at the asylum. The relieving officers used to boast that they weren't the old-fashioned clogs because the inmates at the asylum had started making them with modern Gibson soles. Gibson soles didn't make them any better in Mary's eyes.

'You can't see anyone for three weeks. We've got two of the registrars on quarantine for a fortnight, and then after that it's a waiting list.'

Reenie blurted out, 'But they can't wait to be married three weeks! This is an emergency! They have to be married straight away!'

Mary blanched at the shame of this undignified situation and the anxiety of it all. The receptionist was not sympathetic:

'Well, that's your affair. You'll not get a wedding here this side of May Day. We're short-staffed and there's a waiting list. If you want an appointment to register your intention to marry, then I can get you one appointment in three weeks' time for one party, and . . .' she turned through pages of an appointments diary, 'and the second party could have an appointment to register their intent four and a half weeks hence—'

'Why can't they have an appointment together?' Reenie burst in, thinking she'd seen a more efficient way of managing the matter. 'They could save time by going in together.'

'We don't do that. You have to notify separately. It's a legal requirement.'

Reenie persisted on her friend's behalf. 'Look, this is a very special situation. My friend's fiancé is a Jewish man from Germany and his family are in a lot of danger unless they leave Germany, so Mary has said that she'll marry him . . .'

Mary didn't hear the rest of what her friend said. She was walking out through the front door into the dying light of the late afternoon. She was thinking about the clogs which she had burned as soon as she had got herself a job at Mackintosh's.

The clogs had been made from elm – the wood which coffins were made from – and more than one disgusted neighbour had commented, on inspecting them, that they had probably been made from the scrap they used for coffins in the sawmill at the asylum. Ordinarily elm would be considered too hard a wood for clogs, but if all they had in the sawmill that day was coffin scraps, then it would make sense. Mary hated them for their hardness, and her mother's hardness, and the hardness of her situation.

Chapter Fifty

It was the first day that the factory canteen was allowed to reopen after a drop in the number of scarlatinal infections. Dolly Dunkley had not been invited to join the girls for lunch in the factory dining hall, but she was so eager to boast about her news that she made herself an unwelcome guest all the same.

'We're going to get married in the bridge chantry,' she announced.

'What's the bridge chantry?' Bess asked.

'She means the sweetshop under North Bridge – it's old so it's got a fancy name.' Mary did not sound in a mood to pander to poshos like Dolly Dunkley.

'Can you get married in a sweetshop?' Bess looked genuinely intrigued as she put aside her glossy magazine to interrogate Dolly.

'Well, it's not a sweetshop, it's just got a man in it who's been selling sweets. It's really a thirteenth-century chapel where travellers and monks used to pray; it's really very unique.'

Mary did not point out that there are no degrees of uniqueness. 'And is that all there is to it? You can just march in and demand the shopkeeper marries you because monks used to sit in it freezing their knackers off seven hundred years ago?'

'Well no, obviously you have to have a special licence. I'm eligible to apply for a special licence through my father because he's the Rector of the parish of Stump Cross, and—'

'I think I've just lost interest.' Mary was becoming increasingly frustrated by tales of other people who were safe and well and had all the things she wished that she could have, and who took them for granted. Listening to how easy it was for Dolly Dunkley – of all people – to be married in a sweetshop if she wanted to be, when she herself couldn't be married anywhere at all, was too much heartache. She abandoned her cup of tea and hot toast and pushed her way out of the dining hall.

'You can tell me,' Bess said to Dolly, 'I'm interested.' Bess loved a wedding and liked to hear about the planning of them. It did not occur to her why Mary might have stormed off, but she was used to her sister's changeable moods and knew best that sometimes it was kinder to let her go and vent her temper on her own in peace.

'Well, if you want to be married in a chapel which isn't a parish church – you know, like a school chapel, or something – or even if you're an invalid and you want to be married at home in your sickbed, you have to apply for a bishop's special licence and the bishop of your diocese has his staff draw up this huge certificate and you take it to a minister and he has to marry you.'

'Is that what you're getting?' Bess asked. 'Are you getting a bishop to make you a certificate?'

'Oh no, ours is much grander because Percival hasn't been living in the parish for long enough because he's been abroad, and he was baptised in the Congregational Church not the Church of England, and there was also . . .' Dolly continued listing distinctions in their case which made them special in the eyes of the law, both Tort and Ecclesiastical, but Bess didn't fully understand her again until Dolly finished with, 'Which is why ours is an *Archbishop's* Special Licence. It's *much* grander.'

'And that's for letting anyone get married anywhere?'

'Well, yes, but only if one of you has been baptised or christened.'

'This Arch-rival's special licence—'

'Arch*bishop's* special licence,' Dolly corrected.

'How special is it? I mean, if one of the parties has been christened does it cover absolutely every possible scenario, or is there another kind of licence that's higher than an arches licence that covers more things?'

Dolly was in the mood to boast about how special her licence was going to be, and so she resorted to a facetious hyperbole, never thinking that Bess would take it literally. 'You can't get anything more special than an Archbishop's Licence; it covers *every* eventuality. If you got a special licence for Reenie's horse he could marry a horse in the middle of the Piece Hall and no one would be able to object.'

Bess's eyes widened; an idea was forming which she

247

wanted to take to Diana. She thought that she had solved a problem for everyone and she was thrilled at the idea.

'Diana, you know how you said that arranging a disciplinary for the horses was a headache?' Bess had shuffled in next to Diana at her place on the dinner bench at the far end of the factory dining hall.

'To be clear, Bess. I'm not arranging a disciplinary for the horses themselves, I'm writing a disciplinary policy for employees who allow—' Diana stopped abruptly as she realised the futility of explaining this to Bess when Bess was waving at everyone who was passing their table and not listening. 'Yes, Bess?'

'Well, I think I might know a way that we can make it all right.'

'How's that then?'

'A special licence.'

Although Diana's interest was mildly piqued, she had very low hopes that Bess would be offering a useful suggestion. 'And what's a special licence?'

'It's a certificate Dolly Dunkley told me about. You can go and get it from an archway in the church, and you take it to the vicar and it means that they have to agree to do you a wedding anywhere, even at home if you're an invalid. And it's for anyone, so long as one of the horses has been baptised.'

Diana resisted the urge to knock her own head against the surface of the dining table and instead maintained her look of impassivity. 'Can you try explaining all that again, Bess, but in a different way?'

'Well, I'm not saying who it is, but I think I know who the father of the baby horse is in the factory stables, and

I thought if we got a special certificate to have a wedding in the stables we could marry him to the mare who's having a baby horse and then you wouldn't need to discipline Reenie because the two horses would be married before the foal was born and then there wouldn't be anything wrong at all.'

Diana nodded carefully. 'And who told you that you could get wedding certificates for horses?'

'Dolly Dunkley. She knows all about them because her father's a vicar and he signs them all the time.'

'Of course he does. And she's persuaded you to arrange a wedding in the stables for two of the horses so that the foal won't be born out of wedlock?'

'No, that's *my* idea. I don't want Reenie to get into trouble, because she wouldn't let Ruffian out of his stable knowingly and so it wouldn't be fair for her to get the blame.'

Diana decided to pretend she hadn't heard that and hoped Bess wouldn't tell anyone else because she was still hoping that, even if she had to write the disciplinary policy, she wouldn't have to enact it because they would never find the culprit.

'Look, you can have a wedding for the horses if you're doin' it on your own and don't waste any company time, but don't talk to your sister about it. You know she's upset about not being able to have a wedding herself and this might just rub it in. Do you understand?'

Bess nodded, gathered up her dinner tray and went away to her work taking with her the vital information that might have made all the difference to her sister and their friends if only someone had really listened.

Chapter Fifty-One

Mary and Albert sat side by side in the office of Barstow, Midgley, & Lord. They could tell already that Mr Midgley had bad news for them, but at least he would break it to them kindly. Mary couldn't think how having a solicitor talk to the register office would make any difference – if there was a waiting list then there was a waiting list – besides, her friend Reenie had already ruined everything by telling the receptionist that they were only marrying to allow Albert into the country.

'I've found a synagogue in Bradford; they said that they would conduct the service even though Mary isn't one of their people, but you'd still have to arrange to give notice at the register office in Halifax beforehand or it simply wouldn't be legal. We're back to the same problem again.' Mr Midgley clearly disliked giving bad news to the couple.

Albert was keen not to discount any possibility and asked, 'Our friend Irene Calder suggested that there is a place in Scotland we could go to, on the border . . .'

The solicitor shook his head sadly. 'It wouldn't work. Scottish law is very different to English law. Some couples run away to Gretna Green to be married because in Scotland they have a practice known as irregular marriages. In effect, you'd have to take Mary to Scotland, go before a magistrate or a Sheriff, and tell them that you were living together out of wedlock. You'd then be convicted of having an irregular marriage and fined, but they'd record you as having an irregular marriage and in Scotland that counts as being legally wed from that day on. It might work for a Scots couple, but you need to keep your criminal record spotless if you're to get a permit to come back to England, and being convicted of an irregular marriage would certainly be classed as a conviction and would stain your character in the eyes of the Home Office.'

Albert could not conceal his disappointment. 'But do they not have weddings conducted by blacksmith or some such thing?'

'They have common-law marriage and it's not recognised for permits by the English. The problem we have is that although you can avoid the register office by marrying in the Church of England, they will only marry you if you've had the banns read in your local parish four weeks beforehand, and you'd have to be there at the services.'

'But I don't have a parish; I'm a German Jew. And I don't have four weeks.'

'Precisely, you need to be married in the local register office but they are fully booked for the next three weeks.'

Albert could not comprehend these British idiosyncrasies. 'Couldn't we go to a register office somewhere that is not full? There must be somewhere in England.'

'You still have to give notice in the register office nearest you and you have to have been living in that locality for twenty-nine days.'

At last Albert understood what the solicitor had been telling him and he nodded in sad realisation. 'There is no way that we can marry before the deadline, is there?'

Mr Midgley pursed his lips and was silent a moment; he didn't want to have to say it, but he knew that they had to face facts. 'There is no way that you can legally be married before the deadline. I'm sorry. I think your only alternative is to marry in Germany.'

Mary looked confused. 'But how could we marry each other in Germany if I'm in Halifax?' Her mind was working so much more slowly these days. She was so tired, and it was so stuffy in the solicitor's office.

'That isn't possible, I'm afraid.' Bitterness entered Albert's voice. 'It has been illegal for Jews to marry non-Jews in Germany since 1933. Mary cannot come to Germany.'

Mr Midgley looked pained, as though he was angry with himself for forgetting this important fact. 'Then it will have to be France. You had a permit to travel home through France, didn't you, Herr Baum?'

Albert nodded assent.

'Once you had married in France, it is unlikely that you would have to remain in France and you could immediately reapply for a permit to return to England. And this time, as the husband of a British subject, it would be far simpler. *In theory*. For the moment, however, the extension we obtained for you to allow you to sign a lease is shortly to expire. If you stay in England much longer I don't need to remind you what the consequences might be.'

Chapter Fifty-Two

The decision was made in a haze of exhaustion. Mary
travelled with Albert back to the tiny house where she
lived with her mother and sister. It would not take her
long to pack her things, she had so few of them, but she
had never travelled anywhere and she didn't know
what she would need. She was going to France and she
was frightened, angry, and desperately tired. She knew
that she loved Albert, passionately, and she didn't want
to let him go, but she wanted to take a rest from all this
for a while, just go to sleep and let all the trouble
wait for her to return once more to the fray when she
had recovered her strength.

Mary was too overwrought this time to worry about
what Albert thought of their cramped home with its
inadequate sanitation and even less adequate access to
daylight. She knew that she faced a difficult interview
with her mother, and because it was her mother, there
was no predicting how it would go; she might think

Albert was a dangerous Welshman, or she might find him a new suit of clothes up in the eaves, there was just no telling. Mary was so very weary and she knew that she had to explain to her mother where she was going and why and she couldn't leave without doing that, but a little part of her wanted to steal away like a guilty thing and leave the explanations to someone else.

Mary unlocked the door and she immediately knew that something was wrong. She didn't know how she knew it, but something in the house was in the wrong place. She didn't bother to take off her shoes or her jacket, but just belted up the stairs to the bedroom to find that her sister was not there. Bess's clothes were missing from their wardrobe and a note rested on her pillow – but it wasn't in Bess's hand, it was in Diana's.

Come to my house as quickly as you can. Bess is stopping here. Bring some clothes for yourself.

This was all Mary needed. It was typical of her sister that she would get herself into some trouble or other just as she was trying to leave the country for the first time in her life. And if Diana was involved, then it must be something to do with work; Bess had probably flooded another workroom the way she'd managed to flood the factory crèche when she was running it. Though why this would require her to stay with Diana, goodness only knew. Mary decided that her mother would have to deal with it this time; Mary had been looking after her wayward sister for as long as she could remember and it was time for her mother to shoulder some of that burden so that she could be free to start a life with Albert and his children who were about to become her own.

Mary hurriedly packed a bundle of clothes together with Albert's help and closed the door on her old house. It sent a shiver down her spine. There was something wrong and Mary had that horrible feeling again, the feeling that someone had walked over her grave. Mary had felt it so many times in the last few months, a familiar feeling, like a distant memory, and she had been trying to put her finger on it, but it kept evading her. She thought it smelled like coal tar. She turned her key in the lock of the front door and was just turning her back on the house when she realised all of a sudden what it was; it was a premonition of death. Mary had felt it before when she lost her father and brothers to tuberculosis, and she knew that she felt it now for a reason. She thought it was Albert, that this was a premonition that they couldn't be together, that he would go back to Germany and be killed and that they needed to make the most of their time together.

'Albert,' Mary said as they walked toward the tram stop, 'I'm worried that I've had a premonition that something bad is going to happen to you; something very bad.'

'You worry too much,' he said, and kissed the top of her head. 'What could happen to me? I'm healthy as a horse.'

When Mary and Albert arrived at Diana's boarding house they found the place subdued and unusually quiet. The lights were on and the kitchen below stairs offered its usual welcoming glow of warmth, but there was no laughter; no animated discussion about work or news or courting. Reenie and Peter looked up from the kitchen table when Mary and Albert came in and Mary might have thought they'd had another of their rows if Diana and Bess hadn't been so solemn too.

Mary put down her bundle of clothes on the kitchen table and gave her friends an irritated look. It irked her that they could be making such a meal of whatever passing trouble they were having, when she was going through something far, far worse.

'Well,' she said, 'we can't get married in England and we can't get married in Germany, so the solicitor has told us we have to go to France. I'd pack my bags if I owned any, but I don't, so I've got everything in a bundle and I've got to hope I find something better along the way. I can't find Mother to say goodbye—'

'Come and sit down, Mary,' Reenie said gently, 'there's been a bit of bad news.'

'*You've* had a bit of bad news?' Mary was on the verge of hysteria now. 'Did you not hear what I just said? I've got to go to a foreign country, where I don't speak the language, for a hasty marriage and I can't find a suitcase or me mother!'

Albert tried to soothe Mary, but she would not sit down, and she would not be soothed.

'It's your mother . . .' Reenie said very gently.

'Yes, well,' Mary huffed, 'she won't like it, but I'm of age in a matter of days.'

Diana saw that Reenie's gentle approach was not working and she decided to be blunt. 'No, Mary. She's dead. It was very sudden. Now look to your sister.'

Mary could not take it in. Her mother couldn't be dead – she'd seen her sleeping in her chair only the previous night. Then Mary looked at her sister Bess and saw the red eyes and tear-stained face and knew that it was true.

'B-but how? W-when?' She slumped in a chair at the table, trying to find an answer in the knotted grain of its surface.

Reenie came and sat beside her. 'It was toxaemia, the doctor said. She got the scarlatinal infection and she soldiered on and went to work, but then it turned to toxaemia and it took her right sudden. One minute she was walking around at work, the next she'd dropped and she was gone. He said she wouldn't have suffered.'

Mary shook her head as though she were trying to shake off motes of dust in the air around her. 'But I'm going to France to be married. I need to find her to tell her that I'm going to France to be married. This is all wrong, it doesn't make any sense. I saw her and she was quite all right.'

'Maria, my love . . .' Albert was close beside her now, his hand closing over hers. 'We cannot go to France together. You must remain here to bury your mother. I must return alone.' Mary looked to Albert in desperation and he took her face in his hands. 'You must stay here and look after your sister and I must go and look after mine, but soon – very soon – we will be together again.'

A firm knock at the front door directly above them brought them all to themselves and Diana looked up through the basement window to see if it was important. 'I don't know who he's here for,' she said, 'but that's definitely a policeman.'

Albert rose from his chair and straightened his tie. 'I think he might be here for me.'

'Hang about!' Diana wasn't ready to jump to conclusions just yet. 'What if he's here to tell us all to quarantine, or something like that? He could be here for any number of reasons.'

'If they wanted a policeman to enforce quarantine, wouldn't they have sent a constable rather than a sergeant?' Reenie had a point and Diana conceded it.

'I'm afraid,' Albert said reluctantly, 'that I was expecting something of this sort. I was granted an extension to my permit, but the last one was revoked early and I have had my reasons for expecting this one to be revoked also. It is very likely this man is here for me.'

'Well, Mr Baum,' Diana said, 'you've got a choice to make, and you've not got much time to make it. You can go with him now, or you can hide somewhere and postpone the evil hour. They can't arrest you if they can't find you.'

Albert shrugged his shoulders. 'But where would I hide?'

'Where would *we* hide?' Mary corrected him.

'Here.' Reenie pulled a note pad and pencil from her pocket and scribbled down a message for her mother. 'My family live on a farm out past Stump Cross, Peter can take you. Go there and wait.'

Reenie tried to reassure them. 'We'll take care of Bess and you can still get to France. We'll not let them take you, Mr Baum.'

Chapter Fifty-Three

When Sergeant Metcalf arrived at the old boarding house he could not have anticipated the train of events that his very presence would put in motion. He had asked for Reenie Calder initially, because he would have no evidence with which to make any arrest until he had first spoken to her. This political business was not a matter with which the Halifax Police Constabulary had ever felt any sympathy and none of it seemed like a criminal offence to Sergeant Metcalf or his Inspector, but their orders were their orders, and they were duty bound to investigate. He had tried her family home out at the farm and they had directed him here. He knew Reenie Calder and he trusted that she was an honest girl and he wouldn't need to give chase, so he decided to make this a leisurely interview.

The sitting room of her old boarding house was cosy with warmth from a glowing coal fire in the grate, but Reenie's palms were cold and clammy with fear. She knew this policeman, and she knew that he was a fair man, but she also knew that Mary needed time to get well away and to get well hidden and she was going to have to keep him talking a while.

'Reenie,' it was a greeting which held rather more significance than it might have done from anyone else; Sergeant Metcalf had interviewed Reenie only a year or so ago when she had fooled him into thinking that she was someone else entirely. It had been an unfortunate start to their acquaintanceship and had almost led to her friends being arrested for a crime they had not committed. Reenie wouldn't make that mistake again. She would say as little as she could get away with. She moved a little closer to the fire and said, 'Sergeant Metcalf.'

'Where's Peter Mackenzie, Reenie?'

Reenie's eyes widened and her heart raced; how could he have known that she'd sent Peter to help Albert Baum and Mary escape to her parents' house? Unless he'd been having them watched or overheard everything they had said as she wrote out the note for her mother. It seemed impossible, but it was the only explanation which occurred to Reenie in that decisive moment. Reenie decided to play for more time and hope that this officer didn't have more constables waiting round the corner to swoop on Albert Baum before he could be led to safety.

'Why do you want to know where he is?'

'We've had a communication from another constabulary suggesting that he's about to do something which we both know would be breaking the law. They think he may have *already* broken the law, so tell me where he is, Reenie and this doesn't need to go any further, we can stop it now. You don't want your young man putting himself in danger for foreigners.'

This riled Reenie; she had thought Sergeant Metcalf was better than this, she had thought he'd hold human justice higher than bureaucracy. 'I suppose you've got to do what you think is right and he's got to do what he thinks is right, but it's nothing to do with me.'

'I heard there was a note.' Sergeant Metcalf waited, gauging Reenie's reaction. 'I want to know about the note, Reenie; tell me everything you know about the note.'

Reenie was holding herself perfectly still, terrified of giving something away; terrified that she might glance or turn in the direction of where Mary had gone and give him a clue as to where they were running with Albert Baum at the very moment that he needed time. Surely if he had seen the note she'd written to her mother about looking after Albert and Mary he didn't need to ask all this? He knew where to find Albert Baum, so why was he wasting time with Reenie?

'I don't know what you mean,' she said, with trembling voice.

'Helping someone else to cross the channel for illegal purposes is just as much a criminal offence as crossing the channel for illegal purposes yourself, you know that, don't you, Reenie?'

There was something in his look that seemed like a message or a warning, but as long as they were talking at cross purposes Reenie was never going to understand what he was telling her, because this was not the interview she thought it was.

'I don't know anything about anyone trying to cross the Channel illegally. Mr Baum has been applying for his family to come here on all the correct permits. He's done nothing wrong and his family have done nothing wrong. If he goes to France with Mary to get married it will all be above board because she will be of age.' Reenie had learnt from her last conversation with Sergeant Metcalf that she should stick as close to the truth as she could, as often as she could, and give nothing away which wasn't already public knowledge.

'I'm not interested in your Mr Baum today, Reenie. I want to know if you saw Peter Mackenzie with a note from his cousins saying that they intended to travel to Spain to fight with the International Brigade against the Spanish government over there, and if they invited Peter Mackenzie to go with them.'

Reenie sank backwards into a chair and sucked in a breath; this was not something she would ever in her wildest dreams have thought they needed to fear. They were afraid for Albert and his children; they were afraid for the health of Major Fergusson if the scarlet fever reached the cottage hospital; they were afraid that war was coming and they would soon be cowering below ground beneath aerial bombardments of poison gas; but Reenie had never thought they needed to worry about Peter's fleeting plans to leave for Spain. His caring nature and simple sense of duty had made him consider making the journey, but Reenie had quickly talked him out of it with the help of Diana Moore. Surely the policeman would see that he wasn't a risk any more.

'He did get a note from his cousins, and he did think of going with them himself, but I talked him out of it. He would never dream of going now. He gave away all his travel things to his cousin. He's got no pack or flask or anything. He couldn't go and I wouldn't help him to go. No one has done *anything* to help him.'

'But he gave his pack and equipment to his cousin to take with him?'

'Yes, he doesn't have it any more because he's not planning to leave.' Reenie couldn't understand why the policeman looked so disappointed with her. She hadn't been around enough policemen to recognise the look they gave you when they wanted to avoid some unnecessary paperwork; when they wanted you to tell them a white lie that was convenient to both of you so that they could go away and say that they had checked up on everything they had been asked to check up on, and you could go free and forget it had ever happened.

'So Peter Mackenzie materially aided at least one of his cousins to travel to Spain to fight the National forces, in direct breach of English law?' Sergeant Metcalf took out his pocket notebook with exasperated reluctance. 'Where is he now, Reenie?'

Reenie swallowed a sob as it dawned on her that everything had become worse again because of her. 'He's in the factory somewhere.' She tried to keep some semblance of composure. 'I don't know where. You'll have to find him.'

Reenie knew exactly where Peter was – he'd be at her mother's house, or on his way there, but she could not bear to be honest with Sergeant Metcalf because she was terrified of making everything even worse. She never wanted to speak again. And just as she was telling herself that life could not become any more horrible, a telegram arrived for Diana. Her little sister Gracie had scarlet fever and the Hunters wanted Diana to come at once.

Chapter Fifty-Four

Diana's feelings of guilt came in waves. She could never regret having Gracie, but she could regret not trying harder to keep her. If she had married a violent man she could have kept her daughter, or if she had married a widower with a lot of young children of his own who needed a woman in the house to cook and clean and skivvy. If she had moved to another town and pretended to be a widow herself, she could have kept her daughter. If she had begged, if she had borrowed, if she had stolen – but no matter how many 'ifs' she thought of, she could never have provided Gracie with a life like the one she had now. A life of safety and security. But how safe was it? Only six months before she'd found that Gracie and Lara had been playing with rat poison they'd picked up by mistake and now the pair of them had been exposed to poisoned milk. Was this home really so safe for her daughter? Should she try to take her back? Should she confess who she really was?

Dr Martin re-emerged from the sickroom. 'She's delirious, I'm afraid.'

Diana choked back tears, while Mr and Mrs Hunter asked a tumble of worried questions.

'But doctor, she was speaking to us only a few moments before you were summoned. She can't have been taken badly so rapidly.'

'She's descended into gibberish, I'm afraid. Just unintelligible sounds. Ordinarily we would move her to the isolation hospital immediately, but their wards are full. You will need to telephone a nursing agency and hire a trained nurse to take over here until the fever breaks. I will give your housekeeper the telephone number and I will be here again myself to administer Pentonil.'

Mr Hunter asked, 'Can we go and sit with her now?'

'I think not. The disease is contagious. I would allow her mother to sit with her on the condition she does not see any of her other children for the next fortnight because we must contain the spread of contagion. You must choose one of your own servants to nurse the child in the sickroom, but allow no one else.'

This meant that Diana would not be allowed to see her daughter again. She had known when she allowed the courts to give her for adoption that this was a very real risk, and she had accepted it then, but the life she had made for herself as a satellite of the Hunter family had allowed her to raise her hopes that she need never be separated from her Gracie again. Now she faced the dilemma she had always feared: should she reveal her identity in order to sit by her daughter's bedside? If this was her last chance, if her daughter was certain to die, then she had nothing to lose and everything to gain. But if she lived she'd be ruining her life all over again – the repercussions of her revelation would change everything. Diana had a decision to make and she felt as though it would kill her.

Glancing briefly at the Hunters, Diana cleared her throat and asked the doctor, 'Sir, do you think she will live? Is there a chance?'

'She has an even chance.'

At this Mrs Hunter burst into hysterical sobs and turned to bury her face in her husband's shoulder. He, in turn, stared blankly ahead of him, shocked beyond belief that the little girl they had let into their lives only a year and a half ago and had grown to love deeply, was perhaps about to leave them in the most dreadful way.

'I suggest you keep the house as quiet as possible.' The doctor, Diana noticed, did not give orders to his wealthy patients, only polite but firm 'suggestions'. 'The child will cry out, but it is merely the ravings of the fever and should not be agitated further with chatter.'

'If I promise to be very quiet,' Diana pleaded breathlessly, 'may I see Gracie one last time?'

The doctor looked down his nose at Diana, his irritation ill-concealed. 'Her mother only. And one servant.'

Diana took a deep breath; this was not the first time she had had to confess to being Gracie's mother, but she knew that if she admitted it now, it would be the last. The repercussions of her admission would be felt beyond the sickroom and everyone would know the secret she had kept for so long. But she needed to be by her daughter's side, felt their separation like an agony that threatened to stop her own heart from beating. 'I understand, doctor, but—' Diana prepared herself to challenge this cold old man, but Mrs Hunter interrupted her, mounting an appeal on her behalf.

'You must allow Diana to sit with her too, doctor. You don't understand what she means to Gracie . . .' The good woman choked her own sobs and was at a loss to continue.

The doctor took a dim view of these proceedings and cast a disapproving eye over Diana. He had already judged from her style of dress and manner of speech that she was not of the same class as his paying clients. 'I would like you to see me out,' he addressed Diana with a little more firmness than he might have used with his wealthy patients.

Diana followed the tight-lipped medical man to the front door, down the path through the rose garden, and beyond the gate. There the doctor turned on her abruptly, his lips curled almost into a snarl. 'I have not been told what your connection is to the child, madam, but I suspect I know.'

Diana said quietly, 'She is my natural daughter and she was adopted by the Hunters a year ago. If you're allowing her mother to sit with her, you're allowing me.'

'I am *not* allowing you; I am not allowing you to see her, I am not allowing you to acknowledge her, and I am not allowing you to make the scene which you were so obviously about to make. That child has a very slim chance of survival and the slightest disturbance could be a death sentence. I am not here to decide, like Solomon, which mother has the greater love for the infant; I am here to save her life. If you want your child to have the best chance of breaking the fever you will stay away. However, if your only care is for yourself and your own satisfaction, then I suspect nothing I say will have any influence and you will do your utmost to agitate young Miss Gracie *Hunter*.'

Diana trembled with emotion and tears rolled silently down her cheeks, but she mastered herself enough to ask, 'When will you know if she is likely to live?'

'If the fever breaks. If her raving stops. When she is able to ask for people she knows.'

Diana ground her teeth. There was nothing she could do. Gracie had been legally adopted through the courts and she had no rights to assert. The right of a mother had been legally transferred to Mrs Hunter and she herself had allowed it.

'I would never do anything which I thought might harm my daughter.' But Diana knew that if the doctor had not marched her outside when he did she would have lost all control of herself, flung open the doors to Gracie's room and gathered her up in her arms. Now she knew that she *had* to stay away. Not only was this Gracie's only chance, but this was her only chance to see Gracie again if she lived. This whole precarious situation relied on the Hunter family believing that she was a half-sister, with a half-sister's love, unthreatening and never troublesome.

A cry rang out from inside the house and Diana and the doctor whirled round to see what was the matter. The front door was flung open with a bang and there was Edward Hunter, eyes wide with excitement. 'Didi!' he shouted down through the quiet rose garden. 'Didi! She's calling for Didi! She wants Diana! She's not delirious! She was calling for Diana!'

Chapter Fifty-Five

'I think Peter's going to be sent to prison.' Reenie crumpled down into a seat at the family dining table which had become the centre of so much family drama and delight over the years.

'Whatever for?' Mrs Calder acted as though this were not only ridiculous, but also highly offensive. Any charge against Peter Mackenzie must be false, there was no doubt in her mind of that. Reenie might get herself into trouble by accident, but Peter was safe as houses.

'He tried to go to Spain. Well, he was going to go to Spain, but then he just helped his cousins by sending them the things he'd bought to take with him. They were going anyway and he didn't think he'd be doing any harm!'

'What would he want to go to Spain for?' Mr Calder was completely nonplussed. 'They're at war over there, it's no time to be visiting Spain.'

'He was off to fight the fascists. He was going to join

the war.' Kathleen said it with a certainty and a resignation that suggested she'd seen this all before, despite the fact that she was thirteen and had never travelled further than Wakefield. 'Well, if he gave them anything to help them on their way he's definitely for it.'

'I don't understand!' Mrs Calder was as shocked and distressed as if Peter were her own blood relation. 'I thought the fascists were the ones in the wrong. I thought the lads going off to fight them were the heroes.'

'You don't read the papers, Mother,' Kathleen had taken the opportunity to peruse publications of every political hue when she was minding the shop on Saturdays. 'There'll *probably* be war, and it will *probably* be against the fascists of one or other of the continental countries run by them; it could be Spain, it could be Germany, and I wouldn't rule out Italy or Rumania – but it isn't war yet. Just now the law says anyone who goes over to fight them has gone rogue and gets hard labour in an English prison if they're caught trying to go, so Peter's for it.' Kathleen did not change her matter-of-fact tone when she saw how her family were taking this news. She turned to her elder sister. 'Reenie, how bad is it? What proof have they got he helped anyone go to Spain?'

'That's the worst part of it, they only know what he was planning because I told them myself! I thought they were fussing about us planning to get Mr Baum's family over from Germany and I was just keen to explain they'd got the wrong end of the stick, so I told them Peter had been planning to go and join up, but then he changed his mind, and I tried to prove he'd changed his mind by telling them he'd given away his travel things and then the next thing I know that was what swung it

– they'd got him on a charge of aiding and abetting on my say so!'

'Who's they?' The cogs in Kathleen's mind were turning. 'You haven't been and said this in a magistrates' court already?'

'No, I said it to Sergeant Metcalf, and now—'

Kathleen shook her head. 'Doesn't count.'

Mrs Calder huffed in irritation. 'I'm quite sure it does count. Now, if you don't mind, Kathleen—'

Mr Calder interrupted eagerly, 'Hang about, have you got a clever way out, our Kathleen?' Mr Calder knew that each of his children had their own peculiar talents and he was not averse to making the most of them.

'It only counts if she gives evidence in court and she can avoid that one of two ways: she can either run away to Timbuktu so's they can't find her to tell her to say all she knows in the magistrates' court – or she can marry Peter.'

'How's that?' Mrs Calder was ready to hear a solution to their problems which chimed in with her own dearest wish. 'How would a wedding help keep Peter out of trouble?'

'Well, it wouldn't because he'd be married to our Reenie and that would be trouble for life, but it would mean they couldn't ask Reenie to repeat all she said in court and then they've got no evidence he's done owt wrong. If Reenie's the only evidence they've got and she gets married to our Peter, then it's all square.'

Mr Calder nodded in enthusiasm as he began to catch on to Kathleen's idea. 'A wife cannot be compelled to give evidence against her husband – oldest trick in the book.'

Reenie blanched. 'Are you certain of this? Would marrying Peter really save him from being arrested?'

Kathleen shrugged. 'It wouldn't give him immunity from all crimes for life – for instance, if he steals a policeman's helmet in a year's time they'll still pinch him for it, but in this instance it's your best solution. Under English law a wife cannot be made to give evidence against her husband and they can only prosecute Peter if they get you to give evidence in court *before* you've married him. If you marry him before he gets put up in court then they'll have to drop the case.'

Mrs Calder managed to look pained, hopeful, and dispirited all at the same time; the weight of worry a mother carried was as constant as it was complex. 'But there'd be no time. Weddings don't happen as fast as that – you need four weeks at least to have the banns read and if they're going to have Peter up at the magistrates' court it will be a day or two at the most.'

'You want a special licence.' Kathleen heaped a good dollop of steaming mashed potato onto her plate nonchalantly. 'That girl who's been banging on about getting married in the sweetshop said she's getting one.'

'But that's just because she's getting married some place irregular,' Mr Calder said.

'You can have a special licence for either; sometimes it's for people getting married in a hurry, sometimes it's for people getting married on the quiet, and sometimes it's for people getting married in a chapel, not a church. I read up on it when that Dunkley lass started throwing her weight around about *my* shop. I didn't fancy letting her have her own way without a fight.'

'Yes, but she can have a special licence because she's

a vicar's daughter and she's got fancy connections; it would be different for our Reenie, surely?' Mrs Calder felt a clawing terror at the thought of hastening her own child's journey into adult life, despite simultaneously wanting her to have the security of a marriage to a nice lad like Peter.

'You had us all christened at Stump Cross, didn't you?'

'Well, yes, of course I did.'

'Then that's all you need. Reenie needs to see the vicar, then go and see the bishop, then fill out a form. It's two forms if Peter wasn't christened.'

Kathleen shovelled a forkful of chicken-and-ham pie into her mouth happily as the rest of her family sat staring in silent shock; could it be that the very decision Reenie had been struggling to make was now the solution to all her problems? Or was it merely the beginning of more? There was so much to think about and so little time to do it with care.

Chapter Fifty-Six

Ruffian was restless. His mistress had left him that morning in his stable at the factory with a little hot mash and a pat of reassurance. After that Reenie had gone down to the parish church on a borrowed bicycle in the pale dawn light. The parish church was no place for a horse not known for his continence and although Reenie was sorry not to have had his warmth on her journey and his moral support on her big day, she knew leaving him in the safety of the stables was for the best.

It promised to be an unseasonably hot day and a thick mist was rolling off the river and up through the valley. It was dark in the stable and Ruffian, like a dog careful of his master, was fretting to see the face he knew best. The stable door was closed and latched, but – as was Ruffian's habit when he chose to roam – he nudged it on the other side and it swung open, the screws in the hinges sliding out of their crumbling sockets in the sandstone doorframe, the stable door itself pivoting with a creak

274

on the long-suffering latch as it did every time Ruffian left his stable on his own. And as it rattled open it revealed a now dangerously thick fog; Ruffian was not deterred by it.

Horses often know their way home, but this horse always knew his way to his mistress. Ruffian kicked a hoof, pulled back his head, and yanked his makeshift bridle free of the bonds which had held it to the post just inside the door. He turned right at the entrance to the stable yard, and made his way ploddingly through the unseasonable darkness.

Reenie and her mother had made the nerve-racking visit to the bishop's office and obtained the necessary licences to allow Reenie and Peter to be married – with her parents' permission – in the parish church at Stump Cross. There had been a rush the day before to find a curate who could perform the ceremony in the empty church in the middle of the week, and then efforts to move Peter all over town so that he wouldn't be found at his boarding house. Peter must have sent a telegram to his parents to tell them that he was being married at short notice because a parcel arrived from them by special delivery addressed to Reenie.

'It's very beautiful.' Reenie did not sound convincing as she laid out the expensive satin dress with matching fur cape which had arrived wrapped in tissue paper inside a gilt-edged box.

'Oh, aren't they kind,' Mrs Calder said, her voice strained.

Kathleen was the only Calder who was ready to speak her mind that day. 'It's all right, but you'll not get any more use out of it after this, and as there's to be no one much at the wedding and no photographer, you might as well wear your overalls as something fancy.'

'*Kathleen!*' Mrs Calder did not want to admit the truth of this. 'A wedding doesn't need a lot of people to make it special and this will still be a very special day.'

It would have been clear to any passersby who saw Ruffian plodding up the Bailey Hall Road toward the parish church that he was a horse on a mission; however, the cloak of fog which concealed him prevented any passerby from noticing him; stopping him; rescuing him from the danger of the road he trod without lamps or human guidance.

An omnibus, its lamps lit and its conductor blowing a whistle to alert passing traffic to its passage, clattered past Ruffian so closely that the McVitie's advertising boards on its side scratched along Ruffian's flank. Ruffian plodded on. This was his town and he would find his mistress.

'I'll have to leave Ruffian behind, won't I?' Reenie had accepted that there would be a lot of changes to her life when she was married; she'd be forced to leave her beloved job at the factory, to leave her family, to leave her friends – it would all be worth it to save Peter from prison, she told herself. But leaving her oldest friend, leaving faithful Ruffian, that would be the hardest of all. They had seen one another through thick and thin and Reenie was only too aware that time was not on their side; Ruffian was a very old horse and these were his last days. By marrying Peter and going away with him to an army barracks, she was consenting to miss Ruffian's final days. It was likely that their last goodbye would be sooner rather than later.

'You'll be able to come back and see him; he'll always be here,' her father had said, knowing only too well that Reenie's visits would be few and far between as an army wife. 'Why don't you take him down to the factory and give him one last day at the stables? He likes it there, it'll be a treat for him on your wedding day.'

Reenie liked the thought that if her old friend Ruffian couldn't be at the ceremony he could at least be nearby. It would be a solace on a day that she was more anxious about than she could tell anyone.

Ruffian had narrowly avoided three potentially fatal road accidents since he had slipped his bonds in the old stables and trudged out in search of Reenie and it could only be a matter of time before a lone horse – invisible in the fog – met with tragedy. Ruffian was plodding doggedly in the direction of the busy junction at the bottom of Horton Hill. This was the junction which met the metropolis of train tracks, the junction which teetered over the brink of a precipice of the canal basin, the junction where Bess had nearly lost her life in the car accident which had destroyed their beloved factory. This was the worst place in Halifax for a lone horse in these conditions. Motor cars with headlamps straining to break through the fog hammered on their horns to alert other road users to their presence as they sped dangerously round corners while horses pulling wagons whinnied and shied at the noise and had to be restrained by their masters who walked beside them, cursing whatever duty required them to make their journey that day, and a chaos of pedestrians wriggled up and down the pavements, arms out in front of them, feeling for obstacles and men.

In the midst of all this stood Ruffian who had reached the edge of the junction and whose only way forward led beyond it. Braving the noise and confusion which younger horses refused to be led through, he lifted his ancient hoof and then stopped dead. Something was holding the ugly old nag where he stood and his ears pricked up. If Reenie had been there she'd have recognised that look in his eye and she'd have known that he wouldn't be able to resist it. Somewhere, the slightest of breezes was carrying twin temptations to Ruffian: the aroma of apples and sweet, sweet hay.

Ruffian turned back the way he had come and plodded south; he could smell the gifts his mistress usually brought him and he would follow their scent to her.

Chapter Fifty-Seven

'You are doing this because you love me, aren't you, Reenie?' Peter had become increasingly worried about his intended, and as they snatched a moment alone together, out of earshot of her parents, Peter took the opportunity to see how the land lay. 'Because I know you and you don't seem happy. I don't want us to be married if it will make you unhappy. I only want—'

'It's not you making me unhappy; I promise!' Reenie couldn't tell him her real fears. She wasn't marrying him because she was *in love* with him, she was marrying him because she loved him enough not to want him to go to prison. The guilt of what she'd done weighed on her; she had told the police sergeant that he'd helped his cousins go to fight in the civil war in Spain and if it weren't for her he'd be free. This was her doing and only she could remedy it. There were worse reasons to marry and she told herself that if she was miserable then she deserved it. There was no one to blame but herself. 'I'm just sad it's all such a hurry. And we'll have to leave the factory and our friends. That's all.'

'You know I only want you to be happy, Reenie, don't you?' And Peter meant it, because he loved her.

'I know. And I promise I'll be happy when I know that you're safe.'

Ruffian had crushed several flowerbeds on his journey out of the town, but nuisance though he was, he was less of a nuisance than he would have been on the public highway. Ruffian had trudged through the garden of the lady mayoress (where he had drunk the contents of her birdbath); churned up the gravel drive of a prosperous carpet manufacturer (where he had knocked over a half dozen milk bottles and a pat of butter which waited on the step); and crushed a Wendy house belonging to some children who were mercifully absent. Ruffian's luck was wearing thin and, after escaping the dangers of the town, he now came up against the worse danger of the country: a shotgun. Ruffian was not easy to see in the fog, but his destruction of the gardens could be heard and ill-tempered Squire Curran had convinced himself that he was being besieged by poachers, burglars, or worse. Old man Curran had seized his shotgun and run onto the terrace which looked out over the garden where Ruffian now walked in innocence.

The fog had cleared a little and, as Ruffian trudged toward the scent of apples, he began to emerge in Squire Curran's field of vision. 'Marjorie!' Curran shouted through the open French windows behind him. 'Turn those lights off! I want to see the blighters! I want to see the whites of their eyes!'

Old Squire Curran raised his shotgun to his shoulder and squinted down the sight at the horse which he was convinced was an advance guard of vagabonds coming to turn his orderly home into a circus of sin. His finger slid over the steel trigger of his favourite Purdey game gun and he paused a moment to wait for the horse to come just a little closer. That pause proved to be fatal for the squirrel who was scurrying through the budding oak behind the horse. At the moment of Squire Curran's pause, three things happened: a breath of wind brought a fresh blanket of fog between Ruffian and his would-be assassin; a fresh waft of apples drew Ruffian quite suddenly in a different and unexpected direction; and Mrs Marjorie Curran took her irascible husband to task and threatened to confiscate the decanter again if he didn't give her that gun and stop interrupting the broadcast of the Ovaltineys on the wireless. His shot had missed the old horse the first time, but Ruffian panicked and Squire Curran ignored his wife and did not go into the house.

Reenie's plan to marry Peter to save him from prison could only work if they were married before he was arrested, and that was not by any means a certainty. Unbeknownst to Reenie, as she was standing outside the church, Sergeant Metcalf was getting on his bicycle and going out in search of the young couple. News had reached him of the hastened nuptials and he was determined to reach them before they could sign the register.

Ruffian was moving a little quicker now; the aroma of apples and hay was stronger, and the angry man with the noisy weapon was still in pursuit, shouting a catalogue of threats through the fog at the scoundrels who he supposed were leading the horse away.

In Ruffian's limited experience, Reenie Calder was the source of all the apples in the world and these would surely lead him to her and must be close now. Despite his age, despite the dark, despite the fog, despite the man with the gun and all the odds, Ruffian began to gallop. It was not a steep hill at first, but all the hills in Halifax start like that for a pace or two; Ruffian knew the incline well and would usually pace himself for a heavy climb, but not this time; he left no energy untapped and, hell for leather, he bounded up and away.

Ruffian might not have known it, but he had almost reached an ancient seat of sanctuary; he was galloping toward the garden of the immense rectory of Stump Cross and, hanging from their solid oak front door, were the apples he sought, part of a magnificent Easter wreath.

Ruffian arrived at the rectory gate breathing hard, but not spent. He was going to take the apples his mistress had left for him and then he was going to fetch his mistress and take her home. This premature night – as the early morning fog must have seemed to him – was full of dangers and he wanted to know that she was well out of it. He stepped backward a good few paces from the garden wall and then took it at a gallop, jumping in time to clear the garden wall and to land on the rectory lawn. It was not a showjumping manoeuvre he would ever allow his mistress to know that he was still agile enough to perform, but he could not see her which meant that she could not see him. Ruffian trotted quickly to the door of the rectory and seized an apple between his few remaining teeth and tugged. The Easter garland to which it was attached pulled free of the door-knocker and flicked back around Ruffian's neck like a wreath. Ruffian was left with one loose apple in his mouth and several around his neck for later which suited him well and he lifted his head to sniff the air for the hay he knew was also there somewhere and then galloped in the direction of the Stump Cross churchyard, leaping over walls and fences as the knowledge that his mistress was waiting spurred him on.

Chapter Fifty-Eight

The curate – who had been a little nervous of the unusual licence and the cloak-and-dagger nature of the ceremony – was turning to the page of the marriage service in the Book of Common Prayer. His life at the parish was not as exciting as his brother's missionary life in China and he longed for adventures to write home to his mother about and this was the stuff great epistles were made of. The Calder family had been lucky to get the assistance of this young man because another vicar might have felt irritated at the rushing about, the common licences, and then the chopping and changing of minds; not so the young Reverend Roberts. This whole drama was writing itself in his mind – and although he was itching to get to pen and writing paper, he was also desperate for the scene not to end.

The churchyard of St Agatha of Stump Cross was not a modest example of its genus. Some churchyards hide themselves away behind dense evergreens; others offer an embarrassment of marble memorials; still others cram crooked headstones into tight chaos with seemingly no room for grass to grow between them.

St Agatha's boasted a rolling lawn and a lofty prospect. The rich wool merchant who had sponsored the construction of the neo-gothic monstrosity had wanted to be certain that he would be seen by the good Lord when he went into church and so it was built on a mound, with not a single headstone to block the view from the roadside of the massive front door.

On this murky and misty morning, one lone beacon stood out on the prow of the churchyard lawn which jutted over the public highway: the life-sized and fully illuminated statue of St Agatha. It was towards this landmark – bright with paraffin storm lanterns – that Ruffian the ugly old nag was cantering, the spring garland swinging loosely from his neck, and – some way off in the distance down the way – an angry squire was in pursuit.

Ruffian could not clamber up the sandstone wall which held up the embankment of the churchyard and he trotted up and down the wall for a moment or two before finding the gate. It was open and it was a matter of paces before Ruffian had found what he sought: a quantity of good hay resting in a packing crate, cleverly weighted down for him with a collection of weighty summer-flowering bulbs so that it would not be blown away; this was the type of practical thoughtfulness which marked out his mistress. Ruffian bowed his head to the packing crate and tugged at the hay a little too roughly, causing the bulbs to scatter to the ground in all directions.

The absent gardener who had left the bulbs unattended would certainly wonder what had been about.

The act did not go unwitnessed, however; from a few hundred yards down the hill Squire Curran caught sight of the beast under the swinging light held out by St Agatha and took aim at Ruffian again. This time he took off the ears of St Agatha, but still didn't hit the criminally destructive horse.

Ruffian was startled by the shot, but it only served to drive him in the direction of those other lights further into the churchyard; the lights inside the church itself. The lights which must surely lead him to his mistress.

At the sound of a horse's hooves hitting the church door, Reenie's heart leapt. She would know that broken-down old knacker anywhere, and unless she was very much mistaken her Ruffian had broken his bonds in the factory stable and was even now waiting for her outside the church. She squeaked an 'Excuse me!' to the curate and to Peter and then ran to the church doors before Ruffian could kick off some important oak carving.

Peter followed her to the church doors. 'What are you doing, Reenie?'

'I'm letting the horse in before he kicks the place down.'

'You can't bring a horse into a church, that's blasphemy!' Peter looked back over his shoulder to where the curate was waiting with Reenie's family and hoped he couldn't hear them. 'Why is your horse at the church door? I thought we agreed he'd have a nice day down at the factory stables having a big feed? A church during a hasty wedding really isn't the most convenient place for an incontinent horse.'

Reenie had wrestled with the huge iron door latch and was pushing the door open with her shoulder, careless of the expensive dress and smart fur cape she was wearing. 'I *did* leave him there, but he must have got away. It won't take me five minutes to tie him up outside.' Reenie stepped out into the mist to see Ruffian waiting for her, loyal as ever. She could have hugged him, but she knew that this was not the time. 'Give me a minute and I'll—'

Reenie was interrupted this time not by a horse, but by a squire with a shotgun.

'Who are you? What are you doing with that horse?' The somewhat out-of-breath old buffer made his questions sound like an accusation, which in a way they were.

Reenie was at a loss to answer. This day was not going according to plan, and although it had been her own plan she found that she welcomed the interruption of a horse and a shotgun so long as the horse kept its water and the shotgun wasn't aimed at anyone. 'It's my horse.' Reenie called out. 'I'm just saying hello to it then I'm tying it up. What are *you* doing?'

'I'm going to take you and the horse into police custody. You'll not get away this time. I've cornered you!'

Peter and Reenie exchanged looks of equal confusion before Peter asked, 'Did you put this lot of apples round his neck?'

'No I did not!' the old squire barked back at them. 'He stole them, and I'm a witness to it.'

Following closely behind Squire Curran was Sergeant Metcalf on his police bicycle and the sight of his uniform brought Reenie back to reality with a bump. 'Go back inside, Peter,' she gasped. 'Go and hide in the vestry.'

'Oh no you don't!' Squire Curran was determined now

to round up whichever wrongdoers had allowed a horse to run roughshod over the gardens of his neighbours. 'You're staying right where you are.'

Sergeant Metcalf coasted in on his bicycle and dismounted alongside the squire. 'Are you the individual who just shot an ear off St Agatha?'

'Yes, I am. I was aiming for this horse, it has just—'

'Good, you're under arrest. Stay where you are and I'll tell you your rights in a moment.' He then turned to Reenie with the look of exasperation he always wore when he spoke to Reenie Calder. 'What's this I hear about a wedding in a hurry, Reenie?'

Reenie pulled herself up to her full height and prepared to do all in her power to save Peter, even if it meant a wedding she didn't want. 'You can't prevent it. We've got a special licence and we're already in the church and that's sanctuary.'

'You're not in the church,' Sergeant Metcalf pointed out matter-of-factly, 'you're outside the church holding onto a horse covered in apples while you argue with a man who has just shot the ear off St Agatha – but that's by the by. I came all the way here, on my bicycle, up some very steep hills and very shortly after my breakfast, I might add, because I heard down at the station that there was to be a hurried wedding, and I wanted to make certain that it didn't have anything to do with that little chat you and I had the other day about Spain.'

Reenie didn't hesitate to stand her ground. 'What if it was? What's it to you?'

'You wouldn't be trying to avoid testifying against someone in court by marrying them, would you, Reenie?'

Peter looked like a rabbit caught in headlights, but

Reenie was still the girl who had been running rings around the local constabulary since she was old enough to talk. 'It's not illegal, is it?'

'No, it's not illegal. But it is damn foolish if you haven't first made certain that you *are* going to have to testify in court at all.'

Peter's eyebrows shot up. 'Reenie, you told me that he'd told you that . . .' His voice trailed off as he realised that this was another mess of Reenie's making.

'If I may?' Sergeant Metcalf interjected, his patience sustained a while longer, possibly by the influence of St Agatha herself. 'My Inspector was sent a request by another constabulary who thought you, Peter Mackenzie, might have given material assistance to individuals seeking to illegally cross the channel for the purposes of interfering in a foreign war, contrary to English law; to whit, your cousins. My Inspector told them he would investigate and sent me to do so. I asked my questions and I returned to my Inspector and I gave him my verdict. And do you know what my verdict was?' Sergeant Metcalf got no answer, so he asked directly, 'Do you know what my verdict was, Irene Calder?'

'No, Sergeant Metcalf,' she whispered.

'My verdict was that it was all *kids' stuff*! Not a bit of evidence of anything serious, just all kids' stuff.' The policeman looked from Reenie's fur cape, to the horse covered in apples and then gave her a withering look. 'Our report is final. I'm saying this once and for all: there is no evidence of any crime which it would be in the public interest to pursue, and I will not be burdened with any paperwork on this occasion. Do we all understand each other?'

'But what about the gardens?' Squire Curran barked out. 'They've been driving that horse all over my lawn and I saw it steal those apples!'

'Did you really?' Sergeant Metcalf asked without surprise. 'I'll be getting you to come down to the station to give a statement then. But for now, give me that shotgun, there's a good fella'.' Sergeant Metcalf arranged shotgun, man, and bicycle, then cast one more look of disappointed irritation in the direction of Reenie Calder and headed off in the direction of the station.

Reenie looked at Peter, all her bravado lost now that she realised what she had done. 'I'm sorry, Peter. I really thought he was saying that he was going to arrest you when he found you.'

Peter gave a sort of nod and, taking patience from St Agatha, said, 'All right, you go and tie up the horse and I'll go and explain to your parents. They'll want to know why their horse is here at least.'

Chapter Fifty-Nine

'I'm not giving my blessing.'

The curate looked up eagerly from his service book at this new twist in the tale. He had always thought the father looked jittery. 'Er, but you're still giving your *permission*, aren't you Mr Calder?'

'No. I withdraw my permission; she's not signing anything. No one's taking my Reenie away.'

'It's too late, Dad, it's all arranged.'

'It isn't too late; I signed nothin', and I'm not signing nothin'. You're too young to do this without my say so and you haven't got it.'

'But Arthur,' Mrs Calder pleaded, 'we talked about this. We agreed that in the circumstances, with a war coming . . .'

'We agreed she needed to be kept safe and provided for, and that there was no harm in hastening the inevitable. But look at her, Annie, she doesn't want this. She's not happy. What use is survival if she's so unhappy?'

'Reenie, love,' Mrs Calder used her softest voice for her daughter, '*are* you unhappy? Do you think you'd be unhappy if we let you wed a little early with a war coming on?'

Reenie flushed red and her voice caught in her throat as she looked at Peter with a helpless desperation. The curate knew that look, he'd seen it before. It was the look of a lost sheep who is waiting to be told where they must go. In his grandfather's day the vicar was there to enforce the wishes of the bride's father – to tell her to obey the men in her life and marry the groom she had been chosen for – but times had changed for the better; this was the twentieth century, he could listen to his flock, he could be a force for good.

'I will need to speak with the bride and groom alone in the vestry.' His voice had a chirruping quality, like an eager little garden sparrow.

'Are we in trouble?' Reenie managed to croak out.

'No, not at all, not at all.' The curate herded the young couple towards his robing room. 'This way.'

Peter looked shocked, but hurt at the same time. There was none of the relief one would have expected to see from a young man who had recently evaded prosecution and imprisonment. His heart was broken.

'I'm very sorry, Mother.' Reenie sat at the table in the church vestry, hands wringing a handkerchief. 'I only said I'd do it to make Peter safe and then, when I knew he was safe, I just couldn't go through with it.'

'It's all right, love, I understand.' Mrs Calder put an arm around her eldest daughter's shoulder and squeezed her affectionately.

'I'm glad you do, because I'm not sure why I went to all the trouble to reading up on licences and banns and whatnot if it's all to be for nothing.' Kathleen's irritation might have been motivated by her disappointed realisation that she was not, after all, going to get a bed to herself at home.

'Oh, Kathleen! Can you show a bit of understanding for your poor sister? She's had a very trying day.'

Mr Calder tried to encourage his younger daughter, while also sounding very serious and solemn. 'You did well, Kathleen. It was a lucky thing you finding that bit o' knowledge about licences. We weren't to know that we didn't need it, but at the time you gave us peace of mind. It was very lucky having you around.'

Kathleen was further put out. 'Luck had nothing to do with it! I've been researching canon law and I happen to know a lot about it.'

Reenie sniffed resentfully. 'Well, if you know so much why don't you find a way to help Mary and Mr Baum get married? They're the only people who really should get married and they can't and it's not fair.'

Kathleen went to take up a seat on the vestry window ledge. 'Oh, that one's easy. I could have them wed first thing Sunday morning if they're not fussy about the decor.'

Reenie sat up sharply, 'Kathleen, what do you mean?'

'It's easy; they can have a special licence same as you – except theirs would have to be an *Arch*bishop's, not a Bishop's Licence because Mr Baum hasn't been baptised into the Church of England and doesn't want to be – and they can jump the queues at the register office and be married Sunday.'

'Are you being serious? Can they really? I mean,

would the register office marry them with a licence from a church?'

'No.' Kathleen smiled a wicked grin. 'They'd have to get married in my shop.'

'How's that?'

'Well, you can't go expecting Mr Baum to be married in a church, that's not fair on him seeing as he's by way of being of the Abrahamic persuasion. And you can't get them into the register office. But an Archbishop's Licence lets you get married in a chapel – *any* chapel. It's good for hospital chapels, school chapels, even old chantry chapels what have been turned into tobacconist sweet-shops. You got to have an ordained man from the Church of England to sign the register and make it legal, but you can do it easy enough. You just need someone to let you into the chapel and I don't think you'll find any other chapel in the town which is so entirely free of Christian symbolism. So really, it's up to your Mary and your Mr Baum if they want to go ahead because I'm ready any time; I've got the keys.'

'Why didn't you tell us any of this before?'

'Well, you didn't ask, did you?'

'Reverend Roberts, would you be willing to conduct a marriage service for a Jewish gentleman and his fiancée in a sweetshop if we can get the proper licences?'

The eyes of the enthusiastic curate lit up at the thought of the letter to his mother and his missionary brother this would make. 'Rather!'

'Where's Diana?' Reenie asked, as she threw her jacket down onto the back of a chair at the basement kitchen table. It was still an oddly welcoming sort of place, despite all the sadness which surrounded the house for them now. Mrs Garner, their old landlady was gone, and Bess and Mary were grieving, but the range was always warm and the cats were always glad to see her.

'She's gone to see if they'll let her visit her sister Gracie. She's made a little improvement but Diana hasn't seen her yet.' Mary looked worse than ever as she nursed a teacup and gazed out of the skylight at the street above. Reenie wondered how much she had slept since her mother had died, or if she slept at all these days.

Reenie rubbed the ear of the tortoiseshell cat which jumped up to greet her. 'I wonder if Gracie and Lara have still got the cats we gave them? We gave them the two siblings to this cat, you know.'

Mary did not have a fondness for cats. 'I shouldn't remind Diana of that at the moment if I were you. Cats can spread scarlet fever.'

'Can they?'

'That's what the newspaper says so perhaps that's how they caught it. It doesn't bear thinking about, does it?' Mary tried to look a little less despondent and asked, 'Was it Diana you came to see?'

Reenie bit her lip. She knew what she wanted to say, but after she had caused so much trouble already with her well-meaning bright ideas she was afraid of making everything worse for her friend. Could she really suggest something so ridiculous?

'Reenie?' Mary asked again, 'Did you come to see Diana?'

'Is Mr Baum here at all?'

'No, he's gone to see the solicitor. Reenie, what is this about?'

Reenie took a deep breath for courage and then said, 'Now, I don't want to get your hopes up, and I know that this is going to sound very odd, but I've talked it over with Peter and with my sister and with my parents – and they all think this is going to work.'

'Think what's going to work, Reenie?' Mary asked suspiciously.

'We think we can get you a special licence to be wed, and we think we can get you wed this Sunday.' Reenie clarified, 'To Mr Baum, of course! There's just one thing, though: are you fussy about where you get married, like the building?'

Mary was clearly beyond caring. 'We'd get married on the number seventy-eight bus if it meant an end to all the madness.'

'That's good, because this is almost as bad as the bus! I've spoken to Kathleen, and I've spoken to a curate, and if we get onto it sharpish we can get you married in Kathleen's shop. It's all legal, like, because it used to be a chapel, but we don't think we'll be able to get the cigarette advertisements taken down because Mr Hebblewhite's broke his ladder. What do you think? Do you want one last try? Can you face it?'

Mary shook her head. 'I wouldn't even know where to start.'

'That's all right, because I know what to do. I've just had a special licence drawn up myself so I can help you arrange the whole thing. It might not work, but it seemed like a last chance, and well . . . I couldn't do nothing, could I?'

Chapter Sixty

Percy Palgrave had not been offering Dolly a great deal in terms of future happiness. Granted, he offered her an escape from a situation in which she was determinedly making herself unhappy and he offered her a kind of odd validation by giving her an opportunity to tell people that there was someone who thought highly enough of her to marry her, but beyond that, what was he really offering? A union which had begun with bickering and was based on a mutual dislike of work and a hope that the other would take on the burden of working so that they did not have to. In the case of Percy, it was work of a domestic nature he objected to in the immediate term, and then he had hopes that he would become a kept man when Dolly came into her inheritance. Dolly's plan was of a similar kind; she wanted to live the leisurely life of a colonial wife while Percy earned the money for servants who would both slave for her *and* give her a feeling of social superiority. Neither of them had any appreciation for the personal qualities of the other and so it was a shame that, when the inevitable happened, Dolly Dunkley could not see what a favour Mary had done her by scuppering her plans to be married.

It happened on an afternoon when both Mary and Percy found themselves waiting outside the Women's Employment Offices, listening to the corridor clock tick. Mary was waiting to see Diana and Mrs Wilkes about a short leave of absence while Percy was waiting to collect Dolly to take her out to the Army and Navy Stores to buy some of the things they would need for their new lives in Burma. Percy vaguely knew that Dolly worked in the factory offices, but he hadn't paid sufficient attention to precisely which office she worked in and so he had not realised that he was meeting her in a department by which she was not employed. If he had asked her directly, he'd have discovered that she was being formally reprimanded for telling some impressionable factory girls 'not to bother with quarantine', and that she intended, at that meeting, to tell her superiors in no uncertain terms to stuff their job and then to flounce out to her waiting fiancé who was whisking her off to a new and glamorous life in the Far East.

'Hullo.' Percy attempted to mitigate the boredom of waiting for Dolly by making conversation with the only other person present. 'Do you work with my Dolly?'

Mary was irritated and showed it. 'I'm Mary Norcliffe. I *used* to work with Dolly.'

'Ah, yes, I've heard lots about you.' Percy decided not to say that Dolly had said nothing complimentary. 'Heard a lot about you from my fiancée, Dolly Dunkley. Don't s'pose she's mentioned me. Percy Palgrave, Burmah Oil

Company?' He added those last three words with the quick, clipped delivery of someone who has grown used to the idea that their employer impresses people.

'I hear you're to be married in a sweetshop.' Mary did not try to keep the resentment out of her voice, though she knew she should have done. She was just too unhappy at the injustice of it all, and all her worry about Albert and his family was weighing heavily on her patience with the rest of the world.

'Well,' Palgrave coughed an odd sort of faux chuckle, 'not really a sweetshop. Although, might make a funny story one day, s'pose.' He was thinking of it already as a tale that he would regale the other First Class passengers with on his voyage back to Burma with his heiress bride. 'Really a thirteenth century chapel. Frightfully rare finding one still standing. Quite an honour to be first couple to wed in it. Expect the papers will want a snap.'

'And saves on decorations.' Mary was blunt by nature, but she was not in a mood to look for opportunities for diplomacy that day. Reenie might still be encouraging her to hope that she and Albert could themselves be married in this little sweetshop everyone was talking about, but Mary couldn't bring herself to believe it. People like Dolly and Percy got to bend the rules for weddings, but not Mary and Albert. 'You could get away with one bunch of flowers for the altar and that would pretty much fill the place up.'

'Doubt we'll get away with just the one bunch. Think Reverend Dunkley will want a lot more fuss for the big day.'

'Well, if you've got the money you do as you please. I bet the Dunkleys will be glad to have one less mouth to feed, even though they'll be losing Dolly's wage, pittance though it probably is.'

Mary's words gave Percy Palgrave pause; like Dolly he was a greedy young man, but unlike Dolly he had good instincts. Mary was quite clearly truthful (if rather rude), and had some close knowledge of the Dunkley family. He would have been a fool to let the moment pass without asking more questions, and whatever he was, he was no fool.

'What do you know about the Dunkleys' situation? I understood the Reverend Dunkley was a Rector not a vicar. He's quite a wealthy man in his own right, isn't he?'

Mary's eyebrows said it all. 'Have you seen how they live? I heard from Reenie, who heard it from their servant, that when Dolly's father told her she had to get a job she nearly threw a fit. They've got nothing but the shirts on their backs. The servants are only paid for by the parish. They'll be right glad she's marrying you. She needs to find someone to keep her before Mackintosh's sack her.'

There was a silence in which Mary knew she had gone too far, but was too upset by her own circumstances to care, and Percy was concerned that he had also gone too far, but in a different way entirely, and feared he might not be able to get himself out. If he broke off his engagement with Dolly now – without a good enough reason – word would get around his social set that he was 'the wrong sort' and it might jeopardise his chances with other girls he met later; and there was not a shadow of a doubt in his mind that he wanted there to be other girls later. All of Dolly's appeal had vanished. He needed to break off his engagement, and he needed to find an excuse fast. He wondered if this young woman might provide an excuse.

'I can see you're a woman who speaks her mind. Good Yorkshire trait. Not how we do things where I'm from, but each to their own and all that. Sounds like you and Dolly haven't rubbed along quite so well and I understand it; not everyone can.' He was doing his best to build a bridge which he could cross. 'But tell me, Mary,' he groped in his weasel mind for something he could use to postpone this all-too imminent wedding while he came up with an excuse to completely escape it, 'tell me as a woman: do you think it's fair of me to expect Dolly to come away with me to Burma so hurriedly? You know her better than I do; you know she has a large wardrobe of clothes and she can't bring them all. Is it wrong of me to expect her to be ready to leave at a moment's notice? Should I give her more time to settle her affairs here, to pack up her little life?'

Mary didn't care a fig, but she was saved the opportunity of telling Dolly's fiancé this in the most forceful terms because at that moment Dolly herself emerged triumphant and red in the face from Mrs Wilkes's ornate oak office door.

With quick thinking Percy Palgrave rose to his feet to greet Dolly and take his leave of his surprisingly useful informant. 'Thank you, Mary. I've appreciated our little chat; you keep up that Yorkshire sharpness. Very refreshing. I'll think on what you've said; quite right.'

Dolly scowled at Mary behind Percy's back as a matter of routine as she followed him away to the factory corridor which would lead them out to the gate and the

301

start of what she thought was to be a glorious new life. 'What was Mary saying to you?'

'Well, she was making me think of you, my sweet.' He reached a quiet stretch of corridor where he thought he might risk speaking of the topic closest to his interests. 'I've been selfish; I see that now. I've expected you to come away with me at a moment's notice, but the life I live out in the colonial office is harsh. We were just talking about your wardrobe and how you need time to decide what you discard before you embark on a new life—'

'But I thought you were taking me to the Army and Navy to buy me all new things so it didn't matter what I left behind?'

This one sentence was enough to make Percy realise that Mary had been right. Dolly had been expecting *him* to buy her a trousseau and he had been expecting *her* to buy him a new set of luggage; this was not a union which could be profitable. They walked past a noticeboard where a freshly pinned poster warned employees to be vigilant against scarlet fever and reminded them of the symptoms to watch for. Palgrave would not even have noticed its existence if Dolly had not attempted to rattle the frame which protected it to see if she could take it down. His eyes scanned the symptoms listed and he decided there and then that it would be politically expedient for him to develop each and every one of them to the most virulent degree and to do it sharpish.

'You know, Dolly, I'm not feeling at all well. I've come over quite shivery and I have a terrible pain in my throat. No, don't come any nearer, I would never forgive myself if I passed on something to you that did you harm. I must go home at once and send for the doctor. I'm terribly afraid this will mean quarantine. You'll be brave for me, won't you, Dolly, if we can't see each other for a time? Absence will have made my heart grow fonder.' Absence, Percy hoped, would also make his mind grow sharper, and he would think of a way to weasel out of the engagement without a dent to his reputation. The emotional scene which Dolly was about to cause would only confirm his belief that he had made the correct move.

Chapter Sixty-One

If Mary and Reenie had been worried that they had come to the wrong address, then the Easter decoration hanging over the door-knocker would have told them that they had arrived at the exalted abode of Dolly Dunkley.

Why Dolly's stepmother had chosen to replace the original garland, Reenie would never know, but the sight of so much good food wasted as decoration offended her even more than it did Mary. The Easter garland was as bright and bold as Dolly had described; twists of young ferns and wisps of white cornflowers had been woven together to hold the apples which set off the contrasting foliage. It was ostentatious and it did not help Mary to feel any less ashamed of her down-at-heel shoes and shabby coat.

A child answered their knock at the door and when Reenie said they were there to see the Rector the anonymous infant bellowed over his shoulder, '*Pa!* There's *people*!' and let them into the rectory hallway to wait on the

304

threadbare rug which gave the lie to the extravagant garland on the door.

The Reverend Dunkley emerged from his study, clutching a newspaper and squinting over reading glasses. 'What's this? What's this? We're not at home to charity collectors; you need to see the—'

'I want a marriage licence!' Mary took Reenie, the Rector, and the anonymous infant by surprise and, what's more, she caught the ear of Dolly who had been sulking upstairs in her bedroom. Mary collected herself when she realised that she had snapped, and said, 'I'm sorry, sir. I . . . it's just that my fiancé needs us to be married very quickly because he is not English and he needs to settle the matter of our marriage before he applies for his next employment permit. We are applying for a special licence and we need your signature to say that I am of this parish and have lived here all my life.'

Reenie produced the papers she had brought in a factory envelope. 'She's got a christening certificate, a letter from the factory to say she's not been away anywhere, and a reference from the rates collector to say he can vouch for the fact she's always at home when he calls and has definitely been resident in the parish for the required time.'

The Reverend Dunkley was about to open his mouth when the thud of angry footsteps running down the stairs made him look upward with trepidation; Dolly was coming.

'What's going on?' Dolly yelled from the stairs before she turned the corner at the landing and propelled herself down the final flight, making the bannisters rattle in their fixings. 'What are *they* doing here? Who said you could come here? This is *my* house.'

'Dolly, dear, these young people have come to see me about a marriage licence.'

'I don't believe it! Reenie Calder called off her wedding and Mary can't get married. Everyone knows that. Whatever they've told you, don't believe them. *She's* the one who told Percy he ought to postpone our wedding!' she shouted, pointing at Mary as she thundered into the hallway. 'And *she's* the one whose horse ate our wreath!' she finished, glaring at Reenie.

'Is this true?' The Reverend Dunkley pulled off his reading glasses to give full scope to his look of astonished disappointment.

'Well, if you will put food on your door you shouldn't be surprised if animals have a go at it.'

The Reverend Dunkley waved Reenie's words away impatiently. 'Not the wreath, girl; the wedding! Is it true that the young woman who wants a marriage licence cannot be married? I must say that, given recent events,' and here it wasn't clear if he was referring to the wedding which Reenie herself had called off, or the suspended nuptials of his daughter, 'I'm minded to preach a sermon to the young people of the parish on the sanctity of marriage, because it appears to me that it is being taken far too lightly.'

Had the Reverend Dunkley kept his voice down while he was saying all this – and not allowed it to rise to a warble of wounded indignation – he might have avoided the following scene, but his own slightly raised voice – combined with the one-woman stampede which was his daughter – brought another actor to the stage: the young Mrs Dunkley. Mrs Dunkley was not Dolly's mother; she was the second wife of the rector, and was a relatively new wife at that. Previously, Mrs Dunkley had been a noticeably pretty young widow in the Reverend Dunkley's congregation with a brood of young children to provide for. The Reverend Dunkley tried to use 'provision for the children' as his excuse for their very short engagement but, truth be known, his own haste was a constant source of personal embarrassment to him. Her appearance at the open sitting-room door changed the direction of the conversation entirely.

'Herbert, my dear, you really must try to keep the noise down, you're quite disturbing the twins.' Mrs Dunkley looked round and gave the girls a welcoming smile. 'Have you come about the Easter egg hunt for the Sunday School?'

'No, madam.' Reenie thought it best to keep it formal even though this woman looked barely older than Mary. 'We're here for a signature for a marriage licence; a special licence.'

'Oh, that's a nice quick job.' Mrs Dunkley would have done well on a factory line with that sort of attitude, Reenie thought. 'There's no need to keep these girls waiting for that, is there, Herbert?'

The Reverend Dunkley didn't like being told how to conduct his profession and wanted an excuse to refuse them. 'I don't think I can, my dear. It's a very busy time and I don't have a moment between now and Whit Sunday when I could conduct a wedding. It will have to wait for—'

'Your curate has already agreed to conduct the service for us.' Mary had an argument ready for any objection; this was her last chance to marry her Albert and she would fight tooth and nail for it.

'Has he really?' This flustered the Reverend Dunkley. 'Well, I don't know when he was expecting to find the church free; we have Easter services, and—'

'He says he'll marry us in that old sweetshop.' Mary had no pretentions regarding the place she was to be wed; all she cared about was that it was legal and quick so that it would keep her Albert safe and give his children and his sister the best chance to come to England.

Dolly – who had been glaring daggers at Mary and Reenie since her arrival – was now apoplectic with rage. 'You want to take *my* wedding! How dare you! You know that was going to be *my* wedding! I'm going to be the first bride in the chapel on the bridge and Percy is going to get our photograph in the paper. Is this why you told him he should postpone our wedding? Were you planning to steal my wedding all along?'

'I didn't tell him to postpone your wedding! I didn't tell him to do anything at all. I'm here for a signature on a bit o' paper and I'm entitled to it by law. You don't own that damned sweetshop and I'll get married in it if I want to. God knows I'd rather just get it over with in a register office, but this looks like the only way. This whole thing is absurd – and no matter how angry you are, Dolly Dunkley, you cannot possibly be as angry as me. So if you don't mind, I want your dad to sign my bit o' paper, and then I want to get off because you are getting on my wick!'

It was an unwise outburst and Mary thought she had scuppered her chances once and for all because the Reverend Dunkley was giving her an odd look. He held out his hand, took the sheaf of papers from Reenie, and disappeared into his study. His absence was so long that

Reenie wondered if they were supposed to leave, but Mary had locked eyes with Dolly whose face was twisted into a nasty, goading expression.

Mrs Dunkley was still waiting at the door of the sitting room, smiling placidly; she reminded Reenie a little bit of Bess in that respect. The difference with this lady, Reenie thought to herself, is that she is only too aware of what's going on around her and she is keeping her household in check and that was no mean feat. Reenie was glad she'd turned up and wondered how long she could keep her stepdaughter from launching herself into a full fist fight with Mary over her right to be the first bride in the bridge chapel. It was surely only a matter of time.

After what felt like an age, the Reverend Dunkley re-emerged with Mary's envelope and some papers of his own that he had added to the clutch. He offered them to both Mary and Reenie, uncertain which he was meant to interact with. 'This is everything you'll need. You must go to the Archbishop's office, mind you; this isn't the licence, this is just the signature you need in order to apply for it.'

'Daddy!' Dolly snarled, not taking her eyes off Mary. 'You can't do this! You can't let her take my wedding.'

'No one is taking your wedding, my dear, it is just being postponed to give us more time to plan. This young lady has just as much right to marry in the meantime as you do. You can't expect the whole parish to postpone their nuptials until your banns have been read. Come along now, let these young people go home and you come into the sitting room, come on, come along.' The Reverend Dunkley appeared to be trying to herd his daughter towards his young wife like someone shooing an angry cat.

'I will be at your wedding, Mary Norcliffe,' Dolly snarled, 'and I will object.'

Chapter Sixty-Two

Diana was watching the clock in her office with her jacket in her hand when Reenie burst in. 'This better be important, Reenie. I'm just about to leave the office to visit my convalescent sister and I'm not in the mood to hear one more person tell me about the mare in foal in the factory stables.'

'It's not the mare, it's Dolly!' Reenie gasped. 'Mary and I managed to get a special licence so that she and Mr Baum can be married this Sunday, but Dolly is threatening to show up at the wedding to object.'

Diana raised an eyebrow. 'You've managed to get them a marriage licence? A real, legally-binding marriage licence to be married in England?'

'Yes,' Reenie insisted. 'I got Mr Baum to check it all with the solicitor and everything. It's all above board, really it is. But it will only work if someone stops Dolly from objecting on the day.'

'What's her objection?' Diana asked. 'Is it legitimate?'

311

'I don't know, she didn't say. She just said that she'd turn up on the day and stop it. You need to do something, Diana.'

Diana didn't take her eyes off the clock on the wall above her neatly cleared desk. It was evident that she did not think this situation was as urgent as Reenie did. 'I'll have a word with her beforehand and make certain she doesn't interfere. However, just now I have a bus to catch and Dolly Dunkley can wait until Sunday morning.'

But Diana was unlucky that day; as she'd been packing up her work to leave, a medical drama was unfolding in another office in which she was to play a part.

Mrs Starbeck disliked people who made a fuss about illness and disliked even more the tendency of Mackintosh's employees to stay at home when they were perfectly capable of coming to work and pressing on. She had first seen what people were capable of when she was a child out in Ceylon where the workers on her uncle's estate wouldn't try any nonsense about taking to *their* beds. Even the women would be back to work in the fields with their new-born babies strapped to their backs just hours after giving birth. Cynthia Starbeck would not be leaving her post for a slight scratch in her throat and a little rise in her temperature. Apart from toothache – which she conceded *was* dangerous – she did not believe in ill health; these things were all about mind over matter.

'I want you to post this memorandum on the notice-board in the Montelimar workroom, Dolly.' Mrs Starbeck pulled a freshly typed sheet of foolscap from her Empire typewriter and thrust it in the direction of the young woman in front of her. 'I'm shortening the dinner hour in their department by one quarter of an hour. If they don't like it they must tell their fellow workers to return from sickness absence and make up the full quota of the work force.'

'Are you quite all right, Mrs Starbeck?' The messenger girl, who hoped to Dickens she didn't look anything like the absent Dolly Dunkley, took the proffered sheet of paper and became even more concerned. 'You look a bit of a funny colour.'

'I'll thank you not to make comments of a personal nature, Verity Dunkley. Please go immediately and do as I've instructed.'

Starbeck was glad to have an excuse to send the girl to the other end of the factory. She was confident that the pounding headache she was experiencing would abate once she'd got rid of Dunkley.

Mrs Starbeck picked up her first piece of correspondence and was seized by a fit of coughing. She fished in her skirt pocket for her clean handkerchief, coughing into her right hand all the while. The deep paper cut was throbbing and hot to the touch, but she had left it uncovered, confident that fresh air would remedy it far more quickly than any mollycoddling. But her head did pound and she felt so parched . . .

Some time passed before Mrs Starbeck awoke, her face clammy with perspiration, her cheek sticking uncomfortably to the blotter on her desk. She was dimly aware of a gathering of people around her, touching her, loosening the collar of her blouse, feeling her pulse.

'How long has she been like this?' The question was asked by someone she knew, a familiar voice. It was her father's voice. No, it was a woman's voice. There were so many unwelcome voices crowding around her peace and quiet.

'She sent me away to put up a notice, but she thought I was someone else, and when I looked at the notice I saw that it was all nonsense so that's when I went to fetch Nurse Munton.'

Someone had turned on her desk lamp and the light was painfully bright. She wanted water and quiet, and she was sure she was on her father's boat and it was rocking from side to side while it sailed through the coalmines on her mother's morning-room rug. The thirst constricted her throat and reached into the throbbing pain in her hand behind her eyes; they were all one.

'I came as soon as I could. How bad is it?' A new voice, a capable voice, another pair of hands, but blissfully cool.

'We've called for a doctor, but . . .'

'No, call for an ambulance. She needs to be removed to the isolation hospital. Don't get too close to her. Have you touched her? Then wash your hands immediately. She has a very bad case. I doubt she'll live through the night.'

By the time Cynthia Starbeck entered the isolation hospital she had lost all sense of her surroundings, or what was being said about her. The nurses considered it a mercy because she was very far gone. There was an open wound on her hand which had become so infected that it had turned green and purulent and her fingertips were a dark purple tinged almost with black and there was a blue tinge to her earlobes and lips. This last symptom was the most worrying for the staff at the isolation hospital; it was a sign that she was developing blood clots in her lungs which would hamper her breathing at best, kill her at worst. There was no doubt that she had succumbed to blood poisoning. The bacteria coughed from her septic throat had entered the paper cut in her hand and now quietly worked away to end her life.

'Can anything be done for this one, doctor?' The night sister who'd attempted to make up a bed for Cynthia Starbeck on a bench in a corridor had a long shift ahead of her and she would need to prioritise her attentions; there were plenty of other patients who needed her.

'I don't like the look of that festering wound. Why don't people come in sooner?' The doctor frowned behind his cloth mask. 'Have it washed and apply a magnesium sulphate paste to draw out the poison. I don't think it's worth giving her anti-toxin; if she were going to develop scarlet fever we'd see it by now. Hmm . . . nasty case of clotting in her fingertips; looks like they might need to come off.'

'Nil by mouth, doctor?'

'Not yet. See if she lasts the night. No sense putting her through anaesthesia if she's on her way out. Notify me at the first signs of necrosis and we'll make a decision about theatre then.'

'Shall I tell the chaplain to notify her family?'

'Yes, I think that's wise. There's very little chance she'll pull through and they'll need to prepare themselves for the worst. They'll need to quarantine either way.'

Cynthia Starbeck awoke from the nightmares of fever to face the nightmares of reality. She was disorientated and weak, but she was fully aware of her surroundings and she was horrified. She lay in a crumpled nest of bedding which was drenched in her perspiration. This was no hospital bed, but some low, creaking army cot pressed up against the wall of a corridor, not a hospital ward or a sickroom. The sounds and smells would have been enough to tell her that she was not alone: this corridor was crowded to capacity with other such sufferers as she.

Mrs Starbeck tried to push the damp bedding away from her, but something about the feel of it on her finger-tips – or rather the absence of feeling – made her look down at her hands.

At first the shock struck her dumb; she didn't under-stand what she was seeing and waived her hands violently in the vain hope that these horrible, alien fingers were not attached to her and could be shaken out onto the floor and away from her. But no matter how she strug-gled to wriggle away from them, these ugly fingers were now her own. What had happened to her while she slept? Who had done this to her? She blinked hard and rapidly but the sight did not change. The tips of her fingers were not only black, but they were beginning to shrivel to sharp little points like the talons of some terrifying bird of prey. Her fingernails, streaked with the same dehydrated blood, now curled over dead flesh. She could feel nothing in them and she began to scream.

'There now, dearie,' a staff nurse hurried to her side, 'don't you wake up the ward, there's no need for that. Nothing to worry about, we'll get you straight into theatre . . .'

Chapter Sixty-Three

There could never have been a good time for the infamous factory foal to be delivered, but that afternoon was perhaps the worst possible time for Diana Moore. It was not only the afternoon on which she was trying to get away to see her daughter Gracie, but it was also the day on which Mrs Starbeck had been removed to the fever hospital. Cynthia's case of scarlatinal infection would put some parts of the factory back into isolation measures after they had only just emerged from them and Diana knew that the work of implementing all this would not only fall to her, but it would fall to her to complete immediately.

Diana had a lot to do and a lot on her mind when she arrived at Mrs Wilkes's office with her clutch of correspondence, and she was so preoccupied that she did not initially notice the visitor in her manager's office.

'Ah, Diana,' Mrs Wilkes picked up her cup and saucer, 'just the girl. You know Mr Parsons from Men's Employment.'

Diana nodded at her opposite number and waited for Mrs Wilkes to offer her explanation:

'Mr Parsons says that they require the assistance of Women's Employment in the matter of the factory stables. The much-anticipated foal was delivered in the night.'

Diana fixed Mr Parsons with a steely eye and said, 'I was not aware that we had any female staff in the factory stables, Mr Parsons.'

Mr Parsons smiled a smug little grin which suggested that his department felt they held a winning card. 'The veterinary surgeon is a lady.'

Mrs Wilkes smiled over her teacup to Diana with a look which suggested that she too thought this was outrageous, but they weren't in a position to argue about it.

'We would like,' Mr Parsons managed to pronounce, through his oily grin, 'an investigation into the lineage of the said foal, a draft company policy, a draft disciplinary process, and a subsequent tribunal to be conducted by your department once the culprit has been identified.' When Diana and her manager did not reply – their false smiles beginning to make their faces twitch – Mr Parsons went on, 'Men's Employment are so busy at present. We are planning the annual golf tournament for the senior staff at the Norwich Factory and we have been requested to commission a solid silver trophy in honour of the occasion. I'm sure you quite understand.'

'Oh, we do, Mr Parsons, we do.' Amy Wilkes's smile was beginning to look rictus and she couldn't sweep the man out of her office fast enough, but she made certain that he did not have the satisfaction of seeing them appear daunted. As the door closed on him, she said, 'Well, Diana, what do you think the odds are that they deliberately hired a lady veterinary surgeon just so they could drop this at our door?'

'Just to be clear, Mrs Wilkes, you're not suggesting that someone in *our* department takes this on, are you?'

'Oh, but of course. In fact, I thought I'd give it to you. It's not often that one has the opportunity to write a disciplinary policy, investigate a breach of it – and then hold a tribunal all in the course of one project. It will be excellent experience for you. I suggest you go down to the stables and see what you can find out. If you're lucky, you might even be able to speak to the vet.'

'So just to be clear,' Diana pinched the bridge of her nose and tried to remain impassive, 'at present we have the Italian fascists helping the Spanish nationalists to bomb Spain; we have a war between China and Japan; we've got unknown submarines firing torpedoes at British ships in the Mediterranean; we've got shootings and explosions in Palestine on public transport; Sir Oswald Mosley has doubled the number of card-carrying fascists in Britain; we've got employees in Germany who we can't bring home; we've got a shortage of women staff while they sit out their quarantine; and the de facto head of Time and Motion is in the fever hospital, but you want me to write a disciplinary policy for any Mackintosh's employee who allows a Mackintosh-owned horse to become pregnant without company permission?'

'Yes, that's about the size of it.' Mrs Wilkes sipped her tea, her little finger tilting upward as she lifted her teacup from its saucer. 'Do you foresee any difficulties with that?'

'No, Mrs Wilkes, I'm sure it will be a most enjoyable project.'

'It will if you handle it correctly. The order of the day is *perfunctory*, Diana. Give them their disciplinary policy on the back of a Quality Street carton and tell them to lump it – we've got more important things to do and we also don't want them to sack Reenie Calder over a horse!' And she winked at Diana.

Chapter Sixty-Four

Dr Georgina Spanswick had a large and genial soul, but like all pioneers she was made of tough stuff. Over a decade before she had been among those first intrepid Englishwomen to gain recognition as veterinary surgeons by the Royal College and the steely determination it had taken to get there had never really left her.

This tenacity notwithstanding, it was a bad time to qualify as a vet; horses were falling out of favour with businesses and for every new client she added to her practice she lost three to the growing trend for cars, vans, and tractors. The trade depression might have slowed the investment in motor vehicles for a time, but it had also squeezed purses so that her patients' owners couldn't afford her fees. Dr Spanswick could have left the profession – she had other options – but she stayed in it for love.

It was a happy accident which brought her to the factory stables just as Diana was arriving there herself.

Dr Spanswick had come out in the small hours of the morning when the overnight stable lad had raised the alarm that an expected foal was now coming, but the mare was in some distress. Dr Spanswick had delivered the foal and if she had sensed a tension among the staff in the factory stables, she hadn't mentioned it, or asked what was the matter; she knew that the staff would tell her in time. She suspected that the uneasiness among the staff was being passed on to the horses and was the reason for the mare's trouble – a rather loud murmur of the heart. These things could often be brought on by nerves and be recovered from with rest and she had come back to check on the situation so happened to be at the stables when Diana arrived and asked her questions.

'Is it healthy? Will it be a good enough sort of horse?' Diana asked the vet. She felt no need to conceal her total ignorance of matters equine or zoological; her job on this occasion was to pay lip service to the Men's Employment Department and to give the most cursory investigation into the parentage of the animal.

Dr Spanswick responded to the questions as though they were the most insightful she'd heard that day. 'He's healthy in body and limb and he's got an inquisitive nature; he should make a jolly sound working animal. Good all-rounder, I'd have thought.'

'And his parentage?' Diana hoped to God there was no way to give an answer to her next question. 'Is there any way of telling who might have sired him?'

Dr Spanswick folded her arms, tilted her head, and gave the foal a look of careful inspection. 'Well, he looks nothing like his mother. He's apron-faced, but he's also jug-headed. He might grow out of that, I suppose, but it's distinctive and I'd have thought it probable that his sire had one of those traits; I've not seen any horse in the factory stables with a similar profile, but I expect time will tell.'

Diana knew that time would tell and it was as well to get it over with there and then to save unnecessary dramatic revelations later. 'Have you ever seen a horse called Ruffian? Lives on the Calders' farm.'

Dr Spanswick squinted her eyes at the foal with incredulity and then her face lit up in recognition. 'Of course! I don't know why I didn't see it before; he has the same sharp withers. Very distinctive-looking horse; unmistakeable.' She beamed a warm grin at the bandy-legged youngster. 'Oh, you are like your papa, aren't you?'

Chapter Sixty-Five

'Your friend from work is here to see you, Miss Starbeck.'
The auxiliary nurse had an irritating habit of allowing
any callers to wander up to Cynthia's bed, regardless of
whether or not they had received an invitation to do so
by the invalid herself. This would not have happened if
she'd still had the money for a private nursing home,
but as it was, Cynthia was doomed to put up with the
loathsome communal facilities at the cottage hospital
run on charity terms by the borough council.

'Look cheerful, Miss Starbeck,' the auxiliary was determined to dragoon her patients into grateful compliance,
'some people would be very glad to have as many visitors
as you have.'

Cynthia did not think herself lucky. She had survived
the scarlatinal infection, but what use was mere survival
if the disease took so much of you with it? The doctor
had explained that the pains in her joints and her head
were likely to last for many months – if they ever went

away at all. It was the nature of that particular strain of streptococcal bacteria which had caused the outbreak; the medical officers had observed the same thing in patients who had survived the Doncaster outbreak. He'd also told her that she was lucky. They'd only had to amputate her fingers and not her hands so the recovery time would be so much shorter than if it had been her hands which were necrotic. She had been so very, very lucky. She would need plenty of rest, of course, but the doctor was sure that her friends and family would take good care of her once she returned home.

'And you'll need your friends all the more now,' the doctor had told her and she'd nodded, pretending to be rich in friends. 'You will need them to do a great many things for you until you can learn to do them for yourself again. But don't worry, in time you'll be able to feed yourself once more, dress yourself, perhaps even write little notes. I think you'll surprise yourself with just how much you can achieve. You've been very, very lucky.'

She should have known what would happen next; the doctor wrote a note to her employers excusing her from work for six weeks – as was customary – but he also explained the nature of her illness and the changes and adaptations which would be required in the office on her return. The letter had fallen on Diana's desk.

Now Diana asked, 'How have you been?' without enthusiasm for an answer, as she pulled the utilitarian hospital chair closer to Cynthia's bed and ushered Cynthia's other visitor closer.

'I've had a lot more visitors than I want,' Cynthia Starbeck said flatly.

Diana ignored the rebuff and went on, 'I've made some

arrangements concerning that other matter we touched on when I visited you yesterday.'

'I can see that.' Cynthia looked to the chair beside Diana where Bess Norcliffe was smiling benevolently.

'I've spoken with the Norcliffe sisters as I said I would and Bess has agreed to come and nurse you when you are discharged from hospital. The doctor has said that you'll need someone to help you wash in the mornings and brush your hair, feed you your egg and soldiers. Bess got used to doing all that for babies when she ran the factory crèche, so she can easily do it for you. You'll have Dolly Dunkley at the factory to take dictation and do your typing, so between the two of them you should be able to function just as before.'

Cynthia squirmed uncomfortably. 'I can't possibly pay for a nurse . . .'

'You won't be paying for a nurse,' Diana said. 'Your room in the boarding house is a room with twin beds and Bess here needs bed and board somewhere while she works at Mack's. Her mother died very suddenly and her sister is marrying a widower with a family, so you would be doing her a very great favour by sharing your room with her and she would repay you by helping you in your recovery. Bess can take the extra bed in your room and I won't increase your rent.'

'What if I don't want her doing all of those things for me? What if I don't want anyone to . . .'

Diana cut in pragmatically. 'Then you'll starve to death in your pyjamas. Just try not to do it too loudly; it will cause a noise nuisance for the other tenants.'

Cynthia felt sick. She had been frustrated enough at having one incompetent assistant under her feet, but now she would be trapped with two of them, and she knew that no matter how much she wanted to be independent, she badly needed this offer of help.

'Very well.' Cynthia swallowed her pride and addressed herself to Bess. 'Thank you for offering to come and help me in my recovery. I'm very sorry to hear of the loss of your mother, and I do hope that you will be comfortable in my accommodation.'

'Oh, I know I will!' chirped Bess, happily. 'I've already been round and filled the wardrobe. I saw your walls were very bare so I've begged pictures off all my friends and put them up on every wall and I've got all kinds of potted plants – I've even taught the cat to sleep on your pillow so it will be warm when you get back. I'm going to make it all just lovely!'

Chapter Sixty-Six

It was a little after dawn on the morning of the wedding and the Quality Street girls had been getting ready to leave Diana's boarding house where they had dressed and slept the night before, as much as any of them could be said to have slept. They were now hurrying to the chapel, via the stable at the back of the Old Cock and Oak in the centre of town where Reenie had stabled her horse for the night. It was an anxious time for all of them, but most especially for Mary. She had asked her sister to look after the wedding ring, but now she could see that Bess was skipping along beside her with it in her hand.

'Bess! What are you doing? Put that in a pocket somewhere safe or something will happen to it.'

'I haven't got a pocket to put it in.' Bess waved the ring around airily, possibly hoping to catch a pocket as it floated by her.

'Bess, I gave you one job to do—'

Reenie cut Mary off mid-sentence. 'Can't you just put it on your finger until we get there? We need to hurry.'

'Oh no,' Bess was admiring the shine of the new wedding band, 'it's bad luck to put it on if you know you're going to take it off again.'

Reenie plucked it not unkindly from her friend's fingers. 'Give it here! *I'll* look after the ring.' Reenie took it and reached inside her coat pocket but then thought about what she was about to do and worried that it might drop out if she put it in her pocket loose. Sometimes Reenie thought too much and had a tendency to be a trifle elaborate; this was one of those times.

'Reenie Calder, what are you doing to my wedding band?'

Reenie had reached into her other coat pocket and pulled out the shiny red apple she'd brought to give Ruffian and now wouldn't and was jamming the ring into its flesh. 'Well, if it's lodged in here and then I put the apple in my pocket, the ring definitely won't fall out of my pocket.'

'And then when you take it out it will be covered in apple juices!'

'I'll give it a wipe for you.'

Mary sighed, 'We don't have time for this.'

This was not the Easter wedding which any of the girls had been expecting to attend. The toffee factory that spring had been a flurry of expectation, educated speculation, and then plain gossip, but the girls on the Strawberry Cream line had all been agreed that there would be wedding banns for one of them before the year was out.

'Well, these aren't the decorations I thought we'd be having.' Reenie poked her head inside the doorway of the church and sighed at the brightly coloured embellishments which had been left there by some other person, for some other purpose. It was a shame they couldn't have done things differently, but the wedding was going ahead and that was all any of them cared about now.

'How long do you think we ought to wait?' Mary was kicking at her shoes because she was wearing them without socks and her feet had slid down to the toe uncomfortably.

'Why?' Reenie asked with just a little sarcasm. 'Did you have somewhere else to be?'

Bess giggled. Bess often giggled.

'What's so funny?' Mary was determined to treat the occasion as a solemn one and her sister's silliness was getting on her wick.

'You kicking at your shoe,' Bess chuckled quietly, just sensible enough that she shouldn't let the curate inside the door hear her. 'You look like Reenie's horse when he's been given a job he doesn't fancy doin'. *He's* always kicking his shoes off.'

'I'm not kicking them off, I'm just trying to get my foot straight. The insole's all over the place.'

All three girls turned to see the curate emerge from inside; he looked more nervous than they did, if such a thing were possible. 'Ladies, this is really most irregular, I do think . . .' The curate's voice trailed off as he realised that he had no objections left to make. It was the other girl he needed to speak to, the one who was beautiful and terrifying.

For months the toffee factory workers had been laying bets on whose the next factory wedding would be. The smart money was on Reenie Calder; although still only just seventeen she had been courting a very sweet Junior Manager from the Time and Motion department for nearly a year and, according to rumour, had been negotiating with him on the terms of an engagement. Reenie's friend, Mary Norcliffe would not have seemed a likely candidate for matrimony a year before, but then life had wrought its changes; Mary was no longer known as 'The Bad Queen' behind her back because her quick temper had given way in response to the kindness she had found in new friendships in the factory, and now that she had been given the chance to work in the Confectioners' Kitchen and work closely with the handsome young widower who ran it, some (including her flighty younger sister) whispered that she might make a suitable stepmother to the Confectioner's two small children.

Meanwhile flighty Bess, still known as 'Good Queen Bess' in the factory because her kindly nature never changed, was possibly the Quality Street girl who everyone hoped would wed; Bess was friendly and obliging to a fault and her sister Mary was convinced that if she wasn't guarded round the clock she would get herself in the family way by obliging rather too much. Mary was clinging to the hope that this latest new home would give Mary's blood pressure a well-earned rest.

Diana Moore was now so old by the standards of the factory girls that no one seemed to think of her in matrimonial terms, and that was the way Diana liked it; being the talk of the town had lost its appeal for her many years ago.

Now the day of the wedding was here and it had come in an unholy hurry.

Reenie was resplendent in a satin gown and light fur cape which had been a gift from her young man's parents when they'd told them they were to be engaged. Reenie was glad of the cape in the chill of the church and she felt sorry for Mary who shivered a little beside her while they waited just inside the nave door. Reenie was not surprised to see that Mary's dress was of a slightly old-fashioned cut; it had echoes of a dress she'd seen Mary wear on another occasion to church, and she remembered how it had transfixed Albert Baum the factory Confectioner; it seemed fitting that Mary would choose something that he would have liked had he been the one to choose it.

'Is she definitely on her way here?' The curate looked anxiously to Reenie; he'd never married anyone by special licence before, and when that fourth, more assertive factory girl had presented herself at the vicarage late in the evening with the letter signed by the bishop of his diocese, he had been more than a little taken aback. He knew the law; he knew that in some rare cases respectable people were married without the four weeks of having the banns read, but those were usually in the case of civil servants who had been working abroad and were only returning to be married in their family church. For people who had lived in the parish this was most irregular. Admittedly, Shakespeare himself had been married by special licence, but the date of William Shakespeare's wedding touched uncomfortably close to the date of his first child's christening. The curate was assured that this was not the reason for haste in this particular case, and he didn't know if this worried him more.

That more assertive factory girl who the curate had been waiting for appeared at the bottom of the steps in a Mackintosh's chauffeur-driven car and made her way quickly up toward them. 'She isn't coming.' Diana did not sound disappointed. 'The wedding can go ahead.'

'Who isn't coming?' The curate found this whole situation most suspicious and he would have raised objections if a very large, ornate special licence signed by his superior's superior had not persuaded him to go along with it. 'Is this a person who knows of some lawful impediment why—'

Diana cut him off before he could waste any more time. 'There is no lawful reason why this marriage shouldn't take place. It was a personal reason and I've dealt with it.'

Mary looked a bit scared of Diana when she said that, but Reenie knew better and breathed a sigh of relief. A spring morning was stretching over Halifax and it was nearly eight o'clock; in just a few moments it would be legally late enough in the day for the wedding to begin.

Chapter Sixty-Seven

The wedding of Mary Norcliffe and Albert Baum was conducted – without flowers or fuss – in the bridge chantry chapel on the banks of the Hebble Brook. The premises were still fitted out as a sweetshop, but the windows were shuttered and for that morning only the place had an especially sacred ring. The nuptials had been hard won, and for that reason alone it was all the more appreciated by the bride and groom.

The curate who had agreed to marry them held the Book of Service open before him and held it out for the wedding band to be placed upon it.

Nothing happened.

The curate gave them a friendly nudge. 'Who has the ring?'

Reenie woke out of a romantic reverie and her hand shot into her pocket to retrieve the band she knew that she had put into a safe place. But Reenie's hand came up empty and she exchanged a horrified look with Mary's angry one. The ring – which Reenie had shoved into an apple in a moment of overthinking – was gone, stolen out of her pocket by a decidedly put-out Ruffian who could not understand why his beloved mistress hadn't handed it over herself.

'No one panic.' Reenie was swallowing hard and looking around her while she thought of a solution to the problem they now faced.

Mary went white. 'When *you* tell me not to panic, Reenie, the first thing I do is panic!'

'It's . . . it's going to be all right . . .'

'What's going to be all right?' Albert Baum was not easily worried, but this wedding had been snatched from him once already and he was terrified that some impediment might still be found to prevent it.

'The ring . . .' Reenie said.

Mary sighed. 'The ring you promised me that you were going to look after and not lose through a hole in your coat pocket . . .'

'I think Ruffian must have stolen it when I was patting him earlier.'

Albert Baum stepped forward. 'Reverend, is the type of ring an essential element of the legal act of marriage; will you refuse to sign the register if we do not have a gold ring?'

'Well, no, the giving and receiving of rings is not a legal necessity, but—'

'Then I think we can supply the necessary. Reenie, turn over that box.' Albert heaved at a crate which they recognised as a Mackintosh's outer. 'If we're lucky we'll find something with foils.'

'What are we looking for?'

'Quality Street.'

'But there are no rings in Quality Street tins! We need something with a ring, like a washer from a tap or summat.'

'No, we need Quality Street. In amongst all this we must be able to find a carton at the very least.'

The girls turned over all the boxes, crates and sacks. Bess found four packets of Lyon's tea and a copy of the American edition of *Vogue*, but they were not what they wanted.

'Found it!' Reenie called out. 'I've got half a carton under the counter, will that do?'

'Chuck us it here.' Mary held out her hands to catch it.

Reenie threw the carton across the chapel to her friend and she seized on it and rummaged for the sweet she needed: the Toffee Penny. She knew exactly what Albert had in mind. He took it from her as though it was the most valuable thing in the world and untwisted the wrapper with careful but rapid expertise and stuck the toffee pat to the inside lid of the carton. The wrapper of golden paper and yellow cellophane he folded over and over to create a golden strip, then tucked the ends into one another to form a perfect band of gold. He held it up gracefully beside Mary's hand, and then said to the startled vicar, 'You may proceed.'

'Repeat after me, Mr Baum: with this ring, I thee wed.'

Albert Baum's eyes filled with tears of happiness at the realisation that they had overcome their last obstacle and that he was really and truly about to gain his dearest wish. He said solemnly to Mary, 'With this ring, I thee wed.' And slipped the toffee wrapper ring onto the finger of his beloved.

Chapter Sixty-Eight

Reenie's mother was getting her wish; she was celebrating a spring wedding in their parlour and she was keeping her daughter at home a little longer. It was not the wedding she had been expecting, but she was delighted with it. When Mr and Mrs Calder had heard that Mary and Albert were going to have a wedding but no wedding breakfast, they insisted that everyone come to the Calder family farm to eat a good dinner with them and raise a toast to the happy couple. Mrs Calder had laid on a feast of roast lamb with mint and tracklements and Mr Calder had chilled some bottles of his best elderberry wine in a trough in the yard. The Calder men had gone hunting in the outhouses for boxes to serve as extra chairs, and the Calder women had chopped extra logs to build up the kitchen range to a roar.

When Reenie, Peter, Mary, Albert, Diana, and Bess all finally arrived at the Calder farm it was mid-morning and they were ravenous. Mary and Albert's faces were flushed with happiness, and their friends were singing loudly and merrily with the pure elation at having at last pulled off the great feat of both getting Mary her wedding, and saving the little absent Baums. Diana Moore, who rode along with them in the back of the waggon which Ruffian had been persuaded to pull, did not deign to join in the singing, but dignified as ever, she had the appearance of one who might be entering into the spirit of the thing on the inside.

The party alighted, Ruffian was rewarded, and after much rejoicing, a feast was enjoyed.

'Well, I'm just glad to have a year where, so far, Reenie doesn't appear to be in any trouble.' Mrs Calder bustled around her assembled guests, serving them all sparkling elderberry wine in a mismatch of beakers, glasses and tankards.

'Was she in trouble last year?' Bess's memory, which was encyclopaedic for the astrological signs of Hollywood movie stars, was short when it came to scandals of which she had been the principal cause.

'Yes, because she was covering up for you!' Mary reminded her younger sister.

'To be perfectly honest,' Kathleen said in a confiding tone, 'I wouldn't blame your sister; Reenie's got a nose for trouble. The three Christmases before she went to Mackintosh's she was in the soup with our Sunday School mistress for everything from lateness to accidentally burning down the privy. I'm only surprised she's having a year off from reprimands.'

'Yes, well, that's quite enough of that, thank you, Kathleen.' Mrs Calder said. 'We'll just be thankful that this year is different.'

Reenie was not saying anything; she was watching

Diana Moore closely. Diana Moore was sipping her elderberry wine with a coolness which Reenie considered to be ominous. 'Diana,' Reenie finally plucked up the courage to ask, 'I'm not in any trouble this year, am I?'

Diana raised an eyebrow in thought and then said, 'Well, there is the small matter of the mare in the factory stables who has recently delivered a foal.'

'Oh Diana, you are a card.' Reenie's father chuckled. 'You had us going there for a minute. I know my daughter can be a bit muddle-headed at times, but I know she'd never be Tomfool enough to let our old stallion loose in a . . .' Mr Calder's voice trailed off along with his confidence as he saw that Diana Moore did not appear to be joking.

'Um . . . I-I was careful with him, Dad, honest; it's just I didn't realise that he could let himself out of the stables he was in at the factory and so there's a chance that he might have—'

'It is a *certainty*.' Diana Moore was impassive.

'Yes, but no one can ever be certain, can they?' Kathleen was ready to find a legal loophole if there was one. 'How could anyone prove that the foal was sired by our Ruffian?'

'Because I've seen it,' Diana said, 'and it is peculiarly ugly.'

Mary laughed so hard and so suddenly that she nearly choked on her elderberry wine and had to be slapped on the back by her attentive new husband. Mary's laughter was infectious and before long even Diana was showing a ghost of an exasperated smile.

'Don't laugh,' Diana tried to keep a straight face, 'it's not funny. I have had to write the words on an official report in the office; I have had to write down that I believe I know the sire of the foal because it's so ugly.'

Peter, emboldened by his beaker of elderberry wine, drew back his shoulders and said, 'It wasn't Reenie's fault, it was mine. I let Ruffian out of his stable and if anyone's going to be dismissed it should be me.'

Albert Baum cottoned on to what Peter was trying to do and joined in. 'No, it was not Peter, or Irene; it was I! I released the horse!'

Mary rolled her eyes at Albert. 'You weren't even in England then! It was last spring that he must have gone wandering.' Then Mary caught a look at her sister and said, 'Don't you start confessing to things, you're enough trouble!'

Mrs Calder was glad that Diana didn't seem too serious, but she was still concerned at this revelation that Reenie was in trouble at work again. 'But joking aside, is there going to be trouble when she goes back?'

'I have been tasked with holding a disciplinary hearing and, as it happens, I have already decided on the outcome.' Diana looked as hard-faced as she did at any other time and Reenie couldn't tell if she should be worried.

'What's going to happen to me, Diana?'

'I'm sentencing you to another year of hard labour at Mackintosh's toffee factory. If you leave in the next year I'll flay you alive.'

'I'm not sacked?' Reenie asked with a mixture of excitement and relief.

'No, because if you leave that would create more work for me, and I'm no fool. Just go and make your apologies to the stable manager and tell him you'll not let it happen again.' Diana appeared to think of something else. 'And for heaven's sake get Bess to stop bothering him about giving them a wedding; horse weddings are ridiculous.'

Chapter Sixty-Nine

Gracie was out of danger, but still convalescing after her illness. She reclined, where Diana could see her from the terrace of her adoptive parents' home, in a wicker chair on the lawn, shaded by a blossoming cherry tree. Lara sat up in a matching chair beside her, throwing a switch up into the branches to make pale pink petals rain down on them and their matching cats besides. The cats, who were not yet a year old, were still playful and fascinated by falling flora, but Gracie's cat was already showing signs of the devoted shadow it would grow to be.

Diana sensed that she was not alone on the terrace and she turned to see Edward Hunter, Lara's father and the adoptive father of Gracie, coming out to see where the children wanted to have their tea; indoors or out. They could have anything they wanted as far as he was concerned.

'Diana,' he said, an uncharacteristic awkwardness coming into his voice, his manner shades of stoical and shades of reluctance, 'I didn't realise you were here. More charity work for my wife?'

Diana hesitated. It was her policy to avoid all lies except the one essential one; the lie that Gracie was her sister. She had to confess that this time there was no excuse related to charitable endeavours, or meeting minutes to be signed. 'I wanted to see Gracie. I've been worried.'

Mr Hunter nodded. 'So have we. She gave us quite a fright. It was a close-run thing.' He paused, debating whether to ask something or not. 'The night the doctor came and he brought you out here with him – the night Grace's fever broke – what did he say to you?'

There was something in his manner which made Diana suspect that he knew, but she couldn't quite tell. Edward Hunter had always seemed like a good and generous man, but if he discovered the truth about her real connection to Gracie, how would he respond? Would he think she had deceived them all through malice? Would he understand that it was the only way she could do what was best for her daughter? Would he condemn her for bringing that daughter into the world in the circumstances she had? Would he condemn her for maintaining their connection with dishonesty? Diana thought for a moment before answering honestly, 'He told me to prepare for the worst.' And in that moment Diana did prepare for the worst, because she felt certain that her secret was out, that the doctor had spoken privately to Edward Hunter and that he was even now preparing to tell her that she was being cut off from her Gracie.

Edward nodded slowly, giving nothing away. 'Yes, I think we all did that night.' He took in a deep breath and looked out across the garden to where the girls waved ribbons above the heads of their cats, and frowned. 'They've settled in well together, those two. We couldn't have predicted how well it would work out after such a sudden adoption, but one can't always foresee everything.' A silence stretched out across the lawn and back again. 'Lydia and I wanted to tell you that we've decided to send them away.'

Diana's heart lurched into her stomach and she felt a cold, cold sensation running up the back of her neck. She remained impassive on the outside, but only because she realised that she could not speak.

'If there is war – and it seems only a matter of time now – there are likely to be shortages of food in towns like this. The countryside would be better for them, healthier. I have family in the Lakes, over near Coniston; we'll send them there. They'll be well away from the noise of any bombing raids and all the things which might frighten them. We'll bring them back here when we think it's safe, but it's better for them to send them away.'

He knew. Of course he knew. How could he not? This wasn't the angry confrontation she had expected, but then they did not seem like angry people. It was typical of his class that they would allude to it, but not make any scene; wait until she was alone somewhere quiet and tell her that they were making a clean break of it. She swallowed, but her mouth was so dry she thought it would choke her.

'Will – will I be able to write to her sometimes?' Her voice came out weak and hoarse.

'Write to whom?'

Tears welled up in Diana's eyes and threatened to

obscure what might be her last sight of her Gracie. 'My daughter, will I still be able to write to my daughter?'

Edward Hunter's expression moved through a moment of mild confusion to total shock. He started visibly and then hurried breathlessly to correct Diana. 'The *cats*. We're sending away the *cats*. You gave them to us, didn't you? We thought you'd want to . . .' His voice failed him as he looked from Diana's horror-stricken face to the face of the little girl in the wicker chair in the middle of his lawn; they were the same, they had always been the same. 'Are you telling me that . . .?'

'I thought you knew!' Diana gasped out through barely suppressed sobs. 'I thought the doctor had told you and you were sending her away because he'd told you. I would never have told anyone if . . . if . . .'

'Dear girl,' the words had the ring of an admonition when Edward Hunter said them, 'dear girl. What were you thinking?'

'I needed,' Diana gasped, 'I needed to give her a better life. I thought . . . I thought it was the only way.'

Edward Hunter looked desperately at Diana. 'What did you intend to do?'

'I don't know,' she said. 'I don't know.'

Chapter Seventy

'You know I have to go away, Reenie.' Peter had leant his dark blue Raleigh Racer up against the side of the factory stables. For a fleeting moment it felt like the old days when he would take his bike apart and she would brush down the horse, except this time there were pannier bags on the Raleigh and a rucksack on Peter's shoulder.

'I don't want you to go away on my account.' Reenie was at a loss for what to do with her hands now that she and Peter could no longer talk by touch. 'You know that, for me, it was just too soon, that was all. We could go along as we did before . . .'

'I can't, Reenie.' Peter swallowed back the pain of his broken heart. 'There's a life I thought I was going to have with you and it's gone – and I don't know how to describe it. It's like I'm mourning for that life we were going to have because it's died, or at least it never got to live.'

'But what if it's just postponed?' Reenie pleaded in spite of herself, because part of her had realised now that she wanted to be free and yet another part of her did not want to feel the pain of losing her closest friend. 'We've got our whole lives ahead of us – we don't need to hurry anything.'

'That's just the problem, Reenie. We're marching to the beat of different drums, you and I. I see that now. I see how much you want to keep your job at Mack's, and how much I want a family and a home. Those things will never work themselves out. There's a war coming in all probability, and if I can't go and fight the fascists in Spain, then I'll get my training in here and get ready to fight them somewhere else. Perhaps when I come back we'll both have changed, or perhaps we won't. I hope you don't change, Reenie. I hope you always love it here, because it's part of what made me love you.'

Reenie shed a tear and sniffed. 'I'm so sorry, Peter. I really am so sorry.'

'Don't be.' He hugged her tight. 'It's all going to be all right.'

Doreen and Siobhan sat side by side on kitchen chairs in Doreen's back garden watching their children play at mud-pie making. It was their first taste of normality together in what felt like such a long time.

'We were all talking on the line at work about throwing you a party, seeing as you didn't die of the scarlet fever.' Siobhan said.

'I don't want a party, I'm exhausted. I want a packet of biscuits.' Doreen gave her friend a wan smile.

Siobhan thought she did look too weak for a party, but also thought she could probably do better than a mere packet of biscuits. 'We brought you Mint Cracknel and Quality Street, but Pearl insisted that you were slimming so you'd only want to sniff the wrappers.'

'Give over! I've had scarlet fever and I want a chocolate and a pint of tea.'

Siobhan laughed; Doreen sounded better in herself, at least, even if she still had a long way to go before she was strong again. 'How are you feeling?'

'Like I've been wrung out and hit on the head with a frying pan, but otherwise I'm all in one piece. What's the gossip from Mack's? Did they have to fumigate my peg in the cloakroom after I fainted?'

'You did more than faint, you were delirious with fever. They shut down the whole line and got the District Medical Officer to give us all throat tests. Some of the minnows refused to have tests or quarantine and the Employment Department threatened to sack the lot of them. It was handbags at dawn on the Caramel Cup line, so you missed a treat.'

Doreen looked worried. 'Seriously, though, was everyone else all right? I didn't give it to anyone else, did I?'

'Three of the minnows caught it, but it turns out they had all three of them been passionately kissing the same lad from Stebbins' farm who also had it, so the jury's out on who they got it from.'

'Did they really trace it all back to Stebbins' farm? Wasn't that just a rumour?'

Siobhan shook her head and tried to swallow a gulp of tea at the same time. 'No they published a report all about it in the *Halifax Courier* and everything; one of the milker's kids had an ear infection. The milker dressed the kid's ear each day, then went down to the sheds to milk the cows. A couple of the cows got infected teats from the milker, and the infection carried through the milk to the schools and the town, and through the Stebbins' kids. It just goes to show how quickly these things happen.'

Doreen held her herself upright for a moment to see what the children were up to, then sank back down into her chair, her head supported with a cushion as she leant it back against the wall. 'Do you think they'll get a fine or something, the Stebbins' lot?'

'No, they're getting a subsidy.'

'They're not!'

Siobhan gave her an arch look. 'I'm not kidding. They're getting a government subsidy to set up pasteurising machines and things in the dairy. I can't believe it. Three dead and they get a subsidy.'

Doreen shook her head in wonder. 'Well, I suppose if it prevents it happening again?'

'But does it, though? There's still posters up everywhere telling us to boil our milk. There's even advertisements in the national newspapers telling everyone they have to boil their milk, not just people in Halifax.'

'That seems like it's a waste of a lot of people's time if it's only in Halifax,' Doreen said.

'Well, it could be anywhere, couldn't it? Or there might be some other bug waiting to get us some other way. I mean, how do we know the danger's passed? How do we really know?' Siobhan thought about the uniforms her husband wore to his job as a hospital porter and worried about the myriad germs which clung to them and posed a danger to all around her.

'The District Medical Officer announced that there had been no new infections for a fortnight running and that meant it was all over. It's over when he says it's over,' Doreen said reassuringly, 'that's how we know.'

Siobhan looked down at her hands, the skin had cracked around the knuckles and was red raw from frequent washing. 'But how can we ever go back to normal? How can we ever live our lives the way we used to? Shouldn't we be keeping the kids at home in case there's more illnesses out there, not just scarlet fever, but other things that might be hanging in the air, or growing in the water? I heard from one of the mums at the school that there are two new kinds of measles. They've been found in Manchester and they can kill a child in under twenty-four hours. Shouldn't we be trying to prevent them before they even happen? Shouldn't we be more cautious than ever?'

Doreen summoned the strength to sit forward and reach out to pat her friend's arm. 'Not unless the District Medical Officer says it's time to do that. We can't live our lives listening to rumours about things in other towns which might kill us. If the District Medical Officer tells me to batten down the hatches, then that's what I'll do, but not before.'

'I don't know how everyone can go back to normal so easily. It's been months. I keep dreaming that the kids are at a party and one of the other kids has "it" – whatever "it" is – and I have to try to protect them, but I can't because no one cares about it except me.'

Doreen reclined against her cushion again. 'You know, my mother used to have that same dream. She told me about it. She had it during the Spanish flu and for months after and she used to wake up crying something awful.'

'Does she still get it; does she still have the dream?'

'No. It went away in the end. It took a long time though, but it went away. Eventually, if you give it enough time, it leaves you be.'

Author's Historical Note

On 15th April 1935 my great-grandmother Connie died from septicemia; she was just twenty years old. Coincidentally, my father and I also both contracted the life-threatening complication when we were twenty. My father contracted his through a scratch on his hand while he was working as a chef in the Café Royal, and I caught a bare ankle on the corner of a sharp box while clearing out the ancient, dirty cellars of my city library. It was thanks to the case history of his grandmother Connie that my father was able to recognise the telltale signs of blood poisoning in both cases and get early treatment to prevent the kind of complications which were once commonplace.

Septicemia is now a much more treatable illness than it was in the 1930s; antibiotics have saved not only countless lives, but also countless limbs. Where a bad case of tonsillitis was a cause for panic and quarantine, it is now more usually remedied with rest, fluids, and banana-flavoured antibiotic medicine. What has not changed is the need to prevent the spread of infections in the first place.

At the time of writing the second draft of this book I found myself – along with the rest of humanity – in the grip of a pandemic. It felt very strange to sit down to write about characters who could shake hands, share a box of sweets, or embrace, when all around me lives had been turned upside down by our absolute need to isolate ourselves. I tried to encourage my characters to continue the normal life which I could not have, but they resolutely refused and so I went back to my research notes for 1937 as a distraction.

It was with a jolt of recognition and a strange feeling of solace that I stumbled on the records of the West Yorkshire outbreak of scarlet fever and septic throat which almost shut down Doncaster. The *British Medical Journal* reviewed the case once it was over and the more I read about it, the more I wondered what would have happened if their efforts to test, trace, and isolate cases had failed. What would have happened if the infection had flared up again months later in a nearby town? What if there had been a second wave in Halifax?

The Doncaster epidemic had started with a dairy which didn't pasteurise their milk. From there it spread to the customers of the dairy, and those patients spread it through coughs, sneezes and touch to the wider population of the town. The local isolation hospital was filled rapidly and some of the TB patients were 'sent home for a Christmas break' to make room for more victims of the milk-borne infection. Staff at the hospital ran out of masks – which were essential when treating this infectious condition – and the local government advised people to avoid crowded places, like cinemas and pubs. Children were sent home from school, government agencies took charge, and the Ministry of Health's own laboratory began testing throat swabs from patients in an attempt to track and trace the outbreak and decide who to quarantine. The parallels with our own position were so numerous that I couldn't help but find a kind of reassurance in knowing our ancestors had weathered the same storm, or at least something with many similarities.

In the case of the Doncaster outbreak they faced a strain of streptococcal bacteria which appeared to be 'of a much more serious type than those normally seen', to quote the *British Medical Journal*. Not only was the fever it caused more serious, but it spread more widely. Adult women appeared to be twice as likely to catch this strain of scarlet fever, and adult males were four times as likely to succumb; the infection even appears to have reached household pets as the *BMJ* mentions the case of an Airedale who suffered. But these are only records of the very worst cases – the scarlet fever cases – because they were the only patients the isolation hospital were able to find room for. Patients who presented with symptoms which were thought to be less dangerous were quarantined at home until they had ceased to be infectious. In another similarity with the 2020 pandemic, this infection left patients with complications long after the infection had left them: arthritic pain went on for months in a way that was unusual for streptococcal infections.

The 2020 pandemic meant the postponement of many things for many people. For my fiancé and me it was a wedding. Postponed or cancelled nuptials and small ceremonies are a continuous theme in this book, and there will be many more contemporary couples who will sympathise with them. Although I cannot direct anyone to a sweetshop chapel in Halifax for a post-lockdown wedding, I can offer one in Rotherham. The inspiration for Hebblewhite's misshapes shop came from a real Yorkshire bridge chantry. Rotherham and Wakefield both boast interesting examples of bridge chantries (and Halifax may have had one which didn't survive to the twentieth century), but it was Rotherham's I was interested in because for a little while in the early twentieth century it was a newsagent, tobacconist, and sweetshop. I decided to take it and put it underneath a real iron bridge in Halifax (which is still standing in all its bold red glory) and to concoct an imaginary campaign to return it to a place of worship. This wasn't such a far-fetched idea, because in Rotherham in 1927 – after hundreds of years of using the chapel as a warehouse, almshouse, lodging house, and gaol – the local people decided to turf out the shopkeeper who was occupying it and hold services there on Sundays.

Weddings have been held in this little chapel and the idea of giving one of these 'sweetshop weddings' to my characters was irresistible. The real Albert Baum, however, was not married in a sweetshop, but his situation was inspired by some real events which were happening in Britain at the time.

It was with a special kind of heartache that I read Louise London's book *Whitehall and the Jews* which describes in detail the hurdles which Jewish refugees had to get over if they wanted to come to London to escape the Holocaust in Germany during the Thirties and Forties.

The character of Albert Baum has – like my cousins' grandfather Al Baum – Polish family, which makes him ineligible to claim refugee status in 1930s Britain. I was astonished to discover just how many Jewish refugees wanted to come to Britain to escape the Nazis, but were refused asylum; I wanted to write about one of them but I was cautious because I didn't want to imply that the Mackintosh's toffee company had any special campaign to rescue refugees at that time; I have seen no archive evidence that they did. Although, given the company's work to rescue children from the Spanish Civil war, and their much later attempt to give asylum to Ugandan refugees, it wouldn't be the most unlikely discovery I've ever made. We will see what the company archives hold when lockdown is lifted and we can all look at them again. Eventually, if we give it enough time, this will all become history.

Acknowledgements

At the close of 2019, during the early stages of writing this book, water started pouring through the living room ceiling. The roof had failed, and an emergency house move loomed. I thought I could still hand the manuscript in on time. Sadly, there was worse to come; my partner's brother Grant died suddenly, and his family were devastated by his loss. His funeral was the last time they all saw each other; by then, the pandemic was already building. My partner Scott (NHS Nurse extraordinaire) was transferred to a Covid-19 nursing team just as the first lockdown began and before we'd even finished unpacking in our new home. From that moment on, we never seemed to catch our breath.

Perhaps this is why the third book in the Quality Street Girls series is so different from the two which went before it. Looking back, I notice that I have kept my characters away from crowded places, and I rarely describe their faces – perhaps because I have seen so few this last year.

The Quality Street Wedding is a different book from the one I had planned, and it nearly didn't see the light of day, but thanks to the patience, understanding, and editorial genius of Kate Bradley, you are reading it. Huge thanks are also due to my agent, Jemima Forrester, who keeps me sane by making me laugh and always being ready to do battle with my imposter syndrome. To Kati Nicholl for copy edits which sing; Lara Stevenson for deadline day support; and all the team at HarperCollins Publishers for their hard work in the hardest of times.

Thanks also to Craig Leach for sharing his memories of scarlet fever; Adam Thompson for going out in search of my bridge chantry; Messers Flowers, Vannucci, and Stoermer for a Pascha gift of substance; my parents for looking up the details of their own Archbishop's special licence; Dr Annie Gray for helping me to put food on the table when I could find none in the shops; J. B. Wilkinson for saving Scott's bacon; both the Authors' Elevenses Club and the Kings Close Coffee Club for their moral support; and all the team at BBC Radio York for their continued enthusiasm for the adventures of Ruffian, the horse.

Special thanks to Mark Kendall, Jonty Joyce, and Alex Cronin for coming to the rescue. I can never thank you enough for all you did.

Penny Thorpe
March 2021

If you loved *The Quality Street Wedding*, turn the page to discover more of Penny Thorpe's wonderful books.

PENNY THORPE

The Quality Street Girls

Three girls. One factory.
A Christmas they'll never forget

PENNY THORPE

The Mothers of Quality Street

Can the factory girls pull together for a very special day?